'he Kid

's on the panel in the building's
hat some kind soul among her
dache that had started in the cab
settled in for the night, pounding just above her right eye. At that
exquisite moment, Kate saw the kid—that ghostly, smudge-faced
kid—sitting on the staircase inside. A one-armed Barbie doll was on
the step beside her.

"Hi, Sweetie!" Kate said through the wired glass, exaggerating the
enunciation of the words to make her meaning clear. "Would you
come and let me in, honey? You remember me, don't you? I live on
the third floor?"

The girl did not budge, apparently still trying for first prize in a
zombie look-alike contest. At first, Kate felt a twinge of concern for
the girl. Why on earth was she out in the hallway so late in the
evening? Kate leaned her forehead against the cool glass and closed
her eyes. When she opened them again, Jenny took the doll into her
lap, whispered something into her plastic ear, walloped her twice
across the bottom, and started up the stairs.

"Hey! Hey, where are you going?" Kate shouted. "Hey, you better
come back here, you little... Hey! Hey, did you hear me?"

And with the little darling thus doubly emblazoned on Kate's
mind, if not yet on her heart, their second encounter ended.

DISCARD

Wings

KATE AND THE KID

Anne Rothman-Hicks and Kenneth Hicks

A Wings ePress, Inc.

Mainstream Novel

Wings ePress, Inc.

Edited by: Jeanne Smith
Copy Edited by: Joan C. Powell
Senior Editor: Jeanne Smith
Executive Editor: Marilyn Kapp
Cover Artist: Kenneth Hicks

All rights reserved

Wings ePress Books
http://www.books-by-wings-epress.com/

Copyright © 2010 by Kenneth Hicks
ISBN 978-1-61309-869-1

Published In the United States Of America

Wings ePress Inc.
3000 N. Rock Road
Newton, KS 67114

Dedication

"To Alice, who read and edited each version, and to our two sons, Brendan and Zach, who cheered us on as well."

One

On the last Friday in June, at three o'clock in the afternoon, Kate and her co-workers at Hiroth Publishing were told to assemble in the executive conference room on the fifteenth floor, the one with the leather chairs and polished wooden table and original Audubon prints on the walls. It was an odd hour for a meeting. Minds tend to wander on the last workday of the week. She, herself, stared out the window at the East River where a tugboat pushed a tarpaulin-covered barge north toward Hell's Gate at stop-action speed. Alternately, she played with her shoulder length blond hair, examining the split ends and fighting the urge to chew on them. She almost didn't hear when Sandy Hiroth made the oft pooh-poohed announcement that the business bearing his family's name would be closing down at 5:00 p.m. that very day.

"Hiroth Publishing wants to thank all of its loyal employees for their years of hard work. With the final paycheck, each of you will be receiving two weeks' severance, along with your accrued vacation pay. Our very best wishes to all of you."

She thought of Roger's periodic warnings that she should find another job. The old-boy, old-money network had been whispering that things did not look good at Hiroth. But Kate chose to believe that management was telling the truth and that one of New York's oldest and proudest publishers had no plans to shut down. As usual, Roger had been right. Kate glanced across the room at her friend, Stevie, from Marketing, who gave a resigned shrug. She had sided with Roger.

"Thank you all very much," Sandy said, smiling as he handed each of them their final checks, one by one. He was tanned from weekends at his country club, relaxed from a recent golfing vacation. He had his stashed away. That was certain. He was going to come through this smelling like the proverbial rose. An old rant of her mother's came to mind: "trust the rich only to screw you."

"They didn't get to be an old money family by giving it away." That was another Carla quote.

The thought of finding a new job in today's economy made Kate's stomach hurt, her head throb, and her palms sweat. How long could she live on the contents of her personal envelope—five weeks of salary? What if she ate only peanut butter and saltines? Or cancelled her landline phone?

The alternatives spun through her mind for the next hour as she packed up her office items, putting some in her backpack and the rest into a box Hiroth would deliver next week. Free of charge, he reminded them. What a guy!

As she was leaving, Stevie caught her on the sidewalk outside.

"Hey, Kate, a bunch of us are going to spend some of this paltry severance on getting drunk. You coming?"

"I don't think so. I'm not feeling so hot."

"Don't let it get you down, Kate. We'll be laughing about this some day. Just stay strong. I'll call you! We'll have lunch next week." She paused. "In fact, maybe you can ask Roger to come. Then he can pay for it."

Laughing grimly, Stevie got into a cab with a few others and they sped away.

~ * ~

Kate trudged home from 42nd Street. The decision was made partly to save the subway fare and partly because a long walk was her personal cure for stress of all kinds. She had planned to write a book on the subject called, *Hike until You're Too Tired To Think: A Pedestrian's Guide to a Sweet Eight Hours' Sleep.*

From work to her apartment on 92nd Street was just about two and a half miles—a nice trek, but what was her hurry? By the time she climbed the stairs to her third floor apartment, she might be able to take a nap. At least her humble abode was dirt-cheap. God bless rent stabilization! And God bless Sheldon Silver.

It was in this state of mild depression that Kate first saw Jenny, who was looking out the window of Mrs. Morley's street-level apartment. The child's six year old body was framed by a set of heavy pleated maroon drapes as in a Victorian portrait photograph. Her dark hair appeared not to have been combed or washed recently. There were brownish smudges on her cheek. Kate assumed she was just one of Mrs. Morley's many granddaughters over for a visit. After a day of serious playing, she looked like she needed a bath.

Their meeting could well have been completely unmemorable. But when Kate forced herself to smile and give a silly sort of hand-wagging wave on her way up the stoop, there was utterly no response from the kid. She didn't smile back. She didn't wave. She just stood there without blinking an eye—a black hole of emotion.

So peculiar was this expressionless waif that a thought flashed through Kate's brain—maybe this was not a living, breathing human being at all. Maybe this shadowy image was a ghost, some sort of churlish spirit, who had wandered off at dusk generations ago to play hide and seek in the tenement alleyways of old Yorkville and had never been heard from again.

"Tough luck, ghost-girl," Kate whispered to herself. "I've got my own damn problems."

Then Kate climbed the stairs to her apartment, turned on the shower, and stood under a hot stream of water for half an hour, pretending that she wasn't crying. Water was free, after all, in the apartments of New York City—even hot water.

She barely thought twice about the little girl on the first floor with the dirty face.

~ * ~

That night was a co-op warming party that Kate had not wanted to attend, even before she lost her job. She had gone to Roger's apartment, hoping for a quiet night that involved only two of them getting very drunk. However, Roger prevailed upon her in his calm and practical way that she found so hard to fight. Maybe she would meet someone who would know about a job, he said. And it would be good for her to get out of the apartment and not dwell on the abysmal unemployment rates and her overall prospects. It was all very sensible advice, and since he hadn't once said, 'I told you so,' about Hiroth Publishing, she found some decent clothes she had previously left in his closet, hopped into the shower with him (another deciding factor), and they were on their way.

The lucky new owner of a three-bedroom co-op in a pre-war building was an old friend of Roger's (whether from an incredibly expensive summer camp, a prep school or a college fraternity, Kate did not get clear). Kate had spent summers keeping cool in the sprinklers at the playground and had attended college on a needs-based scholarship, since Carla's law practice had never made her wealthy. (Now there was an understatement!) And all evening, Kate could not shake the thought that this fellow and Roger were filthy rich—or on the way to becoming even more filthy rich. Like all the other Sandy Hiroths of the world, they didn't have to live from one paycheck to the next. They didn't care that others did. Not their problem. They would cut anyone else off at the knees if their own little castle of contentment were threatened. Then they would smile and hand them a final paycheck and say: "thank you."

Except for the need to bring a suitable present, the party was the same as several others she and Roger had attended together that year. The women were thin, tan and aggressively fit, with impeccably toned small and large muscles. The men were square-jawed and also fresh from the gym. Everyone had a job involving the Internet, or investment banking, or fabulous stock options, *plus* perfect teeth. They were so intense their eyes didn't seem to blink even as they talked and laughed in each other's beautiful faces. They oozed self-confidence. It was as if Kate had wandered onto a soundstage where they were shooting a commercial for low calorie beer, and she imagined that at any instant a voice would cut through the din and yell, "Hey, who's the broad with no job and the flabby inner thighs? How the hell did *she* get in here?"

What did any of them know about bad luck? Or failure? In her twenty-seventh year, she was supposed to be a famous writer of fine novels living on the southern coast of Ireland. There would be sheep in the meadow, cows in the corn, and representatives of *The New Yorker* or *Harper's* flocking to the door to interview her and urge her to write more short fiction. More, Kate! Instead she was an editor, and not even a high-class editor of meaningful books or incisive essays. Not even *close*. For the last five years, she had been the editor of high school and college textbooks, for pity's sake; correcting the grammar and pedantic style of college professors. And now she was an unemployed textbook editor to boot.

To say the least, it was very difficult to "mingle," as Roger had so optimistically urged. She was as likely to stand on a table and announce that she had a particularly virulent strain of herpes as to admit to this Brahmin crowd that she had no job. So she did what she could to survive the evening. With a strong drink in hand, she dutifully made the rounds, concocting various professions for herself as the whim arose. She told one person she was a brain surgeon who limited her practice to Mensa members; another that she was a Columbia University archeologist mining the depths of the Meadowlands landfill. With her glass refilled, she confided to an especially earnest Vassar graduate that she was a CIA intern working on a secret government project to replace experimental white mice with a mammal that was both more numerous in this country and of a sort less likely for the scientists to become attached to.

"And by God, I think we found them," Kate said.

"Really? What?" the woman asked.

Kate bent close, as though fearful the wrong people might be listening, and, breath sweetened by too much booze, whispered, "Lawyers."

Kate erupted in a belly laugh that silenced the entire crowd for a second or two, and the Vassar graduate slipped away. From across the room, Roger appealed to her with a weary look to *please behave.* But Kate was deep in thought about Sandy Hiroth and his house in Scarsdale complete with heated pool, and about being screwed by old money. She grabbed a bottle of tequila from the open bar and spent the next half hour sucking on a lemon and going from small group to small group, interrupting them to say that she was helping a Studs Terkel wannabe write a book on the inane conversation of the *nouveau riche* at cocktail parties.

"Would you all please speak up?"

Dead silence followed. She had lost her audience and there was zero chance of getting them back.

No one appreciates wit anymore, she thought.

Five minutes after she pulled her routine on a group that happened to be near enough to Roger for him to overhear, he was guiding Kate into a cab for the ride back to his place. She was still very drunk, but with the alcohol haze clearing, she was also beginning to realize what an ass she had made of herself. She looked across to where Roger sat rigid, his 6'3" frame crammed into the back seat. He was very handsome, especially in profile, with his short brown hair cut that morning for the party. As she cuddled up to make amends, thinking another shower would be just the thing, Roger kept his jaw a bit too square for a bit too long, staring straight ahead of him at the back of the cabby's neck.

"How could you be so immature?" he asked. His brown hair fell in an even line over his brow. His fingers were splayed over his knees. "Really, Kate. Maybe it's time for us both to be alone for a while and think seriously about our situation. I mean, where are we headed?"

Kate was not one to grovel, even when she was wrong—and certainly not to someone who was destined to be as rich as Sandy Hiroth. At 83rd and Park, the cab stopped for a light and she hopped out.

"Please get back in the car, Kate," Roger said.

"Just doing as you suggested, Roger. And you know what? I feel like I'm thinking better already. Much more seriously. I mean, look at me; I'm not smiling at all. *Plus*, I know exactly where I am headed. I'm headed *home*."

"*Please*, Kate. You are in no condition to walk."

Even the cabdriver could recognize the concern in Roger's voice, but his words were like a red flag in front of a bull.

"Oh, *really*?" She sat on the curb, yanked off her high heels and waved them in Roger's direction as though to say that a person who was too drunk to walk would not have thought to do anything that practical.

"Kate, either get back in the car, or that's it. We're done."

"Stick a fork in it then, Roger."

She hiked up her skirt and lurched unsteadily north toward her apartment. Ten blocks later, with her stockings worn through and the bottoms of her feet in a state of open rebellion, she reached her foyer and experienced one of her life's more difficult epiphanies—that her keys to the front door and to her apartment were still in the pockets of her jeans, which were on the floor of Roger's bedroom where she had expected to spend the night.

She began to press all the buzzers on the panel in the building's foyer, one after the other, hoping that some kind soul among her neighbors would let her in. The headache that had started in the cab settled in for the night, pounding just above her right eye. At that exquisite moment, Kate saw the kid—that ghostly, smudge-faced kid—sitting on the staircase inside. A one-armed Barbie doll was on the step beside her.

"Hi, Sweetie!" Kate said through the wired glass, exaggerating the enunciation of the words to make her meaning clear. "Would you come and let me in, honey? You remember me, don't you? I live on the third floor?"

The girl did not budge, apparently still trying for first prize in a zombie look-alike contest. At first, Kate felt a twinge of concern for the girl. Why on earth was she out in the hallway so late in the evening? Kate leaned her forehead against the cool glass and closed her eyes. When she opened them again, Jenny took the doll into her lap, whispered something into her plastic ear, walloped her twice across the bottom, and started up the stairs.

"Hey! Hey, where are you going?" Kate shouted. "Hey, you better come back here, you little... Hey! Hey, did you hear me?"

And with the little darling thus doubly emblazoned on Kate's mind, if not yet on her heart, their second encounter ended.

Two

Late in the morning of the day after her run-in with the tequila bottle and the kid, Kate put on her bathing suit and went up onto the roof of her building. Positioned properly, her head could be in the shade of the doorway to the stairs, while the rest of her body was in the sun. One of her friends in college, who seemed to know about these things, swore that vitamin D from the sun was the very best thing for a hangover, especially a tequila hangover.

Sally McKean, her neighbor on the third floor, was hanging up a load of wash to dry in the open air. She had let Kate in after her own night of carousing at a neighborhood bar. Until that point, Kate had sat on the front stoop for two hours, cursing Roger and fending off passing guys who could not believe that she did not want to go with them to a party. ("Thank you. I just got back from one.")

Sally made a few extra dollars a month by doing odd jobs for the landlord: sweeping the halls, taking the trash out to the curb, and showing apartments when there was a vacancy. For that reason she had a key to Kate's apartment and opened the door for her, no charge, although she made it a point to tell her that anyone else would have paid ten bucks apiece for the extra keys.

"I'll give them back when I get mine from Roger," Kate had said.

"Don't see that happening anytime soon," Sally replied. "You really freakin' messed things up this time, you dumb-ass."

"Yeah, yeah, yeah."

It was a beautiful June day. Kate lay on a cotton blanket, her thick blond hair wound into a kind of pillow for her head. Three extra-strength Tylenols were doing their work and she dozed from time to time, reminding herself in intermittent moments of wakefulness that writers (and artists in general) were happiest and most creative when dirt poor, and that a sense of personal loss was a *good* thing. By one o'clock, she had nearly convinced herself that kissing both a job and a boyfriend goodbye in the same week was a streak of luck.

"Makes sense to put the freakin' wash out on the line, don't it, Katy?" Sally said. A half dozen clothespins stuck out of her lips at various angles, but didn't interfere with her voice projection. Demosthenes couldn't have done better. "Two and a quarter for the freakin' dryer? Is that nuts? Do I look like I'm crazy? And up here ya got your sun, ya got your breezes..." She paused to throw a clothespin at a pigeon that was flying too close for comfort. "Ya got your freakin' flying vermin."

Kate smiled. The Tylenols were beginning to work on her hangover. It no longer hurt to roll her head. And the pounding behind her right eye was just an unpleasant memory, like her fight with Roger.

"They're actually rock doves," Kate replied, in a drowsy undertone. "A guy I used to know told me that. He said they came over from Europe on ships. Probably there were a few in the masts of the Mayflower."

"Pilgrim vermin. That's great, Katy. I'll definitely remember that the next time one shits on my head."

Sally took a quick run toward the front edge of the building, scaring the pigeon into flight and startling Kate, who tried to master an involuntary shudder. She had a "thing" about heights and the five-story drop to the sidewalk was anxiety-producing for her. When on the roof, she stayed seated or flat on her back and as close to dead center as she could, certain in her psychosis that if she wandered too close to the edge, peculiar things would begin to happen. The laws of physics would be momentarily suspended. A gusting wind would balloon her clothes and carry her away. A brick wall sturdy enough to hold for a hundred years could inexplicably crumble at her touch.

"Freakin' shit-maker!" Sally said.

The pigeon had reappeared with a friend. Even pigeons had lovers.

Sally took a dash at them, sending a chill up and down Kate's spine.

"Jesus, Sally," Kate said. "You know, all you need to do is catch your foot on the tarpaper and over you'll go. I'm not going to clean you up off the sidewalk, either. I'll let the fire department hose you away."

"Real nice, Katy. I forget what a freakin' wimp you are. You should have been around when I was a kid. We used to hang over the edge and drop coal cinders on people. *Ping. Ping. Ping.* Three points if you hit a priest. Five points for a cop. Ten if he had his hat off."

Sally grabbed a handful of pillowcases and sheets, pinning them to the clothesline with a practiced ease. At five foot six, she was two inches shorter than Kate, with a stocky, athletic build. As long as Kate had known her, Sally had been trying to lose ten pounds. Her hair was naturally dark, but she bleached it, adding a splash of color here or there, as the spirit moved her. This week she had chosen purple. It matched her nails perfectly.

Just then, for the second time since Kate had climbed to the roof, the door from the stairwell opened and immediately slammed shut, followed by the sound of small feet racing down the wooden stairs into the building, fast as a drum roll. Kate wondered if there were laws that required a child less than 48 inches tall to be kept on a leash.

"Crazy freakin' kid," Sally said. "All morning she's been at me to come up here with her, and then when I do, all she does is play with the freakin' door like it's the best toy since freakin' Nintendo."

"You mean that little angel is staying with you? What's her name, anyway?"

"Jenny. But most of the time I call her 'Creephead.' You'll understand when you get to know her better."

"I'm not sure I want to."

Kate told Sally about the fiasco the evening before when she had tried to get into the building.

Sally laughed.

"Freakin' good thing for the Creephead. I told her if she ever opens that front door again, she goes straight to the Child Protective Services. Bingo! Doesn't pass go. Doesn't collect two hundred dollars."

"Child Protective Services?"

"What am I supposed to do? Tell me. She snuck out twice that I know of. Right onto freakin' 92nd Street. I tell her, 'one day someone is going to grab your skinny little ass and that'll be the end of it.' But she don't listen. I'm tellin' you, if I ever pulled that crap when I was a kid, my father would've took his belt to my rear end until I looked like a freakin' zebra."

The door slammed again and the footsteps retreated down the stairs, two by two this time. Distant tom toms. The natives are restless.

"Dumbest freakin' thing I ever did, takin' her in," Sally said then, sauntering over to Kate's blanket, thumbs in the loops of her cut-off jeans. She picked up Kate's bottle of suntan lotion and applied dabs of it to her skin, rubbing it in with the sure strokes of powerful hands.

"Her mother, Linda, and me hung out together when we were kids. That's what this is all about... What a beauty she was, Katy! Long black hair down to her ass and green eyes like freakin' jewels. Her legs could make you sick if you tried to compare. But she got more guys into the neighborhood than a free keg, Katy, I swear. Good-looking guys have friends, even if they ain't quite as hot. There was this one guy, Anthony, who was a couple of years older than us. He had a black Chevy Camaro convertible with an engine you could hear coming two blocks away. He'd park at the hydrant and the guys would hop out. Me and the other girls got the spillover, if you know what I mean. Even freakin' Linda could only have one guy at a time."

Sally paused, and Kate wasn't sure whether she was supposed to agree or not. Sometimes, Sally could be sensitive about her looks.

"I know the type," Kate said finally.

"Don't we all... And she was smart too. Did better than any of us in school. Got a great secretarial job when she graduated, with a big law firm, of all things. Learned that stuff too, real fast, and was working for one of the top guys. She was a freakin' whip, God bless her."

"So what happened?"

"Shit happened, that's what. I don't know exactly. My dad used to say that some horses are sprinters and some are made for the longer course. Linda was a freakin' sprinter. She wanted it fast. She wanted it now! She started looking for a way to avoid working for the rest of her freakin' life—waking up and going to freakin' work every freakin' day."

"Please. I'm depressed enough."

"Yeah, right... So anyway, about two weeks ago, out of the freakin' blue she comes to my place with the kid asleep over her shoulder and a bag packed. And she says, 'Sally, old friend. Ya gotta help me out, Sally.' I mean she's practically on her knees in my living room. Says she has to get away for a little while to clear her head. 'Just a few weeks'll do it,' she says. 'A month tops.' Will I take care of her freakin' kid for her? Jesus!! Take care of her kid? 'Linda,' I says to her, 'what in the hell are you *sayin'*?'"

Grimacing, Sally tucked her Tee-shirt under her bra and applied some lotion to her stomach with the same energetic strokes, as though hoping to melt away some of her love handles with the heat of friction.

"I tried to talk to her, but it was no use. And besides, I figured, 'what the hell are friends for? What's it all about if we can't help out a freakin' friend now and then?' She said she'd pay me a few bucks, but fat chance of me seeing any dough. The thing is, Katy, once you get to know her kid, you begin to see why Linda might not be rushing to come back. That's what I've been thinking. Dumbest thing I ever did."

Sally dropped down on all fours, surveying the open area on the blanket before slapping Kate on the haunches to get her to slide over. She folded her arms across her chest, which soon rose and fell in a peaceful rhythm.

"Must be a little hard on the kid, though," Kate said.

"Nah, the Creephead is made of freakin' iron. I'm tellin' you."

"But, Sally. Think about this. You wake up one morning in a strange apartment and your mother is gone. And then your mother doesn't come back. Weeks pass. No word."

"Well, it ain't quite like that. She calls me every once in a while. She talks to the Creephead on the phone."

"Such devotion."

"Did I say Linda was a hero? I don't think so. She's had a hard time. Made some bad choices and they all caught up with her. Grabbed her in the ass. But never mind all that. The point is, this kid's as tough as a life sentence."

Kate heard the creak of the door opening. Sally sat up.

"Hey, Creephead, c'mere and meet your neighbor! Where ya goin'? Hey, get the hell out here!"

But it was too late. Jenny had disappeared down the stairs again. Kate wondered if she had been listening to their conversation, trying to fill in the bits and pieces she didn't understand about her life.

"How old is she anyway? Six? Seven... Sally?"

Kate propped herself on one arm and looked over at her friend. Sally's arms had fallen to her sides, hands relaxed. She was snoring ever so lightly.

Kate rolled onto her back and closed her eyes, breathing to relax herself, as Roger had told her she should in moments of tension. In through the nose and mouth, out through the nose and mouth. Four counts in, four counts out. She thought she might have heard those same light footsteps on the stairs. Five counts in, five counts out. Was Jenny sitting there inside the door again, like some Dickensian heroine, hoping to learn that she had been switched at birth and that her mother was not *really* her mother? Kate had an inkling of what that was like. Growing up, waiting in an empty apartment for her mother to stop working and to tell the clients to go home, there were several mothers on the block she would have chosen over Carla in a heartbeat.

Six counts, in and out. What was it like to be completely alone and six years old? Seven counts. Eight... Ten counts.

~ * ~

Two hours later, Kate was in the middle of a wonderful dream. A well-respected publisher was trying to contact her! It seemed that a manuscript for a novel Kate had submitted years before had fallen behind a desk. An editor looking for a jelly bean had just found it! The editorial board thought it was the best thing they'd read in the last decade. Maybe *two* decades. Now, they were assembled at a large table in a leather and wood conference room, trying to reach her. The phone was ringing, but she couldn't get to it!

Wake up! Wake up!

As consciousness returned, Kate became aware of a one-armed Barbie doll six inches away from her nose, hopping up and down on its stiff plastic feet as though it needed to go to the bathroom. A young girl's falsetto voice accompanied the hopping in perfect rhythm,

"Your phone's ring-ing! Your phone's ring-ing! Your phone's ring-ing!"

Why this should matter to the little sweetheart and how come she was not with Sally were two of many questions that swept through Kate's mind in the intervening seconds. But Kate wound up concentrating on the doll, which seemed to have had a change of clothes and was dressed for the beach. Her bikini as well as her little sandals were bright pink, and hanging from her one good arm was a pink plastic bag that matched her pink terrycloth robe. Held from behind by two small fingers, the doll seemed to have walked to the spot herself.

"Thank you, Jenny," Kate said. "I appreciate your help."

She closed her eyes, but the doll started jumping up and down on blanket, a bit too close to her nose for easy sleeping.

"My name isn't Jenny," the doll said. "It's Miranda. *Her* name is Jenny."

Kate looked at Jenny, expecting a smile, but the girl was as serious as a hanging judge, except for the fact that most hanging judges don't dress in pink from head to toe, and Jenny's outfit matched her doll's item for item.

"I see. I'm very sorry. I had no idea."

"That's okay," Miranda said sweetly in that high-pitched voice. Jenny's mouth barely moved. It was a little eerie.

The telephone stopped ringing, and Kate wrapped herself in the blanket and curled up for another twenty winks. It was a bit chilly. The sun had slipped beneath the line of the tall apartment buildings on Lexington Avenue and thrown the rooftop into shadow. Kate hoped that, if left to her own devices, the Child of Gloom might quietly go away and haunt some other corner of the world.

Unfortunately, the phone was of some vital importance to Jenny. As Kate watched from the corner of her eye, the girl took the doll by its one good arm and rapped its head smartly on the roof.

Ouch! Kate thought.

"Bad girl!" Jenny hissed. "*Bad* girl! She missed the call."

If any doubt remained that the doll was a miniature version of herself, it vanished when Jenny scowled at Miranda, gave the doll's hair a hard yank, and said that if she kept *this* up, she'd be spending the night with Mrs. Morley.

"Hey, now, wait a minute, Jenny," Kate said. "This is not Miranda's fault. I mean, one of the biggest reasons for me turning off my cell phone and coming up onto the roof today was so I could *avoid* answering the phone. It's bound to be Roger—this guy I know—and he's just going to ask me when it would be convenient for him to deliver my toothbrush and clothes and things from his apartment. So, he can wait. I mean, we just broke up last night. Not that it was really sudden. Roger has been telling me for a month to please stop insulting his rich yuppie friends. Okay, two months. Who's counting?"

Kate's voice trailed off as she realized she was talking to a six year old and that the finer points of her monologue were probably being missed by Jenny, who was staring at her with a certain lack of comprehension. Miranda was perched comfortably on the girl's knee, the doll's unmoving plastic features bearing a startling resemblance to Jenny's, the way long-married couples look like each other. Someone had even applied greenish-yellow paint to the doll's eyes. Still, it was oddly satisfying to have any audience at all.

Kate sat up.

"Bless you," she said. "You don't even know what a yuppie is, do you?"

Jenny's expression did not change. However, the doll nodded 'no' in response to the question: Miranda didn't know what 'yuppie' meant.

"Well, listen to me carefully, because this is important. A yuppie is a person who doesn't ever feel sorry about being rich. *I* say this spiritual deficiency links them to the generations of Eisenhower and Hoover; *they* say it's a state of grace. Really. This is all true. Someday, I'm going to write a book about it. I'll call it *Yuppies and the Puritan Ethic: From Oliver Cromwell to George W. Bush.*"

At this, Jenny nodded sagely. She knew what a book was.

"Time to get going, I guess," Kate said. "Nice talking to you, Honey."

Kate gathered up her blanket, lotion and thermos, and couldn't help but notice that Jenny followed her closely across the roof, matching her step for step through the doorway and onto the stairs.

Then the phone in Kate's apartment rang again, and all sense of order was lost.

"Your phone's ring-ing! Your phone's ring-ing!"

The girl raced down the stairs, stopped at the bottom and ran back up, poised to lead the way down again.

"No, no, no," Kate said. "Haven't you been told never to run for the telephone? It's a *rule*. You have to approach a phone slowly or it'll stop ringing the instant you get to it. Really. I could write a book about this too. *How to Slow Down When They Want You to Hurry*."

Holding to her advice, she calmly put the key into her lock, walked across the living room and ripped the phone off of its cradle with a splendid flourish.

"Buuuunnnnhhhh," the dial tone said.

"You see," Kate said. "Just imagine how stupid I'd feel right now if I'd run for the darn thing."

She left the receiver off the hook and didn't even glance at her cell. She was sure it had been Roger calling, and she had as much desire to talk to him as she did to move to the suburbs tomorrow and begin having babies. As an accomplished lawyer, he was as comfortable on the phone as Brer Rabbit in his briar patch. She, on the other hand, needed body language to convey her message. *A lazy tilt to the head and a bored but amused stare would be perfect*, she thought, *to express the confident ease with which she was meeting the future without him. Man-less. Her fate. Her mother's fate.* Losing a boyfriend was mere grist for the mill of life. There was a book in there somewhere!

Then she turned and saw that Jenny was making Miranda go "tip-a-tap-a-tip" on the end table with her little doll feet, trying to draw Kate's attention to the fact that on the floor was an unstamped envelope. The lack of postage meant it must have been delivered by hand, probably by a messenger at Roger's firm, she thought, until she saw that it was a re-used envelope with Sally's name and address on it.

She tore it open.

'Dear Katy,

I dint want to wake you up. The freakin' babysitter canceled. Believe it?! I figured you wunt mind. Jenny *loves* peanut butter. See ya at 10.

Sal

Frankly, Kate 'dint' believe it.

"The heck with this," she said. "That cheap so-and-so is probably trying to save the cost of Mrs. Morley's babysitting."

She picked up the phone and dialed.

"Hello?" said Mrs. Morley in her wavering soprano voice.

"Hello, Mrs. Morley this is Kate from the third floor."

As Kate waited for the words to register, she stole a glance at Jenny. That was a mistake. Tears glistened in the child's eyes and threatened to overflow down her cheeks. And all the while, Jenny was holding Miranda by the throat, squeezing with every bit of her strength and whispering, ever so softly,

"Don't you dare cry, you Creephead! Don't you dare!"

"Hello?" Mrs. Morley said. "Hello?"

Kate took a deep breath and thought the matter through. Jenny's mother had dumped the kid with Sally. Sally had dumped her with Kate. It should make no difference ultimately in the moral order of the universe if Kate were to dump the child also, this time on Mrs. Morley. It might even be a life lesson. Do as others do to you.

Then Kate made the mistake of looking at Jenny again. Her little fingers were turning white around the doll's throat. A single tear had created a winding rivulet across the smudge on one side of her face.

Was she no better than a yuppie? Kate thought. A Sandy Hiroth?

"Okay, okay. It's only one night."

"Excuse me?" said Mrs. Morley.

"Nothing. Never mind. You shouldn't expect logic from someone who just lost her job. I'm an artist, after all. A writer. Sort of."

"Is this a prank call?" Mrs. Morley asked as Kate hung up the phone.

Jenny seemed confused, but at least she had stopped trying to strangle her doll. That was a good thing.

"We'll have to do some shopping for dinner," Kate said. "And that means we'll have to figure out something for the two of you to wear over your bathing suits. It's getting cool out. Okay?"

Jenny held Miranda up in front of her and dipped the doll twice by way of assent. Kate was beginning to understand why Sally had some problems with this kid.

"First, though, I'm going to take a shower. So you just sit and entertain yourself for a while. I have some magazines over in the corner."

Kate went into the bathroom to start the water. She was about to step into the shower when she heard what sounded like a security gate opening. How could that be?

She pulled on a robe and felt her jaw drop to the floor as she reached her bedroom and saw Jenny crawling out the back window onto the fire escape.

"No, no, nooo!" Kate screamed, but as she reached the window, she could go no farther. She was paralyzed, overcome by her fear of heights—by the familiar sensation of falling over the railing, of slipping through the thin metal slats, which would yawn apart for just that purpose.

With a tremendous effort, Kate was able to stick her head out far enough to see Jenny disappear into what must have been Sally's bedroom window next door. It had never occurred to Kate that they shared the same fire escape. And the thought would not have made the slightest bit of difference. Only demented people walked on fire escapes.

Her stomach did somersaults as she remained rooted to the spot. Finally, Jenny scampered back with matching slacks and sweatshirts for herself and Miranda.

Slightly nauseous with relief, Kate rested her head on the windowsill. Then, after Jenny changed into the new clothes and dressed Miranda, the doll's plastic feet tapped out another short rhythm on the night table.

"Would you please help Jenny?" the squeaky voice said. "She can't tie her shoes yet."

Jenny was smiling shyly. Why? Was she aware how absurd it was that she could navigate a fire escape but not tie her shoelaces?

Kate stopped trying to figure that one out. The girl's smile had transformed her. Suddenly she was quite pretty, the more so because she was incredibly shy. No doubt she resembled her mother. Her pale green eyes had a touch of yellowish brown in them. They were like low-grade jade, polished to a shine. Her dark hair needed to be brushed.

"Of course, I'll help her, Miranda," Kate said. "Any friend of yours is a friend of mine."

Three

After Kate took a shower and got dressed, she sat across the kitchen table from Jenny. Miranda was propped up on the surface.

"Okay, guys, now here is what I've been thinking. It's been a very nice day and it looks like it's going to be a very nice night and I can't see slaving over a hot stove and eating inside. You both agree?"

Miranda nodded her little doll head, but Kate waited, glancing at Jenny. Finally, she nodded her agreement as well.

"Excellent! So I'm thinking a cookout would be nice over in the Park. Hot dogs on buns. Maybe some relish and pickles for a veggie. Potato chips to supply a starch. A good rounded meal? You like that kind of stuff, Miranda?"

"Oh, yes," chirped Miranda. "And Jenny does too!"

"Then what are we waiting for?"

Kate found a battered duffel bag to hold the food they would buy. Then she made a stop in the basement for an abandoned grill she remembered seeing a month or so before, during a visit from the telephone repairman.

At the supermarket, Jenny pushed the cart with Miranda sitting in the baby seat. She had no preferences for the hot dogs and buns, but she picked out a sweet relish and kosher dill pickles and a brand of potato chips with ridges. Red grapes were a late addition to the list. As they cut down aisle three to the cash registers, Kate stopped short.

"Oh, wow," she said, looking at a display of marshmallows, graham crackers, and chocolate bars. "Do you guys know what a s'more is? A s'more is better than food. It is ambrosia of the gods. I know what I'm talking about. It will be one of the recipes in my book, "*Not Just Food.*""

Jenny looked a little lost. Miranda was tilting her head slightly in confusion also.

"Trust me on this, guys. You will love them. Now, Miranda! Give me five, my friend."

Kate held up her palm and hit it against the doll's plastic appendage. Then she did the same in Jenny's direction, and before the child could think about it, she had jumped up and slapped Kate's palm.

"Yeah!" Kate said.

"Yeah!" said Jenny.

They walked over to Central Park and entered at 90th Street, where there was a minor delay while Jenny and Miranda ran up and down the curving steps to the reservoir twice. Then they were on their way again, heading south along the Park drive. At the Metropolitan Museum, they took a right at the first path and after a very short walk, turned off into a kind of meadow with tall trees on each side and a chain link fence and the 86th Street transverse road serving as the northern boundary. At this time of day there were still people strolling everywhere, and they could hear the sounds of teams playing on the basketball courts beyond the trees to the west.

Then Kate noticed a sign that she had never seen. Among the list of prohibitions was a rule against fires.

"What does it say?" Miranda asked.

Kate looked around for rangers or cops.

"It says that any cooking fires have to be over there right next to the transverse road and behind those pine trees. So, I'll set up the grill over there and you gather some wood. But don't get any that's green or rotten. They'll catch us by the smoke."

Jenny stopped with a puzzled expression.

"What do you mean, Katy?" Miranda asked.

Kate had never liked being called Katy. It reminded her of an insect. But the pet name seemed to roll off the kid's tongue.

"Never mind. It's from a song Joan Baez used to sing about making moonshine while the moon shined. I'll play it for you later. Go on! Dry wood!"

Jenny and Miranda raced off with a plastic bag.

"How big?" a voice called.

Kate was not sure whether the girl or the doll asked the question, and that seemed like progress of a sort.

"An inch thick or smaller."

Jenny picked up a branch that was the right width but about eight feet long.

"Is this okay?" she asked, staggering toward Kate like a drunken flag-carrier. Then she lost her grip and it fell, breaking into pieces.

"Perfect," Kate said.

While Jenny was searching for more wood, Kate saw a pair of men standing near the fence at the transverse road, but fifty yards deeper into the park, partially shielded from view by a pair of fir trees. She thought at first that they were two gay guys seeking solitude. But then she noticed one of the men take something from a small pack at his waist and give it to the other man, who handed him a wad of money.

At that point, the man with the pack turned and Kate stepped back out of sight behind some bushes. He was tall and on the thin side but with the wiry build of someone who works out regularly. The sallow color of his skin didn't hide the fact that he needed a shave badly. His dark shaggy hair fell almost over his eyes, which were hard little nuggets of brown, darting around in his head. Jenny returned with a bag of twigs and Kate crumpled some newspaper in the grill and stacked the broken kindling into a teepee-like structure. Still a bit worried, Kate glanced again toward the place where the man had stood. She was relieved that she did not see him and that he apparently had not seen her or Jenny.

When the wood caught and was burning hot, Kate took two hangers from the duffel bag and bent them straight, slipping a hot dog on each and showing Jenny how to hold them over the flame. While Jenny did the cooking, Kate spread a blanket on the grass, opened the jars of pickles and relish, and speared two buns with another hanger. The rolls were toasted just as the hot dogs began to split and drop juice hissing into the fire.

"Well done, Jenny and Miranda. Well done! Now we feast!"

Kate loaded the buns, lathering on the relish and ketchup for Jenny and relish and mustard for herself. Then, they sat and munched away in silence, interspersing mouthfuls of hot dog with potato chips and pickles and fruit punch and grapes. It tasted good, and was the perfect post-hangover dinner as well. *Babysitting is a piece of cake*, she thought.

"Oh my God," she said when Jenny was done. Guess what?"

"What?"

"It's time for s'mores!"

She lanced the marshmallows onto the hangers and instructed Jenny on how to cook them until golden brown on the outside and the consistency of pudding on the inside. Then she put part of a Hershey bar and the hot marshmallows between two graham crackers, causing the chocolate to soften and the mixture to squeeze out at the first bite. A look of pure bliss crossed the girl's face. They each had another, and a third for luck, huddled slightly on the blanket while they gobbled the delicacies down.

Kate sighed, patting her stomach appreciatively.

"You know, guys, I've found that it takes a few women alone together to have a really good time eating. You'll see I'm right when you get older. All of your best food experiences will be with women. I don't know exactly why. But I suspect it's something our mothers taught us and our grandmothers taught them: Never let a man see you eat a lot, or he'll think he can't afford you, or that you'll grow into a blimp, or devour him, or smother him, or sicker stuff than that, if you want to listen to this old bird, called Freud. But you don't want to do that, do you?"

Jenny had been trying hard to follow. She wrinkled her nose and shook her head so seriously that Kate laughed.

"Good girl. Gimme five! It's a rule to remember: 'Never listen to an old bird!' It's like, 'do not take candy from a stranger' and 'don't trust a man who says he loves you on the first date.' There are others, but they can wait until you are older, along with the exceptions to the rules. Which is another book I'm planning: *Every Rule and Its Exception.* Kate paused. A smile crossed her face. "Roger told me he loved me on our first date. He wasn't trying anything funny either. He was just saying good night and blurted it out." She paused again. "I don't know why I fight with him so much. He's really the most decent guy I've ever known. Maybe it's because he's so wealthy. My mother hated rich people with a passion. Maybe it wore off on me. Hmmmmmm."

Just then, Kate noticed that the man who had been selling drugs was seated on a bench near the basketball courts. She thought at first that he was simply waiting for a new buyer, but after a few minutes she realized he was keeping an eye on her and Jenny, although trying not to be too obvious about it. *Why?* she wondered. He couldn't be worried that they had witnessed his transaction. Yet there was no question that he was scrutinizing the two of them very closely and, as time went on, making less and less of an effort to hide his interest.

It was also clear that Jenny had seen him too. Her gaze was locked hard on the ground at her feet. She had picked up Miranda and was holding her tight.

"Do you know that man over there?" Kate asked.

Jenny glanced in his direction quickly, too quickly to determine anything. She shook Miranda's head in the negative. It was clear that she was lying.

"Can we go?" Miranda asked.

Kate put the fire out with a bottle of water and threw the garbage into a trashcan. In another minute she had packed up their things and slung the duffel bag over her shoulder. Jenny's fingers clung to Kate's shirt, loosely at first, then harder and with an increasingly annoying tugging motion as they started walking out of the park.

Kate stared straight ahead of her, but every few seconds Jenny turned to look back.

"He's following us," Jenny said, nearly forgetting that she only talked through the doll. Her hand slipped off of Kate's shirt and she seized it again, resuming her grip.

"Don't worry. Just ignore him. He's a bozo."

They maintained a moderate pace along the sidewalk by the Metropolitan Museum of Art. He kept half a block behind them.

From time to time, Jenny giggled nervously.

"He's a bozo," she repeated in the squeaky Miranda voice. "He's a bozo!"

At Fifth Avenue, they turned south toward the front of the Metropolitan Museum.

"Where are we going, Katy?" Miranda asked then.

"You'll see."

As they reached the row of cabs waiting outside, Kate grabbed Jenny by the hand and hopped into one that had a clear space in front of it. Out of the corner of her eye, she saw that the man had started running toward them.

"92nd and Lexington. Hurry!"

The cab driver turned to stare at her, puzzled by her tone.

"Move it!" Kate shouted. "That guy is chasing us!"

This time the cabby understood. Their pursuer ran up to the car and as he tried to open the door on Jenny's side, the cabby put the gas pedal to the floor and took off, throwing both Kate and Jenny against the back of the seat. Jenny screamed. The man slammed his fist on the trunk and ran after them, but the cab made the first left toward Madison Avenue, tires squealing as it raced down the street. The man continued running until they made another left, heading uptown.

"That should take care of the bozo," Kate said calmly, although her heart was pounding inside her chest.

Jenny looked out the back window, nodding solemnly. Then she took Kate's hand in hers and held it against her cheek for the rest of the ride to 92nd Street.

Four

Back at the apartment, Kate found that Sally had called while they were out and left a message on the machine, saying that she expected to be home very late and asking if Jenny could spend the night. Mildly annoyed, but too tired to care, she found a t-shirt that fit Jenny as a nightgown and gave her the extra, unused toothbrush that was a parting gift from her last dentist visit.

While helping Jenny wash her face, Kate realized that the smudge mark was not dirt at all, but a bruise.

She ran the tips of her fingers over the area.

"How did you get that?" Kate asked.

"Jenny was running in Sally's apartment and fell," Miranda told her. "She's very clumsy."

~ * ~

The only real bed in the apartment was a nice old brass beauty that Kate had purchased for twenty dollars at the Holy Sisters of the Poor Thrift Shop on 96th and Second Avenue. One spring afternoon, she had stripped a hundred years of paint off the burnished metal while Sally had reclined on the roof and questioned her sanity.

"You know, there was a reason people started painting the freakin' things," Sally had said.

The act of giving Jenny her bed meant that Kate would be spending the night on the convertible sofa in the living room. That piece of furniture was also purchased at "The Sisters," but was not quite the bargain the brass frame had been, since it had springs pushing up through the so-called mattress like so many tree roots. Kate only slept on it when friends from college visited. Those events were, thankfully, not numerous.

Like any kid sleeping in an unfamiliar place, Jenny was up at first light. She crept into the living room and sat cross-legged within a few inches of Kate's sleeping form. When Kate stirred, Miranda's plastic face was pressed gently against her cheek.

Smack.

"Hi, Katy!" Miranda said in her high-pitched voice.

"Hi, Miranda!" Kate replied in the deepest *basso* tones she could manage without harming her vocal chords.

Jenny giggled. Miranda danced with delight on the mattress.

"Say it again!"

Kate sat up, swinging her legs over the side of the sofa.

"Hi, Miranda! Wasamatta?"

Jenny giggled harder than before, but then Kate noticed that Jenny had changed her clothes again. Her pink shirt had a bright yellow flower on it, which matched smaller yellow flowers on her pink shorts. Miranda wore a new matching outfit also, yellow with a touch of pink.

"Girls," Kate said very seriously now. "You didn't go out on the fire escape again, did you?" The answer was obvious, both from the downcast look on Jenny's face and from the fact that Miranda also turned away in apparent shame. "Please, no more walking on the fire escape? Okay? Please? Will you promise me that?"

"Yes, Katy," Miranda said sweetly. "And Jenny promises too."

"Okay. Now tell me, is Sally back yet?"

Miranda shook her head. Jenny did not seem particularly saddened by the fact.

"Then we should start thinking about breakfast. And I know just the place."

Ten minutes later they were standing in front of the donut counter at a bakery on Lexington near 86th Street. Jenny picked one with chocolate frosting and sprinkles. Kate got one of the jelly-filled variety.

On the way back, they passed a fruit stand and Kate began to feel guilty about giving Jenny something so nutritionally barren for breakfast. Don't kids need fruit?

She picked up a container of strawberries two ninety-eight a pint. Ouch. She put it down and looked at the blueberries. Three forty-nine!

Jenny was watching her. Miranda danced on the wooden edge of the fruit stand rack.

"Fresh fruit is a rip-off!" she said in what sounded like an imitation of Sally. "The canned stuff is just as good."

Kate put the strawberries and blueberries in her bag and paid for them.

"You shouldn't be eating canned fruit," she said. "They probably use corn syrup. The stuff is like poison."

The words were barely out of her mouth before she realized she was sounding just like her own mother, Carla. In that one respect, at least, she had been a good parent. There was always fresh fruit in the refrigerator, even if Kate usually had to eat it by herself.

Back in her apartment, she went into the kitchen and began to wash and remove the stems from the fruit. She put the donut on a plate and arranged some of the strawberries and blueberries into a face (half a strawberry being a nose and the other half lips, with blueberry eyes and beard). Then, she heard a muffled cry and Jenny came running in to her.

"What happened?" Kate asked.

Jenny didn't answer. She just shook her head.

"Did something scare you? What's wrong?"

In the living room, the curtain at the front window was pulled aside. Kate looked out, but saw only the usual dog walkers on the street below.

When she returned to the kitchen, Jenny didn't seem any more antsy than usual. She was sitting at the table on the edge of her chair. The girl's eyes were wide as saucers at the sight of the fruit face.

"Is this for us?" Miranda asked.

"Of course it's for you," said Kate.

She couldn't help wondering what had frightened Jenny so much, but was distracted by the sound of two voices in the hall. Opening the door, she saw that Sally had arrived, and had brought with her a somewhat rotund young man wearing a t-shirt from Steamfitters Local No. 231. Jerry, as she was calling him, may or may not have been drunk when he and Sally first met the night before, but he was definitely in need of a strong pot of coffee now. Sally, herself, had had her fair share of beer, and was struggling first to get her key into the lock, and then to steer Jerry into the living room. Both of them were laughing all the while.

"Kate, this is Jerry," Sally said, when she saw her at the open door. "Kerry, this is Jate."

They laughed even louder at her fumbled introduction, bending over at the waist and staggering to stay on their feet, which also struck them as wildly amusing. They were having so much fun that Kate had to smile herself. When Jerry fell onto his rear end and let out a loud fart, she began laughing almost as hard as they were.

Kate went into the hall to help. She and Sally each took hold of one of Jerry's arms, and on a count of three, hoisted him to his feet. Smiling good-naturedly, Jerry kept his balance, but Sally's face suddenly became very serious. Kate looked in the direction of her gaze and saw that the drug dealer who had chased them in the park the night before was standing at the top of the stairs.

"Hi, Sal," he said. "Long time, no see."

"Yeah," she replied. "Can't say that bothered me a whole lot, Tony."

Sally gave Jerry a gentle shove through the door of her apartment and he managed to make it to the couch where he lay down for a rest. He was soon snoring.

Sally remained in the hall.

"I should've figured Linda would leave the kid with you," he said, swaggering toward her. "The bitch does have her patterns of behavior. I should know that better than anybody, as many times as she cheated on me. Right, Sal?"

"Whatever you say, Tony."

"Whatever I say? I say, 'where's Jenny?'"

"She's around," Sally said. "Why do you want to know?"

"I came to take her back home," the man said.

"Linda left her with me, Tony. You know I can't just let her go."

"I know you ain't got no choice, Sal. That's what I know."

"Who *are* you," Kate asked finally.

"Katy, stay out of this, huh?" Sally waved her hand at her; however Kate ignored the warning, crossing the hall to stand beside her.

"Stay out of this? We ran into this guy in the park last night and he nearly scared Jenny half to death. Plus, I saw him sell somebody drugs. Right in Central Park."

"Katy, *please...*"

Anthony turned toward Kate. His one hand was deep in the front pocket of his sweatshirt. Sally put an arm in front of Kate, but she brushed it aside.

"I'm not scared of him," Kate said.

Anthony pulled his hand out of his pocket and in the same fluid motion flipped open a knife that glinted inches from Kate's face. The blade was thin and long and seemed to vibrate in the air. She eased backward.

A smile curled the edges of his lips.

"I know you ain't scared of *me*. You must be allergic to metal or something, right?"

"Leave her alone," Sally said.

"Be quiet, Sal," he replied. "I'm just admiring this lady's skin. Beautiful skin, don't you think? Not a mark on it anywhere. She could be doing commercials, this lady."

Kate was positioning herself to kick her right foot into his groin, but the door opened and Jenny raced down the hall to them.

"Daddy, no!!" she screamed.

The girl wrapped her arms around the man, trying to push him away from Kate.

The smile broadened across his face as he gave way to Jenny's efforts.

"Hey, Peanut. Where's your little friend, Goober."

"Is this man your father?" Kate asked "Sally, is this true?"

Sally nodded. Jenny couldn't look at Kate. She kept her face buried in the man's midsection.

"C'mon, kid. Let's pack up your things." He flicked the knife shut and placed it in his pocket. "I want to get back home. Me and you got a lot of catching up to do."

"She doesn't know where Linda is," Sally said. "Nobody does."

"Yeah, okay. I figured that would be the line. So let's pretend I believe you. But Linda knows where you are, right? And soon she'll know where the kid is, won't she? You will tell her for me, huh, Sal? For old times' sake."

Sally nodded.

"I'll tell her. Give me a few minutes, I'll pack her things."

"Don't bother yourself," the man said. "We'll take care of it. Not that I don't trust you or anything."

Jenny held on tight to him as they walked through the front door of Sally's apartment, but there was no affection in the embrace. She glanced back at Kate once and seemed barely to recognize her. The doll was held in her right hand, the head squeezed inside her fist.

"I'm calling nine-one-one," Kate said. She turned to go into her apartment. Sally grabbed her by the arm.

"You ain't callin' freakin' nine-one-one! Even if you get a cop to come down here, you think he'll still have the knife on him? Best case, they'll just take him to the precinct to cool off, maybe. He's out in two hours. Believe me, Katy. And he'll get another knife."

"I'm not *scared* of him, Sally."

"Yeah, I know, but that don't mean you shouldn't be. This is not somebody you're used to, Katy. It ain't freakin' karate class at the Y. Tony is crazy. And his friends are even crazier. You got to stay out of this."

"You think Jenny should be living with a drug dealer?"

"What I think don't freakin' matter, is what I'm sayin'. He's her father. You ain't, and I ain't either."

"You saw how scared she is of him. You should have seen her last night when she saw him in the park."

"Katy, listen to me." Sally put her two hands on Kate's shoulders. "This is Linda's problem, not yours."

"Well, let's tell her what's happening, then."

"I keep telling you, I don't know where she is. She'll contact me."

"When? A week? A month?"

"A couple'a days. I don't know."

"Then give me his name and address. I don't know who I'm going to call, but I'm not going to let Jenny stay with that guy. If the cops won't go over there, then I'll call the child welfare office. There's got to be somebody in this city who cares about this."

Sally stared at her for a moment, made a face, then shrugged.

"His name is Tosca. Anthony Tosca. He and Linda lived in a place on 85th between Columbus and Amsterdam. I don't know the number. It's a brownstone painted pink. North side of the street in the middle of the block. You can't miss it if you go over there."

"Wait a minute. Is this the guy you were talking about yesterday with the big black convertible?"

"Yeah. Like I told you, shit happened."

"That's not exactly surprising when you go out with a drug dealer."

"Maybe it wasn't so freakin' obvious what he was at the time."

"Why, did he have MD plates?"

"I don't have time to explain Linda to you right now, okay? She made some bad choices. Maybe he was one of them."

"I'll say."

Kate turned away.

"Wait a sec, will ya?" Sally called. "Will you hold off this freakin' stupidity of yours for a couple of days, at least? Give Linda a chance to call me. Sunday is usually the night. Okay? Will you be that smart, at least?"

"No. I can't let this happen."

Kate continued toward her own apartment.

"You freakin' jackass!" Sally shouted after her. "If the cops take her, they ain't bringing her back to me, you freakin' idiot! A judge will decide where the kid goes. You think you know so much, but I bet you my next freakin' month's salary you never spent the night in the child welfare office, waiting for them to place you in some group foster home. Didja? And I guarantee you've never been inside one of them homes, huh? You know what they *smell* like? You know what the *kids* are like in one of those places?"

Kate hesitated. She felt as though she had been punched. It had simply not occurred to her that the custody of the city might be worse than the custody of a drug-dealing father.

"Okay," Kate said. "I'll wait until tomorrow."

"Not enough, Katy. Give me forty-eight hours."

"You're just wearing me down, aren't you? You figure that if enough time passes, I'll move on to something else."

"That wouldn't be the worst thing that ever freakin' happened. But that ain't it. I'm just trying to get you to stay out of this long enough for people to arrange things themselves. She's Linda's kid. Give her a chance to deal with Tony without cops and the freakin' city and social workers and all the freakin' rest."

Kate stood at the open door to her apartment. Inside, she could see the table where the plate of fruit still remained, uneaten.

"Fine. I'll hold off on doing anything. But let me know as soon as you hear something from Linda. Will you do that? I'd like to talk to her myself."

"You got my word on it."

Five

After her talk with Sally, Kate slammed the door of her apartment shut and left the building. It was a nice day with a clear, pale blue morning sky. She thought the East River was a good destination. She could enter Carl Schurz Park at 90th Street and follow the promenade along the river to 60th without a traffic light to halt the flow of her steps. The fact that the FDR Drive was only a few yards from the walking path was both a bane and a blessing. There were the exhaust fumes to worry about breathing. But the rushing of the tires on the asphalt had a soothing effect. It was like white noise that blocks out any other sound and allows the mind to roam unimpeded. After ten or fifteen blocks, she figured, the frustration would melt away. At the end of the hike was a small playground with a dog run. That might even be good for a smile.

Maybe at that point she would see the ultimate wisdom of what Sally was saying. This was not her problem. Later on, she would call her friend, Stevie, and make a date for lunch or dinner. Stevie would talk some sense into her for sure. Kate could see the look of sheer incomprehension on her face. "You *what*?"

Kate had crossed Third Avenue and was continuing down the next big hill to Second when she became aware of a cab driving slowly beside her, matching her speed. She was sure it was Anthony, intending to taunt her, and she kept her gaze fixed on the sidewalk ahead. Sally's warning and the thought of him holding the knife inches from her face caused a shiver of fear to rise up her spine. "You're acting unreasonably," she told herself, but couldn't stop a tear from crossing her cheek.

Then she heard Roger's voice.

"Kate! Hey, wait up!"

The cab pulled over to the curb and she kept walking, so it pulled ahead again.

"Hey, c'mon, will you?" Roger said. He was hanging out of the window like a teenager on a Saturday night. "What are you doing?"

"Just walking, Roger. One foot in front of the other. Down this hill. Maybe up another one before the day is over."

The cab pulled ahead of her by a few yards. By the time Roger paid, she was ahead of him again and regaining control. He ran a few paces to catch her and fell into step. They had reached Second and turned south with the traffic before he spoke.

"You know your phone's been off the hook, right?" he said. "And your cell phone's turned off? It's not an accident or anything. I mean, I've been trying to get you for two days. Nobody's *incommunicado* for that long without it being intentional."

"Thirty-two hours," she said.

"What are you talking about?"

"We last saw each other at twelve-thirty on Saturday morning. We're just working on the thirty-second hour."

"Kate..."

"Just trying to be accurate, Roger. Think clearly, and all that."

"Okay, I should have seen that one coming."

He had followed her step for step when she crossed Second Avenue at 90th Street and continued East. Even with his long legs, he was having trouble keeping up with her pace.

"Where are we going anyway?" he asked.

She took a deep breath and let it out, counting three strides to inhale and three to exhale. It felt good to walk at a fast pace. And it didn't hurt that Roger was walking beside her and had used the word "we" to refer to the two of them. She didn't want to lose him. The thought was almost unbearable to her. But why? Was it because she really loved him, or because the thought of being alone in her apartment, looking for a job at this stage of her life was terrifying?

And why did she do things to push him away?

"I thought I would go over to the East River," Kate replied. "And walk down into the sixties. I figured eventually I'd go see this really hot guy I was with the other night and apologize for being such a royal ass."

"Anybody I know?"

"Very funny."

"I was actually trying to be serious. I've thought this whole thing through with some care. I'm the one who made you go to that stupid party even though it was the last thing you wanted to do."

"You're wrong, Roger. I was rude, and there's really no excuse. And here you are acting like it was your fault. I kind of wish you would scream at me. Call me vile names. Make me suffer a little."

"I'll tell you what," he said. "I promise to hold this over your head for the rest of your life, and throw it in your face at opportune times. Okay? Can we move on now?"

He took her hand and squeezed it. She smiled and squeezed it back.

"Deal."

They reached First Avenue just as the light was turning from yellow to red and she broke into a run, dragging him across with her. A long block loomed to York Avenue, and yet another to East End. Roger's head swiveled about, looking for a cab.

"Do we still have to walk?" he asked.

"We don't have to, but today I would prefer it."

"The thing is, I don't have a lot of time. I heard from the partner on this new case I'm working on that we have to go out to San Francisco later today. The plane leaves at four from Newark. He's picking me up at two."

"Don't worry. The exit at Sixtieth is thirty blocks away, only a mile and a half. At fifteen minutes per mile, we'll make it in twenty-two minutes. We'll be at your place in twenty-five, tops. A cab would take ten. And you still have five hours to pack."

She thought she heard a small sigh escape him. But he didn't say another word, simply matching his strides with hers, until they had reached East End and crossed over to the wrought iron gates of the park.

"What happened last night, Kate?"

The question was unexpected.

"What happened? What do you mean? Nothing happened."

"Yes it did. You were crying when I first caught up to you this morning. I saw the tears on your cheek."

Instinctively, her hand raised to her eyes, then dropped to her side.

"It was the wind," she said.

"Right. And I'm the sun. And the moon and the stars and the rain."

"Well, that *is* true, Roger."

She turned left onto the broken asphalt path that leads up a small grassy hill and comes out on the East River Promenade. He had to take a few extra-long strides to stay with her.

"You have to tell me what's going on, Kate."

He held on to her hand tightly in case she tried to pull away again. She didn't.

"Okay," she said.

They continued for a couple of blocks more, past Gracie Mansion, past a cement court where a street hockey game was in progress. The sounds of wood smacking concrete and boys yelling filled the air, and then faded behind them. Finally, she spoke.

"I know this is going to sound crazy, but really and truly not much of anything happened. I played babysitter for a six year old who is staying with Sally. Her name is Jenny and we had a little picnic dinner over in Central Park. We came back... She has a doll named Miranda, and she does all of her talking through the doll, like a puppet. It's kind of funny and irritating at the same time."

"Well, why were you crying?"

"She's staying with Sally because her mother is off somewhere. And we ran into this guy in the park who turned out to be her father, and he came by this morning. The son-of-a-bitch doesn't care about her one bit, but he took her away from Sally anyway, just so her mother will have to contact him. God knows why. He's a drug dealer. Did I tell you that? We saw him in Central Park selling drugs like they were pretzels with extra mustard. Jenny was scared to death of him. What kind of life is that?"

"A shitty life, Kate. A real shitty life."

He stopped walking and gently guided her off the path. Then he embraced her and kissed her with a tenderness that melded gradually into passion. When he released her, he was smiling, and she smiled back.

"What was that for?" she asked.

"I love you," he said. "And for thirty-two hours I've been worrying that you might go out to a party or a bar or someplace and meet someone who would realize what a great thing he has found with you. So I'm very happy to hear it was only a kid. I think I can deal with a kid."

"You should have met this kid."

~ * ~

That night Roger called Kate from San Francisco. The flight had been uneventful and Roger and the partner in charge of the case had had dinner with the client. More meetings were scheduled for after dinner. He had broken away to go to the bathroom and stepped outside the restaurant to call her. She was still feeling the glow of their reconciliation and of the several leisurely decadent hours they had spent in his bed before he had had to rush to pack and get downstairs to the waiting limo.

But Roger knew her well and soon the conversation moved seamlessly back to Jenny. He told her that he had been thinking about the girl and her father, and maybe it wasn't as bad as it seemed at first blush. Just because the guy makes a living selling pot in Central Park doesn't mean he's evil. Some perfectly normal people sell small quantities of drugs, just to cover expenses.

"I don't think you have to worry about the kid," he said. "Sally gave you some good advice."

"I appreciate what you're trying to do, Roger. But believe me, the guy is a shit. He pulled a knife on me with his daughter standing there."

She regretted telling him that the moment the words left her lips.

"For the love of God, Kate! Now I completely agree with Sally. Stay away from this jerk. Stay far away. In fact, if you want to listen to me, you should leave that dump and live at my place while I'm away. Come on, Kate. I insist. It's time you gave up that apartment anyway. You'll move in with me. Call a mover on Monday. Put it all on my credit card. Case closed."

"This is so romantic, Roger. You're ordering me to live with you. Dare my trembling heart expect an order to marry you next?"

"If I thought you would listen to me, I would. Yeah. Marry me, Kate!"

"Sorry. My mother told me never to accept marriage from a man right after a major argument. Or in the middle of one. Wait at least a month."

"Since when do you follow Carla's advice?"

"When it's convenient. Just the way she always followed her own sayings."

An edge crept into her voice that was heard and felt even three thousand miles away.

"Okay, I'm sorry I brought it up. But this is not a joke. The guy's dangerous."

"The point of the story wasn't him, Roger, or me. It was Jenny."

"I understand that. And I'm sure she's a nice kid. But maybe you'll excuse me for being a little more concerned about you than about a little girl who you took care of for essentially one night. I mean, I don't think I'm particularly cold-hearted, but I don't understand your attachment."

There was a long pause then. She could hear people walking by on the street in San Francisco, a car's horn, a woman's laugh.

She had wondered the same thing and hadn't come up with an answer. But thinking about the girl with her one-armed doll made her smile, and almost cry.

"Yeah. I've known her a very short time. And I realize it's odd that she's stuck in my mind. I don't know how to explain it, except that she's a really nice little kid with a big bundle of problems."

"There are a lot of kids out there who have rough lives, Kate."

"I guess there are. But I met *this* one. And we just connected in a really nice way. I'm worried about her, I guess. I'm worried because it seems like no one else is."

"She has a mother, Kate," Roger said gently. "And *that* is why I agree with Sally. I don't think you should view this as your problem. You fulfilled your obligation already. You stepped up for her when she needed someone. But you can't sort through the kid's whole bundle of problems."

He was right. She knew he was right, and yet the image of the girl remained.

"Everybody should have someone who worries about them, Roger," she said.

"I agree, and I hereby appoint myself your worrier. Will you please move down to my place?"

"Tomorrow. I promise. I'll *think* about it."

"You're very difficult, do you know that? It must be why I love you."

"Then I'm sure you wouldn't want me to change."

She heard a slight, exasperated sigh. She knew he was smiling, and that made her smile. She curled up in her bed, missing him.

"I have to get back to work," he said. "So, good night, my love— my darling Kate, who always wins the arguments but thinks she wouldn't be a good lawyer."

"I will never be a lawyer, Roger."

"I know. Something to do with your mother, I suspect."

"Can we please leave Carla out of this?"

"Your wish is my command, my love, as always. But I think she's already in it."

"Goodnight, Roger."

~ * ~

The next morning, Kate spent her time reading through the want ads in the *New York Times* and picking out likely prospects. There were very few jobs in publishing, and those few were in editorial positions she had never worked in. Still, she printed out resumes and addressed envelopes and mailed them before breakfast.

She was at the table in her apartment when she heard Sally's door open across the hall. The sound of two sets of shoes and intermittent giggling announced that Jerry had spent the night. Then there was a knock at Kate's front door.

"Hi, Katy. We were just leaving for work, but I wanted to tell you that Linda did call me last night. She says to thank you very much for your help. She really means it, and that she will take care of this with Anthony. Okay? Did I tell you this was going to work out okay? Huh?"

"What did she say she was going to do?"

"Katy, what do I look like, a freakin' Columbo? I didn't cross examine her, you know."

Beside her, Jerry belched appreciatively.

"Heh, heh. Freakin' Columbo. That's good, Sal."

"I was just wondering, that's all," Kate said. "Is she going to take Jenny herself? Is she going to bring her back here? She's not going to leave her with that guy."

Sally asked Jerry to wait a minute, then took Kate by the arm and led her down the hall a few yards.

"Yesterday you were freakin' worried because Linda wasn't around to watch out for the kid. I told you I would try to get word to her, and I did. Linda knows all about what's going on and she says she will handle it. I can't do better than that. And neither can you. If she messes up, that's on her. It ain't for you to say. You understand, me? She ain't your kid."

"Of course, she isn't my kid. I understand. I was just curious, that's all."

"Curiosity killed the cat, Katy," Sally said then. Her right hand was on Kate's elbow. She squeezed it hard. "Let it be," she whispered.

~ * ~

It was still early after Sally and Jerry left. The sky was nearly cloudless. The humidity was low. Kate telephoned her friend Stevie from Hiroth Publishing. They had played tennis together occasionally at the courts in Central Park and Kate thought it would be fun to have a game in the middle of the week when everybody else was working. Afterwards, she was hoping to persuade Stevie to take a walk down to the Boathouse for a late lunch or early dinner. Generally, Stevie was not one for walking. ("That's what cabs are *for*, Kate," she would say). But what else did Stevie have to do, now that she and the rest of the Hiroth Publishing crew had lost their jobs?

Plenty, Kate soon found out. Stevie was starting work the next day at a magazine called *New York Today.*

"I was just going to call you, Kate," Stevie said. "I was hoping we could have a bite next week, once I've gotten settled in. Can't take those long lazy lunches right away, can I?"

Stevie laughed at the idea and Kate did also, although she was sure Stevie had never taken a lunch that was either long or lazy. Forty-five minutes was the longest they had ever had together and that was interrupted by two calls on her cell phone. Once they had gone to a Mostly Mozart concert together and she had spent the intermission talking to a printer's rep.

"I can't believe you have a job already."

"You're the one who told me about all the rumors. I've been working on this for months. How is Roger, anyway?"

"He's good. We had a fight. But we made up."

"You must be out of your mind to ever fight with him."

"People have said that."

"I'm serious, Kate. A nice guy *and* a lawyer for a big firm. Do you know what they make?"

"Babies and a house in Westchester with a heated pool?"

"Oh, the horror! The horror!" Stevie whined mockingly. "Uh oh, I have a call coming in."

"I'll let you go. I know you're busy. But congratulations!"

"Thanks, Kate. I'll call you. And if anything opens up here…"

"You'll know where to find me. At least until the money for rent runs out."

"You'll find a job in a week, Kate. Trust me. And I really am watching out for you here. I spoke very highly of you."

"Thank you, Stevie."

~ * ~

Kate didn't have it in her to call another supposedly jobless co-worker from Hiroth Publishing just yet and had no idea who else among her coterie of friends might be unoccupied during normal working hours. But it was too quiet and too lonely for her to spend a nice summer day in her apartment. So she put on her bathing suit under her clothes, packed a bag with a sheet, a towel, a wonderfully trashy novel Sally had lent her, and what was left of her suntan lotion, and went off to the subway at 86th and Lexington. She had transferred to the A at Fulton Street and the cars had emerged onto the elevated tracks before she remembered the last time she had made this trip.

Corinne had been a freelancer for Hiroth Publishing. She was somewhat older than Kate, with beautiful features and long straight black hair and the very calm demeanor of an artist who has found her niche. She had lived in New York all her life and had a rent stabilized apartment on the Upper West Side. It had been summer and very hot, and Corinne had invited Kate to go swimming with her.

"Some of the best beaches in the world are just a subway ride away," Corinne had said. "One token."

With Corinne leading the way, they had taken the long ride on the A Train to Beach 67th Street, avoiding the crowds of Rockaway Park with its rides and Coney Island atmosphere.

They had gone in the water several times that day. Then Corinne had sat in her low beach chair and sketched boats passing in the distance and people lying on the sand or walking along the jetty. Kate had worked on a sand castle decorated with pieces of drift wood and sea gull feathers, and shells for doors. When she looked up, she saw that Corinne was drawing her.

It had been a thoroughly pleasant day, until they got back to Corinne's apartment and her new friend offered to apply lotion to the red areas on Kate's back and across her chest, including the parts that had not yet seen the sun. Politely, Kate had declined, and over a slightly awkward dinner, Corinne had confided that since Carla was Kate's mother, she had just assumed...

Sorry. Just one more way that daughter was not like mother.

Kate had wanted to come to this beach with Roger. But every time she raised the idea, he laughed it off. An hour on the A train? Did she like inflicting pain on herself?

It was difficult to explain. Perhaps Carla's deep distrust of wealth and of people with wealth had permeated to her soul. But even with a job, Kate had wanted to see how little money she could live on, just in case things didn't work out.

Today she took the same route she had with Corinne. The beach was nearly empty. She swam for an hour out beyond the line where the waves broke. She emerged exhausted and lay on the sheet with her arms and legs aching and her heart pounding and the sun hot on her skin. It was exactly what she had wanted.

~ * ~

She waited for the lifeguard's last whistle before she started home again. By the time she got to the Fulton Street stop, she persuaded herself that getting off the A train and having to switch to the No. 4 was a mistake. The connecting tunnels would be airless, hot and crowded. All the benefits of the day would be lost in a half hour elbow-to-elbow with successfully employed commuters. Instead, she decided to stay on the A to 59th and then switch to the local. At 86th she could catch an air-conditioned cross-town bus.

It wasn't until she actually came out of the ground at the 86th station that she admitted to herself that she was going to walk by Anthony's building, just to see the place. She was not prepared for what she found.

The northward march of the yuppies had so far missed this building and the ones to either side. Someone had indeed painted the place pink, but that was many years ago. Much of the exterior was peeled down to the original brownstone. The old stonework looked as though it had a rare skin disease.

Clearly, the building was slated for demolition. Weeds grew in the sidewalk cracks and at the edge of the building's front wall. Boards covered the windows on the first and fourth floors. Beside the front stoop and in the corners of the steps were broken bottles and piles of trash. Above the door, which hung open and askew on a single hinge, was a sign announcing the name of a relocation agency that was finding the tenants new "homes." In a matter of a month, Kate guessed, this building and the two that adjoined it would be rubble in a landfill in New Jersey. Condominiums were in this block's future.

Anthony would move on to a neighborhood with more buildings like this one, and Jenny would be dragged along with him.

She was still standing across the street when she saw two young men come out of the entrance. The one who seemed to be in charge was Hispanic. He wore a white short-sleeve t-shirt that displayed a well-muscled set of shoulders and more tattoos on his caramel-colored skin than she could properly appreciate. His dark, curly hair was recently cut. The other man was black. Long dreadlocks fell down his back and were tied in a loose ponytail. A gold necklace glittered around his neck, matching the single hoop earring in his left lobe. The black guy carried a package.

They both got into the back seat of a new model BMW that had been double-parked with the engine running. The instant the door closed, the car took off. It was not possible to see through the tinted glass. Were they watching her watch them?

Kate took a deep breath, crossed the street and went up the front steps of Anthony's building. In the foyer she saw that L. Gilmour and A. Tosca shared apartment 3B. She started up.

The hallways smelled of urine. The stairs creaked. Roaches scurried into the walls' cracks as she continued. She hoped there would not be any rats. She wasn't sure she would have the courage to keep going if she saw one.

On the third floor she found the correct door. If there were any question, it was dispelled by the mail lying on the floor. Mixed into the usual "occupant" letters were a series of legal notices with Linda's name on them. Several summonses had been taped to the door. They all had threatening words printed in bold and capital letters.

American Express. MasterCard. Visa. Bloomingdales. Macy's. They all were fed up with good old Linda.

"Final notice. Your credit may be affected."

It was laughable until she happened to look at some of the names and addresses more closely. L. Gilmour, President, L. Gilmour Corp. Ms. Linda Gilmour, Gilmour Services. She imagined they were all phony. And suddenly she wondered if this is what made Linda disappear so abruptly on Sally. Was she running from the law, or already caught and in jail?

The upper lock had been removed on the apartment door, and as she peered through the hole that was left, the door swung open.

She almost turned and ran.

"Hello!" she called.

The apartment was filthy. Bags of take-out food were on every empty surface. What furniture there was seemed on the verge of collapse. She heard a slight rustling and a little gray mouse raced for a corner where it disappeared under the molding. She could handle a mouse.

"Anthony? Jenny?"

She walked into the living room. A slide-through kitchen was off to one side. Beyond, she could see a door to a bedroom.

"Jenny?" she called again.

Then she saw Anthony lying on the floor with a rubber hose tied around his arm. The needle was still stuck in the vein. A droplet of blood was drying on his skin. There were red marks on his wrists. A few feet away a leather belt lay on the bare floor. In a flash of recognition, she remembered the two men who had left. Had they done this?

She put a finger to his wrist. There was a pulse, but barely.

Quickly, she looked in the bedroom and the bathroom, calling out for Jenny over and over. In a dresser drawer she found an envelope with the girl's name printed on the front. She stuffed it in her pocket.

Jenny's clothing was still in a suitcase inside one of the closets. Then she had an idea.

Carrying the suitcase, she went back out to the hall and raced up to the roof. There, she found Jenny in a corner with Miranda.

"Katy!!" the girl cried in the familiar voice of the doll. "Oh, Katy! I told Jenny you would come. I told her!!"

"Come on," Kate said. "I have to get you guys out of here."

"Is he dead, Katy?"

"No, he's not dead. Not yet anyway. Please, let's not talk about it now. Let's just go."

She ran down the stairs with the child. At the foyer she paused. She couldn't even say why; just to look out and see if anyone was watching.

She was at the corner of Central Park West before she found a phone booth. She didn't want to use her cell.

Cursing herself, she dialed 911.

"There's a man who gave himself an overdose at fifty-two West 85th Street. Apartment three B. Please hurry."

"And who is this?" the operator asked.

"A bystander," Kate responded. "An innocent bystander. And if you keep asking questions, this guy is going to die!"

Then she hung up.

While she and Jenny were still waiting to get on the 86th Street cross-town bus, she heard the siren. It was a quick response. EMS on the job. She wasn't sure whether she felt good or bad about that.

Six

Kate dropped Jenny off with Sally as soon as she returned from Anthony's apartment. The transition was made easier by the fact that Jenny had fallen asleep in the cab on the way home, completely exhausted from the prior two days. Kate told Sally that she had found Anthony unconscious, the apparent victim of a drug overdose, and called 911, but she was too tired herself at that point and too confused to even attempt to give more of the details.

"Maybe I should have stayed there until the ambulance arrived," she said. "Maybe I shouldn't have just taken Jenny with me. I can't believe I just took her."

She was genuinely mystified by her actions. What was it that had caused her to climb the stairs of that horrible building and to grab the kid and just run, without thinking of the consequences either for herself or the child?

"Go on home and get some rest," Sally said. "You look like you're ready to keel over yourself. I'll let Linda know what happened. Don't worry about nuthin'."

Kate nodded, but remained standing in the hallway outside of Sally's door, frozen by her fatigue and what had just transpired. Sally put her hand on Kate's shoulder at the base of her neck and gave her a quick massage that was rough and tender at the same time.

"Hey, ya did good, Katy," she said. "Ya did the right thing. Welcome to the freakin' real world."

~ * ~

Later that evening, Sally knocked on Kate's door.

"The bastard survived," Sally said. "I was just down at Roosevelt Hospital. Freakin' EMS got to him just in time. Couldn't you have waited five more freakin' minutes to call?"

"You would have done the same thing."

"Don't be so sure what I would have done."

"He's Jenny's father. I couldn't just let him die there."

"If you knowed him a little better, it wouldn't have been so hard. He's a lowlife druggie. He thought he was cheatin' the feakin' world, but he made the mistake all of the dealers make sooner or later, he started trying the merchandise himself."

"Did he get Linda hooked?"

"Nah. Linda never did cocaine or heroin. She likes booze too much. Her mistake was ever taking up with the guy. He was a pretty boy. Always dressed real good. Beautiful car. I told her all the pretty boys are the jealous type. But she wouldn't listen. She was hot for him. Early on, she thought it was kind of cute. It proved how much he loved her. If Tony saw her talking nice to some guy, the guy better watch out. Big time. But then, it just got worse and worse. Maybe it was the drugs. Maybe he's just a freakin' crazy man. He started slapping her. Then he used his fists. Put her in the hospital once, at least that I know of. That knife of his will be next. Of course, now he says he's over her. He told me that tonight. But I know he ain't."

"Wait... You talked to him?"

"Yeah, for a minute or so. Linda asked me to. And you know what? This'll show you what a piece of shit he is—he wanted me to go up to the apartment and hide his stash for him until he was out. I told him, 'No freakin' way.' Can you imagine him asking me to do that? He knows I work for freakin' law firms. He tells me I'm just a freakin' bookkeeper, what am I worried about? Piece of shit! If I get picked up with a stash of dope, I'm dead meat. I'd lose all my freakin' jobs. But that's the way the pretty boys are. Everything is for them. Anyway, the cops probably found it. They're always looking to make a buck off somebody's stash."

"I think someone else did, Sally. Just as I was arriving at his building, I saw two guys coming out and getting into a BMW with tinted glass. One of them was carrying a package."

"How do you know they were coming from Anthony's apartment? You ask them?"

"When I got upstairs, I saw a belt lying on the floor near to Anthony. He wasn't wearing one. And his wrists were red, as though they had been bound. I think they tried to kill him and wanted it to look like a drug overdose."

Sally hesitated a moment. A hint of a smile appeared grudgingly on her lips.

"Okay, Sherlock. That's exactly what happened. Anthony says he thinks he knows the guys. They've been trying to cut in on his territory. Now, do yourself a big freakin' favor, okay. Forget everything you saw. Don't tell Anthony. Don't tell Linda. Don't tell anybody."

"Do you think he's coming over here again?"

"No. They worked it out. Everything is agreed. Jenny's with me again."

"Just like that?"

"Anthony has other things to worry about right now, Katy. He don't need a kid getting in the way all the time. Plus, some part of him really loves Linda. After he put her in the hospital, she didn't go back to him, and now he keeps hoping she and him are getting back together someday. So they talked and made some arrangement. She'll keep in touch. He likes to know where she is. Likes to be able to talk to her."

"That doesn't sound good. He wants to control her. That's what jealousy is all about—control."

"I never said he was any freakin' good. What I *said* was it was a shame he ain't in the freakin' morgue right now."

"So Jenny's back with you until Linda returns. And when will that be? Is she in jail, or just on the run?

"What the hell are you talking about?"

"There were all kinds of summonses taped to the door and envelopes with bills and legal notices. Some of them were to Linda, care of some phony business. More than one business."

"How do you know they were phony? Maybe Linda did try to start something. I told you she was a great typist. Her hands were a freakin' blur when she was working."

"This was more credit cards than anybody gets legitimately, Sally. She's in trouble. Maybe the police are after *her*."

"Oh for Christ's sake."

"You did know about this, right?"

"Know, shmow. How the hell did you think she bought that stuff for the kid? A freakin' trust fund? You thought maybe her name was Linda freakin' Trump? Huh?"

"I didn't think she was a thief."

"A thief? The banks send her freakin' cards in the mail. They practically beg you to use the things. They send those freakin' checks five at a time... so she did like they wanted. She used 'em. It ain't a big deal, Katy. There are no cops after her."

"Then what the hell is really going on here, Sally? If it isn't the cops, who is after her? Why is she hiding from her own daughter?"

Sally hesitated. The theme song from *The Simpsons* could be heard through Sally's front door, meaning Jerry was home. Still, Sally whispered.

"I understand what you're saying, but you're so far off, Katy, it's not even funny. There's nobody *after* her."

"Then what is it? I think I deserve to know what's going on, Sally. Especially after today."

"Okay, okay. Look, I would have told you, but she didn't want the kid to know. She made me swear."

"What? Swear what?"

Sally hesitated, glancing up the deserted stairs. Her fingers tugged at her right ear lobe. Then she took a few steps away from her apartment door and Kate followed.

"She's pregnant," Sally said finally.

"Pregnant!"

"That's it. That's all."

"Jesus Christ... Make some sense, will you."

"I am, if you'd freakin' listen to me. She's pregnant and she won't have an abortion. There it is. End of story. I told her she was crazy. 'Not me,' I said. 'I wouldn't.' Going through all that just to..."

"Just to what?"

She squinted at Kate in the dim hallway light.

"Katy, what is this, your dumb time of the month? That's the whole point of this. She can't keep the baby. She can barely afford to keep Jenny. Get it now? She was starting to show and she didn't want Jenny to see her. Do you want me to write this down?"

"But..."

"Don't start in with the twenty questions routine again. I don't know what makes her freakin' tick. She asked me to do her a favor and I am. That's all."

"Then she's in New York. Where? I want to talk to her."

"I don't know where she is."

"I don't believe you."

"That's the God's honest truth, Katy. I swear on my mother's eyes. She calls me pretty regular, and every once in a while she stops by late at night. Looks in on Jenny asleep. Gives her a kiss. Leaves a little present. That's it. I don't need to know more and I don't want to know more. And neither should you."

"Do you tell her how Jenny is when Linda's not here? Being lonely all the time can't be worse for her than knowing about the baby. Have you told her that?"

"Of course I tell her. Over and over again like a freakin' broken record. She doesn't want the kid to know. And anyway, they won't let her keep the kid with her."

"What?"

"That's what she says. I don't know. Sometimes I think she's for real and other times I think this is just another one of her cons. You know, there was a reason she and Tony got together once. Each of them thought they were freakin' smarter than anybody. They were always looking for a con, some angle to get some dough without working for it. Maybe now she's just thinking of it as a little vacation from the kid. Who really knows? I mean someone out there is giving her free room and board until the baby comes. Fresh sheets. A sunny room with long, lacy curtains in the windows... Look, I'm sorry, she's an old friend. She ain't perfect, but you can see why I wanted to help her out, right? You see why I couldn't tell? I mean, it's not something she's been wanting to advertise."

Kate suddenly felt extremely tired. She leaned against the wall, trying without success to imagine herself in Linda's situation, so desperate that she would have a baby and give it away. Sally stood beside her, quiet and solemn in the pale yellow light of the hallway.

"I'll tell you something else, though, Katy. Much as I wanted to help her, I don't think I can do this much longer. I mean, you've seen the kid. Imagine her twenty-four-seven. You see what it's like for me."

"Yeah," Kate said, rubbing her eyelids to drive away the fatigue that weighed them down.

"I mean, nobody can take this kid's shit forever. Her own mother's gone. Think about that, Katy. I mean let's be honest here. Her own mother *left her*. That's the bottom line. I mean, if she couldn't hack it with the kid, why am I busting my rear end? Why should I put up with this shit? Do you know what I'm saying?"

Kate nodded, but couldn't bring herself to say 'yes.' She wanted the conversation to end and felt a swell of relief as the door to Sally's apartment opened and Jerry came out.

"Hey, Sal! What the hell're you doing out here? The kid is still up and making so much noise I can't watch TV."

"Turn the TV down and tell her to go back to sleep before I paddle her rear-end good."

"I can't hear the fuckin' thing if I turn it down."

He turned away, irritated, and went back into the apartment.

Sally gave Kate a look and rolled her eyes.

"He never heard of freakin' earphones." Then she called out after him in a falsetto, "Coming soon, honey-bunny!"

Jerry slammed the door in response.

"C'mon in with me, Katy, and say goodnight. Okay?"

She took Kate by the hand and led the way into her apartment. In a small room off the living room, Jenny was lying on a cot, the covers pulled up over her head and arranged so there was an opening to breathe through. The top of Miranda's hair was just visible inside the opening.

"Jenny?" Kate whispered. The child stirred. "Miranda?"

"Oh, Christ," Sally said and walked back into the living room, leaving them alone.

The sheet and blankets were peeled back slowly so Miranda's little doll face emerged, her black hair tousled as though she had been roused from a deep sleep.

"Hi, Katy!" Miranda whispered, hopping gently back and forth in greeting.

"Sally went over to the hospital, Jenny," Kate said. "Your... your dad is okay. I just wanted you to know."

There was silence for a minute or so. It seemed much longer. In the distance she could hear the opening of a rerun of Seinfeld on the TV.

"He's not my father!" a small, nearly imperceptible voice said from deep inside the mound of covers.

"What did you say? Jenny? Miranda?"

The doll bounced on the bed to emphasize the words.

"He's *not* her father. They tell her he is, but he's *not*. She *knows* he's not."

"But Jenny."

"He's not! She knows he's not!"

"Okay, I'm sorry. I didn't mean anything bad. Try to go to sleep."

"Do you believe her, Katy?" Miranda asked. "Do you?"

Kate gently moved back the covers until Jenny's round face was visible at last. Her brow was deeply furrowed, waiting intently for the answer, more serious than a six year old should ever be. Had she herself ever been so serious?

She kissed the child on her forehead, once on the left, once on the right, once in the middle.

"Yes, I believe you," she said. "And I won't let him take you over there again."

Jenny was quiet. Her eyes searched Kate's. Then she lifted up Miranda and pressed her against Kate's cheek and made a kissing sound.

"Goodnight," she said.

Seven

Those parting words to Jenny kept Kate awake long after she returned home and crawled into bed. The fact was that she had no power to deliver on that promise and should not have made it. Kate remembered the many times she had been disappointed in her own youth, believing that her mother would tear herself away from one or more of her wonderful, hard-luck clients, only to be told that whatever event was scheduled would have to be "put off," adjourned *sine die*, as Carla would say in her attempt at lawyer humor. The people she served were the exploited, the defeated, the beaten. How could anyone ever compete with such neediness?

But maybe Jenny at age six was more adept than Kate had ever been in recognizing how undependable the words of adults actually were, including the words of the adults we love the most, and most especially those we want desperately to love us. Wasn't that at least a part of the message Jenny was sending when she refused to talk? Engaging another person in conversation requires a certain level of trust, and Jenny did not have enough of that emotional commodity to spare anymore. So didn't it follow that she had probably already forgotten Kate's rash commitment—ignored it the way that Kate had also begun eventually to discount Carla's promises to her about the time they would have together in some perfect future moment?

The thought of Jenny lumping Kate together with the other adults in her life caused Kate to sit up in her bed. But it was probably better that way. There was so little Kate could do. She got up and fished in her dresser for the envelope she had taken from Anthony's apartment and in the dim light of the end table lamp, she read through the contents for the second time that night. Then she put it into the pocket of her jeans. She had a plan for the next day that might help Jenny. But once she had fulfilled her promise to the extent that she could, Kate was determined to take the advice of Roger and Sally and mind her own business, avoid future entanglements with the child, let Linda take care of her kid! So resolved, she went back to her bed, and soon after her head hit the pillow, she was finally able to sleep.

~ * ~

The next morning she was up early and on her way before anyone in the building stirred. Her primary task was to visit the unemployment office as everyone had urged her to do for the past several days. Deep inside she believed there was a good reason for delay. Until she started looking actively, she could tell herself it would be easy to get another job. Until that first New York State check came in the mail, she wouldn't have to worry about the payments eventually stopping.

She walked to the unemployment office, taking a favorite route down Lexington Avenue. Here it was possible to imagine what the city must have been like when it was still a working class town and men went to jobs in factories along the East River and below 42nd Street, before Avenue 'A' became 'East End' and names such as Soho and Tribeca entered the vernacular.

Lexington had its doorman buildings, but none was taller than twelve stories. There were townhouses also, but most of them had been carved up into apartments during the Depression. And virtually all of the buildings, even the tenements, had been designed with the apparent belief that a facade was not just a wall with a door and windows in it, but something important. Stone carvings were everywhere: a Nemean lion at 91st, a helmeted Athena a block farther down, half-naked Aphrodite at 87th, an eagle at 82nd, cherubs singing at the Church of St. Jean Le Baptiste at 76th[h] and the motley crew of heads at Hunter College whispering commentary on the passersby. It was a welcome distraction from anything, and especially from the business of being without a job.

Like a long-avoided trip to the dentist, Kate found the unemployment office on West 54th to be as bad as she'd expected. Fluorescent lights buzzed overhead and blinked on and off randomly as she shuffled along the "A to L" line. She counted bubble gum blotches on the floor. She tried to decide what color the ceiling tile had been when new. She avoided eye contact. And at long last she was privileged to stand in front of a clerk with a serious passive/aggressive disorder, who first talked so softly Kate could not hear her and then sarcastically pointed out that she had written her address in the wrong space. On the plus side, the walk, the wait and the verbal abuse took up most of the morning.

Emerging into sunlight, she walked to Broadway and turned south, heading for Battery Park. It was a sunny day and a trip on the Staten Island Ferry seemed inviting. The crowds wouldn't bother her. She was sure there was not a living soul among the tall buildings of Wall Street whose job she envied.

At Canal Street, she headed east to Lafayette, stopped for a bowl of wonton soup at the fringes of Chinatown, and continued south again to The Family Court for New York County. Here she planned to perform her last official errand for the benefit of the kid.

On the 8th floor, she entered the clerk's office. She stood off to the side and crossed her arms and tapped her foot elaborately, finally engaging the attention of the chief file clerk, who was busy at one end of the counter. The object of her foot-tapping was a large woman with handsome features, long braided hair and smooth skin the color of a Milky Way bar's center. When she saw Kate, she narrowed her eyes in mock anger, before smiling broadly and walking around the counter to embrace her. Gail Harding had known her for years, since Kate was old enough to deliver Carla's papers to the court for filing. Carla's office in those days was on 14th Street and Kate's pay had been one dollar on top of subway fare. To save money, she had started walking home and discovered Tompkins Square Park and the East Village. *Those were the days,* Kate thought.

"I know you didn't come down here just to see me, honey," she said finally. "But you don't mind if I *act* like you did."

"I'm sorry, Gail. I've been meaning to stop by. But you know how it is."

"Yes, Lord, I do. I haven't seen my own daughter for two weeks, and she lives in my building."

Gail started laughing, eyes closed, shoulders curled inward. Almost as quickly, she became serious.

"I didn't mean that the way it came out, exactly," she said. "I wasn't meaning to talk about you and your mom. I don't go there."

"Don't worry about it," Kate said.

Kate reached into her pocket and pulled out the birth certificate she had taken from Anthony's dresser the day he lay near death in his apartment. She handed it to Gail.

"Does this look real to you?"

Gail placed it on the counter top and smoothed it out. She stared hard at it for a minute, then shrugged.

"The certification's real. You can see how the seal is raised."

"C'mon, Gail…"

"Okay, the father's name is a little off, like it was added later. Maybe yes, maybe no. Happy now?"

"No, as a matter of fact. I want to know for sure whether the name of Tosca is on the original birth certificate on file with the city."

"Only one way to know for sure. Get another copy of the original on file." She shrugged her big shoulders and glanced at Kate. Then she frowned. "Oh, *now* I get it. Now I see why little Kate has come to see her old friend Gail after so many years, after ignoring the courthouse like it held plague germs or some damn thing. Gail's got friends over in the Health Department. Gail'll bend the rules for little Kate."

"It's for a good cause, Gail. I promise."

"Oh, shit. Here we go. Where have I heard that before? Good cause, great cause, *wonderful* cause. Just once I'd like to hear a damned Andersen woman say she needs a favor from ol' Gail because she was backing a *bad* cause. Something *evil.* "

Gail let out an angry grunt to punctuate her speech, but folded the birth certificate carefully and put it in her pocket.

Kate wrote her address and phone number on a scrap of paper and gave it to Gail.

"I appreciate your help, Gail." She kissed the woman on the cheek and they hugged. "And please, if you see Carla, don't tell her about this, okay."

"Now, that's wrong of you, Kate. That's just wrong to be telling me what I can be sayin' to people. I'm a mother. Carla's a mother. Mothers talk, Kate."

"It would be a special favor, Gail."

Gail shook her head and went back to the other side of the counter.

"Okay, if that's the way you want it. But, damn if you ain't just like her!" She picked up a stack of files and put them down again with a loud smack. "*Damn* if you ain't! And just you try to stop me from thinking it!"

~ * ~

Kate kept herself busy for the rest of the day, well away from her apartment building. She had dinner alone in Chinatown and stopped for a movie at 86th Street. It was late when she finally got home and collapsed into her bed for the night. There was no sign of Jenny at Mrs. Morley's window, or on the stairs, and Kate allowed herself a bit of optimism as the waves of drowsiness pulled her into sleep. Maybe the kid's situation wasn't so dire. Jenny's mother was really trying to do what she felt was best for the child. Maybe she would work it out for the best. Maybe Linda would evolve a plan that included Jenny.

That fantasy was over early the next morning.

Kate was making coffee when she became aware of Sally's voice through the wood, plaster and brick that separated them. The fragments were sharp and angry and all but incomprehensible until Sally's door opened.

"What the hell are you doing, Creephead? Put your damned sneakers on. I don't have all freakin' day here. If I'm late, my customers don't like it. And if I lose a customer, believe me, there will be hell to pay."

There was a brief pause. Kate stood just inside her own unopened door. She reached for the doorknob and stopped herself. *Stay out of it*, she counseled herself.

"Every damned, freakin' day," Sally muttered. "Every damned day! You know, Creephead, you are wearing me down to a freakin' stub, here. And if you don't freakin' cut it out, I'm going to do something about it, and you're not going to like it. I mean, you may not like me and you may not like Mrs. Morley, but by God, we will be looking pretty goddamn freakin' good when Child Protective Services takes you back. One phone call to CPS is all it would take, Creephead. You could be in a foster home in twenty-four freakin' hours. Is that what you want, Creephead? Huh? Come on, will ya, move it!!"

After a pause that may or may not have contained an answer to the pending question by a girl, or her doll, Kate heard a new commotion and the unmistakable sound of a light body tumbling down the stairs.

"Jesus freakin' Christ. Are you okay? You're trippin' over your own freakin' feet, Creephead."

Again, Kate put her hand on the knob, but stopped herself. There was a garbled reply in the high-pitched tones that Jenny reserved for Miranda. Whatever concern had crept into Sally's voice vanished.

"Don't talk to me with that doll!" Sally screamed. "I warned you before and I ain't warning you again. Either talk like a freakin' human being or don't freakin' talk to me at all! Believe me, I don't have to take this shit. One phone call and you are out of here, kid. You are gone!!"

The rest was indistinguishable amidst pounding footsteps and echoes as they continued down to Mrs. Morley's, and once her front door opened and closed quickly, and the foyer door slammed shut, the building was serene once more.

Kate took her coffee into the bedroom and stretched out on her bed, listening absently to the sounds of life around her. At 8:45, give or take, Mrs. Hartstein in 2B would bring her swaybacked dachshunds outside, their bellies all but dragging on the pavement as they sniffed and snorted and raised a stubby leg. Shortly after 9:00, Mr. Whitman of 1C—Whitey to his friends—would appear in his battered Stetson and walk, smiling serenely, with his small steps to the neighborhood's several grocery stores and delis, buying an item or two at each and gossiping with the cashiers.

Kate was still in her bed, trying to summon the energy to go around the corner for the newspapers, when she heard Mrs. Morley's lilting grandmotherly voice rising up through the building, becoming more and more clear as she slowly climbed the several flights of stairs. First, Kate could make out the breathy refrain, "Jenn-nnyy! Jennn-nnnyyy." And finally her *sotto voce* muttering in the intervals, "Where *is* that child?" Despite the obvious dangers, Kate had to smile at the thought of Jenny flying the coop again, working through more locks on Mrs. Morley's front door than a young Houdini.

Then the stairs to the roof were groaning, and Kate heard the hinges squeak and the metal door slam and the footsteps circle above. After a pause, instead of two people coming down the stairs, there was only Mrs. Morley, her voice warbling suddenly with panic.

"Je-nyyyYYYY. Je-nyyyYYYYYYYY!"

Fearful herself now, Kate sat up and whirled off the bed, grabbing her sneakers, wondering where she should look first, only to be stopped cold by the sight of a form huddled on the fire escape outside her window—two forms, if you count the doll.

"God bless me," Kate whispered.

Jenny had changed both herself and the doll into matching sun-suits of a greenish-blue and white plaid pattern that highlighted the girl's hazel eyes beautifully. Linda had obviously taken some care in selecting them.

Jenny's pretty eyes begged Kate not to send her back to her child's prison in Mrs. Morley's apartment.

"Come in then, for crying out loud," Kate said, her blood still rushing hard through her body as she pulled open the window, but for fear of the fire escape, not of what Sally would do if she found out. "But you've *really* got to stop this climbing around on the fire escape. Really, Jenny, this is *important.* And if you want to spend the afternoon with me, you must promise not to run away. Okay? Will you promise me that?"

With proper solemnity, Jenny took Kate's hand and clasped it firmly to her chest.

"Thank you, Katy," Jenny said in a sweet, thin voice that was her own, not Miranda's. "I promise and Miranda promises too."

~ * ~

One afternoon. That was the explicit bargain she struck with Jenny and Mrs. Morley and, perhaps, the lingering presence of Roger who, looking over her shoulder, raised a skeptical eyebrow at even this limited involvement. He called her every night, and the topic of Jenny had not been raised. Certainly, she hadn't breathed a word about her trip to Anthony's apartment, or the news that Linda was pregnant. And it was the thought of Roger that prompted Kate to make it crystal clear to Jenny that she was looking for a job very actively, and would not be around every day, or even most days. One afternoon! So where was the harm in it? Why not help Mrs. Morley for a few hours and give the child some needed fresh air? Wouldn't the sunshine be good for Kate too? A hint of a tan would be beneficial for the job interviews she was expecting. Where was the down side?

Jenny, who showed no inclination to speak further to Kate after her blurted 'thank-you,' kept to herself on a fluffy pink towel that said 'Bahamas' on it, and was big enough for half a dozen children. She had a picture book open and was pretending to read to Miranda, emphasizing various points in the story with frequent use of the illustrations. She barely intruded on Kate's review of the want ads except when she reprimanded the doll for some obscure breach of etiquette with a yank of the hair or a whack at its plastic head. Then Jenny would look over at Kate and roll her eyes, as though they were both parents of difficult children.

At 4:30, Kate gathered up her things and announced that she was going to take a shower. She also suggested that, after she was finished, Jenny could take her bath at Kate's apartment for a change. It was an innocuous suggestion. The roof was not a clean place, with the pigeons and the ash belched from apartment house boilers, not to mention whatever was wafting through the air on westerly winds from the refineries in New Jersey. Anyone would have agreed that the girl needed a session with soap and water.

However, as Kate stepped from her shower and left the steamy bathroom—wrapped in a soft towel and feeling luxuriant with the tingle of the day's sun on her skin—she experienced a horrible sense of *deja vu*. A draft of air crossed her ankles and crept up her legs.

Entering the living room, she saw the front door wide open. Its two measly locks had presented no challenge at all to a certain little girl!

"Jennyyy!" she called, trying to remain both patient and calm as she walked into the bedroom to check for her there. She quickly lost her composure.

"God-DAMN-it, Jenny!! Jennnyyyyyyy!!!"

Silence answered and Kate burst into the hallway, pausing to scream the girl's name again before racing down the stairs. Her bare feet left a row of wet footprints as she swung around each landing, taking the turns at break-neck speed. At the last flight she nearly ran over Jenny, who was sitting in the middle of a riser with the doll beside her as though watching a movie on TV.

Kate's momentum carried her past the duo and she spun around to face her, too angry to care that she was wearing only a towel and still dripping water.

"Don't you ever, *ever* do that again!" she shouted, shaking her finger like a weapon and stamping her foot.

Jenny was unmoved and apparently untroubled. The transformation of the sweet-voiced girl from earlier was stunning. Her eyes were those of the zombie Kate had originally seen on these very steps a few days before.

Wild with exasperation, Kate snapped her fingers an inch from Jenny's face.

"Hey! Remember me? The one you promised you wouldn't run away from? Get back upstairs for your bath before I introduce your rear end to the palm of my hand!"

This was a threat Carla had used on Kate in her early years with some success, but Jenny still was not impressed. She didn't move a muscle. Apparently, Jenny either didn't believe that Kate would hit her or didn't care.

Kate pulled the towel tighter around her. What was to be done now? Should she repeat the threat, or perhaps change it to one that she was actually prepared to do, like picking the kid up by the ankles and shaking her hair out?

Help arrived from Mrs. Morley who opened her front door and shambled into the hallway as quickly as her arthritic joints could carry her.

"Oh, dear," she said. "I should have told you, Kate. This is all my fault."

Mrs. Morley motioned for Jenny, and the girl stood up, docile as a baby lamb, walking soundlessly down the stairs and slipping inside the door of Mrs. Morley's apartment.

"Tell me what, Mrs. Morley?"

"The bath, Kate. She just won't do it. It's not you. Only Sally can get her to take one. I can't either."

"But why in the world…"

"Oh, Kate," Mrs. Morley said wearily. "I don't know. Some children get that way. One bad experience in the tub and they won't go back unless you practically tie them up. My third child was like that for months because the water was too hot one time. A neighbor's baby swallowed water once. He fought like a banshee for a year. It happens. And with the foster homes that Jenny's been in, well… Who knows what went on?"

"Foster homes? Is that what you said? When was she in a foster home?"

Sally had spoken of Child Protective Services and foster homes, but Kate hadn't considered that Jenny had actually spent time in the system. She had imagined it was a threat Sally used for effect, not words that had a firm reality to Jenny.

Mrs. Morley shook her head, letting out a breath that was part sigh, part laugh, and part sob.

"Didn't Sally tell you anything about the girl?"

Eight

The next morning, Kate had a job interview, so she was up and on her way down the stairs before she was aware of the tumult coming from Sally's apartment. She paused on the landing one floor below, and could soon tell what was happening.

"Every goddamn TIME!" Sally was shouting. "You smell like a rat's ass. Get in the freakin' water, for the love of CHRIST!! And stop with the freakin' doll talk or I'm throwing it out the freakin' window. Creephead, I swear to God I will."

Kate just shook her head and continued walking down the stairs and out onto the sidewalk. "See, Roger?" she said to his lingering presence. "I did it. She's someone else's problem again. Not mine."

~ * ~

She hadn't been particularly hopeful about this job prospect when she'd sent in her resume. The ad had said the company was looking for someone with experience in trade books, and Kate had never worked with anything but textbooks at Hiroth Publishing. But during the interview, she seemed to hit it off with the editor who was doing the hiring, a woman by the name of Ruth Chandler. Somehow they got on the topic of walking to work, and soon the two of them were comparing the various avenues for sidewalk width, congestion, and visual interest. Ruth liked Park Avenue because it didn't have buses or trucks, but complained about the lights, which were not synchronized

"That's not really a problem," Kate said. "I timed those lights once. They change every forty-five seconds. So what you have to do is start as soon as the light turns and walk each block in just that amount of time, which is do-able. You'll never have to stop for a light. Plus, it's a good pace—twenty blocks to a mile, forty-five seconds each— exactly a fifteen-minute mile. The only problem is, if you walk that fast, you can't look at the fossils."

"Wait a sec. What fossils?"

"The big buildings on Park mostly have limestone facades and some of them have some very nice fossils embedded in the stone. Check out the building on the northeast corner of 72nd Street. And the one just south of Hunter College, a few more blocks down.

"And the lights. You say you actually timed the lights?"

"Do you think I would make something like that up? My boyfriend thinks I'm a little nuts. Actually, on good days, he thinks I'm a *little* nuts. On bad days, he thinks I'm a lot nuts."

Ruth smiled at her and made a note on her resume.

"You're a woman after my own heart," she said.

At the end of the interview, Ruth said she did have a few more candidates scheduled to meet, but she was *sure* that they would be talking again. Kate left on a cloud of well-being, thinking she would soon be rejoining the ranks of the employed.

It wasn't yet noon when she got back home again and knocked at Mrs. Morley's door. Apparently, the altercation with Kate from the night before was forgotten. Miranda squealed with delight at the sight of Kate and bestowed numerous kisses upon her, even before Kate said she was thinking that maybe a picnic lunch in Central Park would be nice.

More news awaited Kate upstairs. Her mail included an envelope from the Family Court clerk's office that she ripped open to find a note from Gail saying, "You were right." Enclosed was a certified copy of Jenny's birth record. The space for the name of her father was blank. Kate had learned enough from listening to Carla hold forth over the years to know that, even if Anthony was in fact Jenny's biological father, with that birth certificate he had no more rights than Kate did to the kid until a judge officially determined his paternity. She was willing to bet that hadn't happened. If it had, there would be no need for the forgery.

"The hell with him then," Kate muttered to herself.

"What is it, Katy?" Miranda asked her.

"Something I have to talk to Jenny about," Kate said.

Jenny's cheeks reddened and she bowed her head.

"It's about your father, Jenny. About Anthony."

"He's not my father," the girl whispered.

"I don't think he is either. But now I have a document—a piece of paper that can help us if he tries to take you away again."

Jenny wrapped her arms around Kate and buried her head in Kate's chest.

"I don't ever want to go back there again, Katy," she whispered.

"Then you won't."

~ * ~

It was a beautiful day, and they soon started on their expedition. The sky was clear and blue with fluffy clouds floating high above the treetops. Once they reached Fifth Avenue and entered the Park, Jenny's mood seemed to soar into those boundless regions. With Miranda cart-wheeling along at the end of her arm, the girl raced ahead and skipped back to Kate again. She looked in every baby carriage. She catapulted onto and off of the benches. She picked up funny-shaped sticks and a brass button and other treasures that caught her eye. At Belvedere Castle, Kate bought a soft pretzel, which they broke up and fed to a contingent of mallards at Turtle Pond. Jenny laughed out loud when Kate told her that the ducks with all the fancy colors were the men ducks.

"Pretty boys," Kate said.

"Pretty boys!" Jenny repeated, laughing again. "Pretty boys!"

A woman after my own heart, Kate thought.

For lunch, they climbed out onto the rocks surrounding the castle and found a shady spot that overlooked the pond and the Great Lawn and the Delacorte Theater. Workers were constructing a set for the next production. Kate explained to Jenny that people came early on show nights in the summer and waited in line with a picnic supper to get the tickets. Jenny and Miranda both agreed this was something they would definitely like to do.

Afterward, they wandered south and east along the paths. They stopped to watch a group of watercolorists painting pictures of the pine trees on Cedar Hill. They ducked under the Glade Arch and checked out the echoes. At 76th Street, they hopped on one foot into the playground, Jenny took a ride on a swing, and they hopped out again. When they reached the Conservatory Water, Jenny's eyes widened at the armada of miniature sailboats and battleships and even a submarine that skulked beneath the water like a crocodile hoping for a meal.

Kate had planned to leave the park at this point and catch a bus back up Madison for home. It was getting late. The crowds were thinning out. The problem was that Jenny was completely enthralled by the water and the boats and the statue of Alice in Wonderland that was big enough for several kids to climb on at once. She pleaded to stay.

"Just a little while, Katy," she said. "Oh please, just a little, little, *little* while?"

It was only the third or fourth time that Jenny had actually spoken to Kate directly and not through the doll. And Kate also remembered the countless times as a girl when Carla had had to hurry back to the office from a playground or a party because a client was coming to meet her and couldn't ever be delayed, even for a little, little minute. Both seemed compelling reasons to spread their blanket out on the hill at the south end of the area. With the slight elevation, she figured she could rest and still watch Jenny, but to her surprise, when she reclined on the blanket, Jenny did not run off to play. Instead, she plopped onto the blanket and nestled her head comfortably against Kate's leg. Miranda was propped against Jenny's small, bony hip.

It was a nice moment in a very nice day. Feeling like they were old buddies, Kate told Jenny about the great interview she had had that morning and how she was confident she'd nailed the job. She'd be back to work soon!

She felt Jenny's head twist abruptly and in her sweet voice the girl asked,

"When, Katy?"

"I don't know. Next week, maybe. Or the week after. The sooner the better. I can't wait to get back into it again."

A taut nod of that little head followed. Then Jenny scrambled to her feet and Miranda said in a squeaky high-pitched voice that she wanted to *play,* not *sleep.* There was an edgy tone to those words that a mother with years of experience might have taken as a warning. However, Kate, with only a few days of parent-for-hire combat training, merely reminded Jenny not to go too near the water and watched while the darling child proceeded to march right down to that exact forbidden spot and stand with one foot poised on the curved concrete edge that surrounded the pond.

"You little rascal, get away from there," Kate murmured. She was smiling until she saw that Jenny's expression was not of cute mischief.

Kate sat up, angrily jabbing her finger toward the water and shaking her head vigorously. Her sign language message was plain, and so was Jenny's response. Holding Miranda out in her left hand and a stick she had picked up in her right, Jenny stepped directly onto the concrete edge as if it were a tightrope and she was the main attraction in a three ring circus.

"Hey!!" Kate shouted. "Get off of there, Jenny!! Hey, do you hear me?!!"

Kate got to her feet and waved her arm in a wide flourish as she had seen done many times by mothers on the beaches of Montauk when their children were going out too deep.

With equal flourish, Jenny ignored her.

"Come here right this minute!!" Kate yelled and started trotting down the incline to the pond.

Jenny's eyes had assumed that vacant zombie stare while she walked along the edge. Her arms were extended for balance; her steps were as precise as a ballerina; she was grace incarnate until her sneaker slipped on a piece of wet paper and she spun, arms flailing, into the air.

"Katy!!" she screamed, then hit the water and disappeared beneath.

Kate raced down the hill to the reflecting pool and reached the edge as Jenny thrashed her way to the surface. Immediately, she jumped in after her, struggling to maintain her balance in the thick muck of dead leaves and dirt that coated the bottom of the pond. She stumbled once and the water rose almost to her chin until she could regain her footing. The girl was coughing and gasping for air when

Kate finally grabbed her and held her tight for a moment, patting and rubbing her back to comfort her.

She waded to the sidewall and lifted Jenny onto the lip of the pool. Jenny was still coughing up water, frightened and contrite, trying to avoid her gaze. Kate didn't think it was the time to say, "I told you so!"

Then, Kate became aware of the smell rising from the water and muck she had stirred up from the bottom.

She held her nose and said in a nasal voice,

"Hoo boy! Sometink 'tink!!!"

Jenny giggled. She looked at Kate and looked away again.

"Sometink tink real bad," Kate continued. "I tink sometink tink so bad we have plenty of room on the bus. What you tink?"

Jenny giggled again and Kate started to laugh, but then Jenny dissolved into tears. She threw her arms around Kate's neck, her body heaved with sobs.

"I'm sorry," Jenny said. "Katy, I'm so sorry!"

"It's okay."

Kate hugged her again and again until the tears and sobbing slowed. Then she lifted herself up out of the water and onto the concrete.

She put her arm around Jenny. They sat for a moment. The girl preened Miranda's hair and tried to wipe off some of the dirt.

"I hate to bring this up," Kate said. "But Miranda's going to need a bath."

"Uh oh," Jenny said then. "Miranda hates taking a bath." She leaned her head and body against Kate. "I'm sorry, Katy. I'm sorry I'm so bad all the time."

"You're not bad," Kate said. "You're a kid. Sometimes kids do stuff that isn't smart. But that's nothing but normal, Jenny. You're just a normal kid."

They got up and turned around to see that a small crowd of mothers and children had gathered.

"That's all, folks," Kate said. "Next show in one hour."

~ * ~

When they arrived at Kate's apartment, Jenny announced it was time for Miranda to take her bath, and that Miranda better be good, or else. Kate paid close attention as Jenny washed Miranda's hair at the sink. In a stage whisper, the girl reassured her doll that she would not pour the water over her head all at once or get soap in her eyes. After that, it was easy. Kate stood Jenny by the sink and washed her hair right there, giving her a towel to hold over her eyes to keep the soap out and pouring the rinsing water into the sink and away from her face. By the time they were done with her hair, the bathtub had filled with water and Jenny and Miranda got in and finished the job by themselves. The girl was clean as a whistle and her hair was combed when Kate walked her over to Sally's apartment.

Kate's own shower took a little bit longer. She had a dinner planned with Stevie and a couple of the other refugees from Hiroth Publishing. The occasion required careful clothes selection, a bit of hair styling, and the artful placement of perfume behind each ear. But Kate was feeling pretty good about things as she marched out the front door. She'd already had the job interview to buoy her spirits, and the afternoon with Jenny, despite the pond incident, had further lifted her mood.

On the whole, an excellent day, Kate thought as she left. A very excellent day.

At dinner, she made the mistake of trying to explain to Stevie and the others why she was feeling so happy. But she was met by blank stares when she told them about Jenny and her doll and how they had met and related their adventure that afternoon in the Conservatory

Waters. Something was being lost in the recounting, she told herself. Maybe you had to be there. But then she began to wonder if the whole arrangement with Jenny really was just odd, a diversion at best until she got her life back to normal. It was foolish to think of it as anything more.

She dropped the topic, but Stevie took her aside in the ladies room.

"Are you crazy?" she asked. "Are you, like, *trying* to drive Roger away?"

"Calm down, Stevie."

"Kate, you're taking care of someone else's kid! She's not even related? Do you think Roger is going to want to spend time with her? He's going to run in the opposite direction, like any other guy!"

'I think you're taking this all a little too seriously," said Kate.

"Maybe," Stevie replied. She took a long look at Kate, peering deep into her eyes as Stevie was wont to do, as though it were really possible to see something in there. "But I don't think so. I think something weird is happening to you. So just do me a little favor, if you don't mind. When Roger starts to run, give him a little shove in my direction. You have my number, right? E-mail address? Cell? I'm on Facebook."

"Very funny, Stevie," Kate said.

~ * ~

The bad news came late the next morning. She was aware that the company was going to be making a decision quickly, and when it was Ruth's assistant on the phone, and not Ruth herself, she knew it was going to be an unpleasant conversation. The words came like a punch in the stomach, a chop at the back of the knees, a swift blow to the kidneys. The meaning filtered through from some distant place to some distant person, not her.

"There were many qualified candidates... Ruth is very sorry... Management decided to hire from within... Budget constraints... Ruth is sure you will be getting a job soon... She said to tell you so... And the best of luck!"

"Best of luck!" Kate thought. *You fucking coward. You couldn't pick up the phone? After you practically hired me on the spot. Got my hopes up? Fucking coward! Oh, hell!*

Kate had believed she was too hardened a veteran of life's trials to cry over a lost job and soon found that this also was not true. Tears rolled down her cheeks in great round drops that she tried to ignore, telling herself that it was demeaning. Grown women don't act like this. They laugh when life turns cruel.

She tried to look at the want ads in the *New York Times*, but could not concentrate. Her eyes jumped across the page. The jobs were the same ones that had been in there the whole week, including the one for which she had just been turned down. WONDERFUL OPPORTUNITY, it said. How many of the other ads were also for jobs that were already taken, beyond her reach, existing just to tantalize her, to rub salt in an open wound.

She washed her face and pulled on her sneakers and was ready to take the mother of all walks when she finally noticed the conversation in progress next door. Sally's bedroom was at the rear of the apartment, just as hers was. With her open window, she could hear most of it.

"I'm getting so *tired* of this!"

Kate listened absently, not so much because she was interested in what exactly Sally might be *tired* of, but in the manner of a person paging through magazines in a doctor's office; that is, to occupy the brain against thoughts of rejections yet to come and new and more painful disappointments. As in a dream, the details of the conversation gradually coalesced.

"It's getting late!" Sally said. "Hurry! He's gonna be here!"

This weekend Sally had planned an excursion to Atlantic City with Jerry. That was why she was home so early. The bus was leaving the West Side around two o'clock to make sure they were all there with plenty of time to hit the slots. Two nights in a great room for the price of one. Enough quarters to cover the cost of the bus ride. A no-limit buffet. It was practically a free weekend. Great, huh, Kate?

Great.

"Put your things in the freakin' bag!!" Sally shouted. Then there was silence followed by an inaudible response, apparently coming from Miranda, not Jenny, and then an eruption, a throaty roar of an Amazon going into battle. "I warned you about that!! I warned you! Give me that freakin' thing!"

When Jenny's high-pitched scream was followed by the sound of shattering glass, Kate knew that Miranda had been thrown through the window and was now lying in the courtyard four floors below.

She went to the front door and stood there for a minute. Her temples were throbbing with a blinding headache. She was determined not to get involved. Not again. *I've got my own problems!*

She opened the door, thinking she would race downstairs and into the street and beyond the sound of voices, of crying, of other people's pain. She was surprised to see Sally out in the hall, hunched over a packed suitcase.

"Stupid freakin' goddamn kid," Sally muttered. "Goddamn her freakin' ass, I warned her about that doll."

"Stop it, Sally," Kate said as calmly as she could. "Please."

She steadied herself against the doorjamb and stepped into the hall.

"She's a spoiled rotten brat. A FREAKIN' GODDAMN SPOILED BRAT!" Sally screamed for Jenny's benefit, but loud enough for the entire building and most of 92nd Street to hear.

"Sally, please take it easy."

"Stay out of this, Kate." She closed the suitcase, locked it and stood up. "Christ, if she'd ever pulled that crap with my mother, she'd've been tasting soap for a month. Six months!! Who the hell does she think she is, anyway? I'm doing her a damned favor, taking her in here. Does she give me a break? Does she make one freakin' minute with her easy? Maybe I really should put her off on the damn city. Let them stick her in a foster home with two dozen other creeps just like her. See if she acts better then."

"Come on, Sally. She's not so bad."

"Oh, listen to the big hero! You take her to the *park*. You take her up to the freakin' *roof*. Try keeping a smile on your face when you cook her dinner and she won't eat it. Or tell me what a great little kid she is when she pisses in her bed and smells up the whole apartment. That's a good one. Does she do that on the roof? Find a corner to sit in and do it in her pants?"

"Enough!"

"This is real, Kate! You ought to try 'real' sometime. You drop in when Roger is gone and you *think* you know what it's like to live like me or like Linda, or a thousand other women like us. Well, let me tell you, if you *did,* you would leave every chance you got. Off with Jerry or some other fuck-up for the weekend. Why? Because it's better than staying *here.*"

She turned and went back into her apartment toward the bedroom. Kate followed.

"Goddammit, where is she?!!" Sally shouted.

She banged open the closet door and pulled clothes out and dumped them onto the floor.

"I swear to Christ, if that kid has left this apartment, I'll beat her so black and blue she won't know which way to lie down."

Kate had seen a window open to the fire escape, but said nothing. Then they both heard the scrape of a shoe on the metal slats outside.

"There!" Sally screamed.

She rushed across the bedroom, and Kate sprang after her.

"You're going to scare her, Sally! She'll fall! Please, she can stay with me until you get back on Sunday. Okay? You go ahead with Jerry and I'll get her back inside. She'll be better by the time you get back. You'll both be better."

Sally shook her head.

"No. I've had it this time, Kate. Up to the eyeballs." She opened the window and leaned out. "Get back in here, Jenny. Now! You get in here or I'm taking you downtown on Monday morning. The hell with you *and* your mother. The city can take care of you. See what you say then, you skinny little snot-nose."

"Please, Sally," Kate said.

"Get in here, Jenny!"

It was silent for a minute. Then the thin, clear voice that Jenny reserved for Miranda came piping in from the fire escape.

"I want to stay with Katy! I want to stay with Katy!"

Sally's arms went rigid, veins bulging on her forehead.

"That's it!! You freakin' little piece of rat crap. You are GONE, SUCKER!!!" She turned to Kate. "Do whatever the freakin' hell you want to do with her. When I get back, I'm taking her to CPS. That's it. She's gone!!"

Sally stalked out of the room, and Kate went after her, watching helplessly as Sally grabbed her bag and hurried off. When Kate got back to the bedroom, the girl was still on the fire escape, tiptoeing close to the edge, looking over the side for Miranda.

"Please, come in, Jenny," Kate said. "We'll have the superintendent next door help get Miranda. Really we will."

Jenny shook her head and stared straight down over the railing at the courtyard below. Kate tried not to think about what Jenny was asking of her. Surely she knew this was not possible.

"I realize the Super's not around *now*. But tomorrow he'll help us. We'll get up first thing in the morning..."

With a quick glance at Kate, Jenny started down the fire escape stairs.

"Jenny, no!! Please wait. Just wait."

The girl hesitated, looping one arm over the railing. Her face was not impassive. Her eyes were not those of a zombie. Her face was alive with pain and confusion and determination.

Kate swallowed hard, then lifted the window open as far as it would go. She took a deep breath. Her arms and hands were trembling as she eased out sideways, her rear-end first, followed by her right leg, her head and upper torso and finally her left leg. She was hoping to act confident, but as she reached the center of the metal slats, she began to shake. A breeze caught her hair. She couldn't breathe. She began to cry. The world was a spinning blur.

Then she felt the girl beside her. A bony little arm was wrapped around her neck. Smooth cool lips were kissing the tears on her cheeks and on her eyes, over and over again.

"It's okay, Katy," the girl said. "We can help each other. We'll do it together, Katy."

Kate opened her eyes and Jenny's face was inches from hers, smiling bravely. She sat beside Kate, one hand in hers, the other on the railing.

Without a word, Jenny extended her legs and then lifted her rear end and moved a few inches. Taking a deep breath, Kate did the same. They repeated the same movement until they reached the stairs. Even then, Kate refused to look down. She kept her eyes fastened at the brick wall to her left, edging down the fire escape one step at a time, feet extended, followed by her sliding rear.

They stopped at the landing below. Three more flights remained.

"I think I'm going to wear right through these pants, Jenny," Kate said. "You're going to be able to see my tush."

Jenny giggled.

"We won't look, Katy," the girl said. "We promise."

"A true pal. 'A person who doesn't look at your tush when you wear through your pants sliding along a fire escape.' That's going in my book of modern definitions."

They started on their way again, Jenny slightly in the lead, Kate concentrating on the process of extending feet, sliding buttocks forward, eyes fastened always on the bricks of the building—red, black, and white bricks, broken and new. She'd never realized how many kinds of bricks were put in the walls. She promised herself that if she survived this trip without a heart attack or a stroke, she would pay much more attention to bricks in the future.

Finally they got to the bottom landing, where she was surprised and somewhat perplexed to see a ladder with a counterweight. They were still about eight feet off the ground, but it seemed close enough to jump.

"I see Miranda," Jenny said. "If you hold the ladder, I'll climb down and get her."

"Oh, no you don't," Kate said. "Number one, you're not leaving me here. Number two, I ain't going back up that fire escape. Number three, I *really* am not going back up that fire escape."

There was no more discussion. Kate pushed and pulled the ladder into position and climbed down first. Her legs felt so weak when she finally touched Mother Earth, she could barely stand up. But she held the ladder as Jenny followed her.

They retrieved the doll and Kate let go of the ladder, allowing the counterweight to draw it up and out of reach. They tried the door to the basement but it was locked. She considered breaking a window, but figured that would just lead them into the locked basement with no prospect of getting into the building. She told herself that if she couldn't think of anything else, she could always start screaming. At least it would be controlled screaming, not the hysterics she was imagining for herself on the fire escape.

Then she noticed the cyclone fence separating the small yard from the back of a large apartment building that fronted on 93rd Street. The door was open to the basement and she could see the laundry room.

"C'mon, Jenny," she said.

She pulled up the edge of the fence and Jenny slipped through. Then Kate crawled after her.

In another minute, they had brushed the dirt off as well as possible and were ringing for the elevator in the basement of the neighboring building. It came and they took it calmly to the first floor and walked out the front door past the doorman.

"Good afternoon," Kate said, careful to keep her rear-end to the wall.

As they got around the corner to Lexington and out of sight of the doorman, she and Jenny started laughing.

"Good after*noon!*" Jenny said in an obvious imitation of Kate.

"Good after-*noooooon!*" Kate repeated.

Hand in hand, they skipped all the way home.

Nine

The next morning there was a knock at the door at a little after seven. Kate was already up, sipping a freshly brewed cup of coffee. She wondered if Sally had come back early, and hoped not. It would mean that things had not gone well. She would be as cross as a hungry bear.

Then she opened the door and saw Roger, adorably unshaven and disheveled after an all-night flight to New York. He was smiling broadly.

"Roger, what a nice surprise!" she said.

Without a word, he dropped his bag just inside her apartment and closed the door behind him. Then he wrapped his arms around her and kissed her on the mouth. She was wearing an oversized man's shirt, her normal sleeping attire, and very little else. His hands slipped under the tail of her shirt and lifted upward.

She pulled away, yanking down her shirt and laughing.

"Roger, stop."

"I've been fantasizing about this entrance for a week solid," he said. "Work with me here."

He tossed off his jacket and started to unbutton her shirt, kissing her as he worked.

Again she pulled away, this time looking over her shoulder toward her bedroom.

"Roger, really!"

"What? What's the problem?"

He was puzzled but still smiling, approaching as she retreated. And then the girl's little face, rosy from sleep, appeared from behind the door to the bedroom. His shoulders slumped.

"Oh, for the love of God," he whispered.

"Jenny, come out and meet my friend, Roger," Kate said. "Roger, this is Jenny and her doll, Miranda, about whom I've told you so much."

"Except that she's living with you. I don't remember hearing that before."

He said this quietly, as though he were speaking to himself, but Kate put her finger to her lips and gave a look in Jenny's direction that asked him to be more careful.

"This is just a sort of temporary thing. Sally has to go away for the weekend. Mrs. Morley wasn't available. Of course, I had no idea that you were coming..."

"I told you I would if I could break free..."

"You said you *might*..."

"I called you late yesterday afternoon, when I found out this was possible. I only have thirty-six hours. Don't you check your messages?"

"I'm sorry. It's a long story, but I've been kind of avoiding the phone for the past twenty-four hours. Then we went to McDonald's and a movie. It was kind of a celebration."

"A celebration?"

He watched as Kate looked at Jenny and smiled and the girl smiled back. A hand came out from behind the door. It held a doll, missing one arm.

"Kate went down the fire escape to rescue me!" Miranda squeaked. "Hooray for Kate! Hooray for Kate!"

The girl marched out from behind the door, with eyes fixed on Kate as though no one else existed in the universe and pressed the doll up against Kate's cheek and made a kissing sound. Kate laughed and blushed and bent over to hug the girl.

"The fire escape?" Roger said, trying not to act like a tight-lipped bastard. It was not easy. "How did you manage that?"

Roger was well acquainted with Kate's fear of heights. There was the incident at the Empire State Building, when she had had to leave. And she'd turned to jelly on the Ferris wheel at Playland and sat rigid for the duration of the ride, eyes closed, fists clenched, begging Roger to either ask the operator to stop the ride or please throw her off and end her misery.

Kate shrugged and blushed again. She looked very beautiful to him. More beautiful than ever, he thought. He felt his mouth soften at the sight of her.

"Well, Miranda had fallen to the yard down there and Jenny was going to go down without anybody and I didn't want that to happen..." She stopped, went into her bedroom, and returned with a pair of jeans that she held up to her face, peering at Roger through the holes worn in the seat. "I wasn't exactly full of courage, as you can see."

Jenny got down onto the floor and started around the room extending her legs and sliding her rear forward, again and again. It was a pantomime that had apparently been repeated often between the two of them but had not yet lost any of its humor. Kate was laughing and Jenny was giggling and it was very difficult for Roger not to break into a full smile himself.

"Sort of like an inch worm," she said.

"But a *brave* inch worm," Roger replied. "Hooray for Kate!"

He wrapped his arm around her shoulder and kissed her chastely on the top of her head. Jenny got up and took Kate's free arm in hers and hugged her as though she were afraid Kate might be taken away.

"So, anyway, Jenny and I are together for the weekend," Kate said. "But that doesn't mean we can't do something."

"As long as it can be done in the presence of a six year old."

"C'mon, Roger."

"Okay, okay. How about if you pack a bag for the two of you and we go down to my place. I've got loads of room and a refrigerator stocked with food. I even have some toys for when my nephew comes over. What do you say?"

"It sounds great to me," Kate said.

She knelt down beside Jenny again. The girl looked worried.

"What do you and Miranda think? I'm sure you would really like his apartment. It has a great terrace, not that I can go out on it. But you and Miranda will. You can even see the river. And we could go to the Park later."

That brought a reaction. Jenny cocked her head and looked at Miranda.

"And the zoo, too," Roger added.

Miranda bobbed at the end of Jenny's outstretched arm.

"He made a rhyme. 'Zoo, too. Zoo, too'."

"How about that?" Roger said. "Zoo, too. Woo, hoo."

"Don't press your luck," Kate said. "Let's get packed."

~ * ~

On the taxi ride to his apartment, Jenny watched the passing streets and buildings as though she were a kidnap victim memorizing the way home. The girl's eyes widened at the sight of a man in a uniform who opened the door for them, and another in the elevator who took them to Roger's floor, but she wasn't moved to speak. And then there was the apartment itself. Roger's mother's cousin had left him a spacious duplex that had been built when space was no object. The entrance foyer was almost as big as Kate's bedroom. The living room could accommodate a game of roller derby. There was a bedroom on the lower floor and two more upstairs, not to mention the den, with fireplace, or the banister that Jenny eyed up for its sliding possibilities. However, as Kate had expected, what really got the kid was the tiled terrace, gorgeously landscaped with trees and flowers, and chairs and benches, and statues of animals and angels. Jenny went right for it.

"Please be careful!" Kate called after her.

"We will!!"

Kate and Roger stood in the doorway as Jenny walked around, exploring, with Miranda clutched to her chest. They were on the twelfth floor and they could see the East River in the distance. A tugboat was pushing a barge south toward the 59th Street Bridge. Jenny watched, transfixed.

"This wasn't my fault, Roger. Sally got really pissed off at Jenny and threw her doll out the window and Jenny was going to go after it herself. I couldn't let her do that."

"Of course…"

"Sally will be back Sunday night and Jenny will move back in with her."

"Sure," Roger said. "And I hear that they're expecting snow in July this year also."

"Oh, Roger."

"Well, it isn't very likely."

"I think she'll have a change of heart. I know her better than you do."

"For which I am grateful, by the way."

Roger had never liked Sally and avoided her whenever possible. He said he wasn't a snob, and Kate believed him, since he was just too good-hearted. But he had never said more than a quick "hello" or "goodbye" to anyone else in the building either. She wondered if some part of him wanted to make it perfectly clear that this was not his world, and never would be. Amen.

"At least don't say anything so Jenny will hear," Kate said. "She's upset enough. At this point, she doesn't know if she's coming or going. She's just been bounced around like a rubber ball."

"By her own mother, Kate. Let's not forget."

"I understand. But I don't have to participate. At the worst, Sally will let Linda know about what's going on and she'll make some new arrangement."

"Kate. That is so unrealistic."

"She'll have to, Roger. Because I can't keep her. Everybody knows that. Really. In a week, something more permanent will be worked out."

"From your mouth to God's ear. Because I hope to be home permanently in a week. And I still like us better as a twosome.

He put his arm around Kate and pulled her close.

"Don't *worry,*" she said. "Everything will be fine."

~ * ~

After lunch, they took a walk over to Central Park, entering at Grand Army Plaza and strolling up the wide shaded path to the Zoo. Once they arrived, Jenny didn't know which way to go first. Her favorites seemed to be the sea lions, until she saw the monkeys. And then there was the polar bear, snoozing in the sun. And what about the penguins, strutting around like they were ready for a formal dance?

They only pried her away with a promise of fresh popcorn, which was sold by a vendor behind the Arsenal building. Kate and Roger bought her a box and then sat together on a bench while Jenny stood on the path, alternately eating the popcorn and feeding it to the sparrows, carefully tossing the broken puffs so that the smaller birds could grab them instead of the pigeons, which had begun to arrive in increasing numbers.

Soon, an amazingly large group of pigeons had gathered around the girl. She waded on matchstick-thin legs through the teeming mass of flapping wings, adding to the sense of her frailty, but with such animation on her face that she was extremely pretty also. Kate imagined that if the birds were suddenly frightened into flight, the updraft could sweep Jenny with them high into the sky and she would disappear. She would be New York's modern-day take on the myth of Ganymede—Jenny Gilmour, popcorn bearer to the Gods.

"She's very cute," Roger said. "But she really does have problems."

"She has to get used to you a little more, Roger. Then she'll talk to you. With me at this point, she's really very... I don't know, normal, I guess."

"I can think of a lot of words to describe this kid. Sweet. Cute. Fun. But I'm not sure 'normal' is one of them. Honestly, I have nothing against her, you understand. But you can see the way she walks, always looking around, like she's worried something is going to happen. She has some deep problems."

"Shhhhh," Kate said, hushing him as Jenny ran toward the two of them with her hands held behind her back, then, with a magician's flourish, handed each a perfectly white pigeon feather.

"Thank you, Jenny," Roger said.

The girl just looked at him warily, then darted back into the throng and began to heave handfuls of popcorn into the air, face glowing with happiness, nearly lost in the chaotic blur of churning wings.

"You see what I mean?" Kate asked. "You see?"

"I'm beginning to," Roger said. "She's as normal as you are, Kate. One hundred percent as normal as you."

From the zoo, they walked north, under the musical clock, and continued uptown to 66th Street where there was a playground with a curving granite slide set into a hillside.

As soon as Jenny saw it, she raced ahead. Kate asked Roger to keep up with Jenny, claiming fatigue as she sat by herself on a bench close to the edge of the tunnel beneath the transverse road. Less than a minute had passed when the person she had been waiting for emerged from the gloom of the underpass.

"Hello, Anthony," she said. "Looking for somebody?"

She had picked him out of the crowds by the way he had stood with slouched shoulders, projecting arrogance. His dark hair had been cut short, and the stubble on his face had not been cut for several days. He was wearing a pullover Tommy Hilfiger sweatshirt from which the arms had been removed. It had a single pocket across the stomach that hid his hands and whatever else he chose to carry there. Despite a slight hollowness to his cheeks, and his scraggly beard, she could see that he had once been very attractive. He still was.

A smirk twisted just one corner of his mouth.

"Hey, I had some business to take care of down this end of the Park. I waved, but I guess you didn't see me."

"I saw you," Kate replied. "But you weren't waving."

"Yeah, well...like I said, I had some business to take care of from my mobile office." He took an iPhone from his pocket. "I got everything I need right here. E-mail, texting, the web— I'm *connected*. All I need is a bench to sit on."

"Or a tree to hide behind?"

"Now, now, Katherine. That's your full name, right? I did a little checking and that's what I was told. Classy name. But you probably prefer Kate. Or maybe Katy. That's what the kid calls you, right?"

"Honestly, what I'd prefer is for you to stay far enough away that it won't be an issue what you call me."

Anthony shuddered as though a strong north wind had slid down the back of his sweatshirt.

"You are a cold lady, Katherine!"

"I'm not joking, Anthony. You're not her father. I have the birth certificate to prove it. If necessary, I'll get a protective order from the Family Court."

"Your mother going to help you with that? What's her name, Carla?" He smiled at her surprise. "Hey, Katherine, I told you I was doing some checking. Funny thing is, your old lady represented my mother once. Got my pops thrown in jail when he smacked her around a little bit. How's that for a laugh, huh?"

"I'll tell everybody at my next cocktail party," Kate said.

She got up from the bench to leave, but he blocked her path, both hands held in front of his chest, palms outward, as though warding off a blow.

"Hey, c'mon, I don't mean nuthin' bad here. Sit down just a sec. We got to talk. I'm not fighting with you, okay? I'm *with* you." He backed up enough to let her through but at the same time gestured for her to sit. When she did, he took the space beside her. She was aware of the odor of an expensive cologne she had considered buying for Roger.

"Seriously," he said. "I've been wanting to talk to you. The docs all said that a few more minutes, I would have been pushing daisies, you know? I don't forget stuff like that, all right? I owe you."

"Don't get too misty eyed, Anthony. At the time, I thought you might be Jenny's father. I know better now."

"The fact remains..."

"Okay then. Stay away from me and Jenny. I'll call us square. And that goes for your minions too."

"What the hell are you talking about?"

"The other day in the park, there were a couple of guys watching me and Jenny. It was pretty obvious, and I didn't like it."

He laughed.

"Maybe they were just checking out a nice looking woman. Ever think of that?" The smile that appeared on his face was charming in its way. She thought of Linda, but didn't respond to his words. "But I will tell you one thing," he continued. "There are lots of people in this city who know Linda, and some of them you don't want to meet. You ask her, next time you see her, about some of the places you should be avoiding. She can tell you."

"Why don't *you* tell me? I haven't met Linda once, yet."

He stared at Kate as though he were a scientist and she were a strange new species.

"Nah, I'll let her do her own talking. But here's a tip for when you do meet the Bitch, okay? You want to know how to tell if she's lying to you? See if her lips are moving."

He laughed at his joke.

"I imagine she might say the same about you. Then what?"

"Then you have to trust your instincts, don't you? And hope you're right."

"Or trust neither of you."

"That'll work. But I'm telling you now, I have no intention of bothering you or the kid. You say I'm not the kid's father." He shrugged. "All I know is what the Bitch told me. Showed me a piece

102

of paper. Said I was the one. Hell, I've been supporting her like she was my own kid."

"Yeah, I saw what a nice place she was living in."

He bowed his head and shook it slowly.

"I'm down on my luck right now, and one of the reasons is that the Bitch owes me money. And I'm not forgetting about it. Okay?" Anger filled his voice suddenly. He paused to calm himself. "But we're getting off the point here, Katherine. Like I said before, I have no intentions of trying to take Jenny, or nothing like that. It's Linda I'm after. Pure and simple. If your and my paths cross sometimes, it has got nothing to do with you. I got no *quarrel* with you. But I ain't ever going to give up my money. You tell the Bitch that, okay? You tell her I'm watching and I'm waiting. You tell her I know what she tried to pull and I'll be ready the next time. You tell her I don't forget."

The cell phone went off in his pocket and he pulled it out and put it to his ear. He listened and looked around the surrounding area.

"I'll meet you in five minutes. Be sitting on a bench overlooking the Wolman Rink. Yeah, watching the ladies roller-skate. I'll call you once I've checked it out. I'll tell you where to meet me next. *Ciao*."

He put the phone back in the pocket of his sweatshirt.

"Business calls," he said and walked away.

Ten

When Kate caught up with Roger at the 67th Street playground, he was standing at the bottom of the slide in the middle of a group of other adults. She told him she had spotted a friend from Hiroth Publishing and they'd been talking. He nodded, seeming transfixed by the never-ending parade of shouting, squealing children.

"It makes me tired just to watch," he said, as a group of them chased each other down the slide, around the bushes and up the stairs to the top of the slide again. Kate couldn't quite believe that Jenny was among the horde and holding her own, even with Miranda in one hand.

"Let's hope it makes *her* tired," Kate said.

Roger raised his eyebrows twice in rapid succession.

"I *figured* there was a reason for this playground bit. You know, you really are surprisingly good at this parenting stuff."

"I'll take that as a compliment."

"I didn't mean it otherwise. It's just, from all that you've told me about Carla and you, I was expecting at least a little dysfunction."

Kate shrugged.

"That's why it's easy for me. I just think of Carla and me in a given circumstance, and then I do the opposite of what she would have done. Works every time."

"Ouch," Roger said.

~ * ~

After a brief consultation with Jenny, they made plans to order in a pizza for dinner, and on the way home Roger rented *Snow White* at the video store. The three of them sat on the sofa with the pizza box on the coffee table so they could watch the movie while they ate. Roger nearly danced a jig when Jenny, with one and a half slices and a glass of chocolate milk in her, curled up next to Kate, gave an existential yawn or two, and started to blink her eyes.

Even then, the problem was that her fatigue could not overcome her fear of being alone in a new bed in this new apartment, and so Kate agreed that she would lie down on the mattress next to her until the girl drifted off. It was a good plan, except that it did not take into account the effects of running after a six year old child all day, or of travel on an all-night cross-country flight. Roger fell asleep at about the point in the movie that Snow White was moving in with the dwarfs. By the time he awoke, the prince had rescued her from a trance. Unlike the fairy tale, however, Kate was so well wrapped in sleep that neither words nor kisses could rouse her.

"Three thousand miles for this," he said to himself as he carried Kate to the big double bed in his room and placed her beneath the sheets. "Six hours in the cabin of an airplane and three thousand miles..."

And as he lay on the bed beside her, he realized what he had been wanting to tell Kate throughout most of the day and into the evening: This is not a fairy tale we are living. Happy endings are not guaranteed. Mistakes of judgment are not forgiven. If a witch cuts you into pieces, there is no magic spell to make you whole again. If the wolf eats you, a woodsman is not available to cut open its stomach and set you and your granny free.

He wondered how that applied to him. More than one friend had cautioned him about Kate. He told them that he loved her and had loved her from the moment they'd first met. But did he? Was that just his personal fairy tale? Love at first sight? Really? Or was it an attempt to justify the one little rebellion he had allowed himself in his otherwise perfectly tracked life? How do we ever know?

One central truth remained clear: In real life, bad choices have consequences that cannot be escaped. There are no "do-overs." If you take in a stray kid, it might not necessarily be good for her, or for you.

"A stray kid, for Christ's sake. Who the hell takes in a stray kid anymore?"

~ * ~

The next morning, they never had much of a chance to discuss Jenny. As the first thin light of dawn slipped through the cracks in the bedroom blinds and they reached for each other as they might have on any other morning, they simultaneously became aware of a 55-pound weight anchored at the bottom of the bed, staring at them with the eyes of a cat. If Jenny had been perched on their chests with a dagger in her teeth, the sight could not have been more unnerving.

"I think I'm having a heart attack," Roger whispered.

Miranda began to jump excitedly on the edge of the bed.

"It's time to get up, Katy," she said, her voice full of a stridency that Kate had not heard for some time. "It's time to go home. Jenny wants to go home!"

"This is Kate's home, Jenny," Roger said calmly.

"No, it's not! Katy lives with me and Jenny on 92nd Street! Tell him, Katy. Tell him!"

Kate lifted herself out of bed.

"Calm down, calm down. Of course, I live on 92nd Street."

"Kate?" Roger said under his breath. "C'mon. This is silly."

She turned to him so Jenny could not see and mouthed the words, "We'll talk *later*."

They had breakfast at a nearby deli. Given the circumstances, it seemed to make sense for Kate and Jenny to return to 92nd Street. That way, Roger could catch an early flight back to California and, perhaps, placate the partner who had not understood why Roger wanted to leave for the weekend at all.

They went uptown in the same cab that took Roger to the airport. Jenny ran ahead upstairs, and Kate and Roger finally had a moment alone together.

"I think you are getting in too deep here, Kate," Roger said. "You've done your good deed. It's time to end it."

"I'm not going for a merit badge, Roger. I'm just trying to help out temporarily. That's all this is. And if you think I'm in some sort of competition with Carla, you are really off base."

"I didn't say that. Don't start getting paranoid on me now."

"I'm not paranoid. You're the one who mentioned Carla yesterday, not me."

"Okay, okay. I'm trying to make a simple point. The girl is not your responsibility. She's got a mother."

"I'm well aware of this. My role is limited. Sally will take her back and that will be that. You think I don't know I have to get a job and go to work? I know all about work. I've worked my whole life. Since I was sixteen, I had a job of one kind or another."

"I know you did."

"I didn't go to expensive summer camps in the Rocky Mountains. I didn't spend Easter break at the Florida Keys."

"This was not meant as an attack on you, Kate. Please don't make it one on me. I admire you for helping out. But I'm worried about you too. I love you, Kate. It's right to worry about the ones you love."

He kissed her and she embraced him in the back seat of the cab, and some of the tension she had felt rising in her began to ease. For a long moment she held him tight, regretting that they had not had any time to be alone and that he was going away again and that she had said those mean things. But the fact was that there was more that should be said, she thought. Much more.

"I love you too, Roger," she said, and got out. And as the car started to pull away and Roger waved out of the window, she yelled after him. "I'll see you next weekend! Just the two of us!"

~ * ~

She and Jenny spent the day close by the apartment building, sunning themselves on the roof, reading the newspapers, making quick trips to the store for food. Kate didn't mention that she was listening for Sally's return, but that was probably unnecessary since she snapped to attention whenever she heard the foyer door open and close and sometimes went into the hall to check, "just in case."

She was confident Sally would take Jenny back. The fact was that her neighbor had a temper that was notorious on 92nd Street. Various tenants had experienced her verbal wrath. Once, the police had to be called when a young lady from down the street had allowed her Golden Retriever to defecate on the sidewalk where Sally was bagging the garbage. However, as apocalyptic as her explosions were, she cooled off quickly. While her adversaries were still wondering if they needed an armed escort, Sally was ready to forgive and forget. She'd petted that dog the next morning while its owner cringed at the other end of the leash.

"Nice dog, hey, Katy?" Sally had said. "*Super* dog. I love goldens."

But the sound of Sally's purple Keds did not resound in the hallways all Sunday afternoon. Nor did she return that evening. And no one in the building had any idea what might be detaining her. A stoop-sitter surmised that she had lost her ticket and was walking home because she was too cheap to buy another one. Someone else suggested that she had been arrested for sleeping under the boardwalk.

No speculation was the equal of the truth, however.

Late Monday night, those size nines finally clumped up the stairs and stopped outside Kate's apartment.

"Kate!" she screamed, pounding her fist on Kate's door. "Kate, come quick! I have something to tell you."

Kate opened the door, still groggy with sleep, and saw Sally, her arm around a somewhat besotted Jerry, steadying him with a kind of headlock as she extended her left hand forward.

"I'm married!" she cried, waving her fingers, one of which bore a gold ring. "We got married yesterday in Maryland, Kate, and we've been celebrating all the way home. Oh, sweet Jesus, I'm a married woman."

Incapable of speech, Kate watched as Sally kissed her man in the middle of his bald spot and ushered him off to 'their' bedroom with instructions to wait for her, as though there were some alternative. Then she let out a whoop that would have scared an Apache, grabbed Kate around the waist, and danced with her up and down the hallway, laughing and shouting at the top of her lungs,

"I'm married. Oh, good Mother of God, I can't believe it. I'm married!"

"It's wonderful news, Sally," Kate repeated back to her. "I'm *so* happy for you."

"He's no Brad Pitt, you understand," Sally whispered. "But he's okay between the sheets, if you know what I mean. And he's got a great sense of humor, right, Katy?"

"Sure he does."

"And that's important, God knows. And he's solid as a rock. I need a guy like that to keep me in line, ya know?" She rolled her eyes upward, threw her arms around Kate again, and squeezed hard.

"I'm *very* happy for you, Sally. Really I am."

But there was something less than enthusiastic about Kate's response.

Sally frowned, squinting at her.

"Hey, no shit, Kate. But if this is your happy face, sad must be a real freaking bummer. Buck up, willya? He's got a great job. Steamfitters have a pension that's out of this world. Twenty-five years and he's free. Full pension with healthcare. *Full* pension."

"It's great. Really it is. It's just such a...surprise. I had no idea..."

"There's some freaking thing bothering you. What is it?"

She stepped back then, hands on her hips. Kate smiled weakly and gestured to the apartment where Jenny still slept with the shockproof sleep of a six year old.

"Oh, shit no, Kate. Don't go there. I told you I wasn't taking her back. And now, well... I mean, you know I can't do it now.

Kate couldn't say anything. She did "know it," but found herself unable to admit the simple fact. There was no way Sally was going to keep the kid now that she was married. She nodded her head. It was the best she could do.

"Well, *Christ*, Kate. I mean, it ain't my fault. I just reached my limit with the Creephead. And now, with Jerry and all... I mean, you can't expect him to want a kid around..."

"I *know*!!"

Kate's voice was louder than she had intended, but the turn of events seemed so unfair: to her, to Roger, to Jenny.

She turned away to try to calm herself and felt Sally's hand touch lightly on her shoulder.

The unexpected tenderness hit Kate hard. She started to cry.

"Hey, it's okay, Katy. Look, I know it ain't easy for you. If you want me to take care of it, I will. The kid's asleep. We'll carry her into my place for the night. I'll call CPS in the morning. Okay? You won't have to have anything to do with it. It'll be over like that. Okay, Katy?"

It sounded like they were taking a troublesome dog to the pound to be put to sleep. Tears splashed on the floor at her feet. Kate shook her head.

"No. I couldn't do that to Jenny. I'll keep her with me until Linda comes for a visit. But I want you to tell her I can't keep Jenny. Promise you'll tell her, because I really can't continue this either. It's begun to affect Roger and me. I can't..."

"Of course I'll tell her. As soon as she comes by."

Kate wiped the tears from her eyes and hugged Sally.

"Congratulations, old friend. I'm sorry for my reaction. I'm extremely happy for you. And I wish you both the very best of luck."

They rocked from side to side, holding on to each other. When they pulled apart finally, Kate saw that a tear or two had formed in the corners of Sally's eyes as well.

"Gotta run," Sally said. "It's still my honeymoon, for the love of Mike. My old man is waiting, and we can't have that. I mean, I'm a freakin' married woman now."

~ * ~

The next evening, during Kate's telephone call with Roger, she lied about the situation with Jenny. She hadn't planned it that way. But he was in one of those overbearing moods he could get into after a day of hard work, a state of mind that she remembered from Carla, in which the law's logic took him over and he carried on a conversation as if he were conducting a cross-examination before a judge and jury, assembling the answers one by one, building his case with unerring logic. 'You're wrong. You see, I've just proved you're wrong with your own words.'

She expected Linda would be making contact within a couple of days—she was due for a visit, according to Sally. At that point, Kate would tell Linda that she had to take her daughter back right away, either to care for her, or to surrender her to Child Protective Services. That choice was for Linda to make, not for Kate or Sally.

Tuesday and Wednesday passed with no word from Linda, and Kate and the kid fell into a routine of going to the 96th Street playground during the day and stopping by the library on the way home to check out books. At night, after Jenny's bath, and before going to sleep, Kate would read to her. She had remembered a futon mattress she had bought for use during an exercise kick and had long ago shoved under her bed. It was the perfect size for a small person to sleep on, and Kate had unrolled it in an alcove of her bedroom that seemed to have been constructed for the purpose.

A small bookcase beside the bed held a lamp and on its shelves were placed Jenny's clothes and Miranda's and, of course, the library books. Jenny's face seemed to shine with delight as she sat there, cross-legged, officious as a hen while she fluffed the pillow for Miranda and arranged the covers over them both.

Later in the week, Roger called. Papers had been submitted and they were waiting for the judge to issue a decision. The lawyers had retired to their rooms, and Roger was in a talkative mood, believing that his time on this case in San Francisco would soon be over.

Kate had been in the middle of reading Jenny a story and asked if he could call her again in a half hour. It would have passed for nothing if she had thought to say she was taking a shower, or on her way out to return a video. But instead she had hesitated, and Jenny asked in the background a little too loudly who was on the phone.

"She's back?" Roger asked. "You took her back in?"

"Well..."

"You never got rid of her, did you? I can't believe this. You lied to me."

"It wasn't exactly a lie, Roger."

"That's a good one. What is 'not exactly a lie'? Is that what they call a half truth?"

"Roger, please. I'm just waiting..." She looked at Jenny who was watching and listening very closely. "Look, I can't talk about this now."

"Well, of course not. God forbid Jenny should ever hear what was really going on in her life. Much better that she continue to be deluded into thinking she has a new mommy."

Conscious of those intent, green eyes upon her, Kate smiled.

"I'll tell her how much you miss her," she said.

Jenny giggled.

"What?" Roger demanded. "What did you say?"

"I love you too, Roger," she said, and hung up.

~ * ~

Later, after Jenny was asleep, Kate went into the living room. She turned off the lights and sat on her window seat, overlooking the street. The night was warm and there was a pleasant breeze. A hint of moisture in the air gave the street lamps a slightly eerie glow. The sidewalks were deserted. The occasional pedestrians seemed especially aimless and lonely tonight, as if they too were passively waiting for the night to unfold and offer an answer to a vexing problem. Kate had set the weekend as her deadline for Linda to find some other solution. The thought of having to tell Jenny that she could not take care of her any more made her stomach knot up like a coiling snake. The phone call with Roger had just increased her tension. Was he wrong to demand that she get rid of Jenny? In her mind, she canvassed her friends and acquaintances—Stevie, Sally, other co-workers at Hiroth Publishing, old friends from college—and all of them sided with Roger, telling her she was a fool to have carried this on so long, jeopardizing their relationship. The only one who Kate was sure would take her side in favor of helping a needy child was Carla. The needy always held the trump card with her. Now wasn't that funny? Wasn't that just an ironic laugh riot!

She heard loud voices from Sally's apartment and decided the honeymoon was officially over. Fragments of an argument survived the mediating brick, plaster and wood. Kate was sure Sally had riled her man. A rather high-pitched voice rose and fell, that she imagined was Jerry's. He was repeating, as much as she could hear, "How can you DO this?!!! How can you fucking do this?!!"

Those words were met by a response that was undoubtedly Sally's, making clear that she had the right to do whatever she felt like, so just "Go SCREW yourself, freakin' ASS-hole."

The fragments grew more disjointed and unintelligible, and Kate was dozing in her seat by the window when she heard the door open across the hall. Sally could be heard saying goodbye to someone, then there were footsteps on the wooden hallway floor that seemed to stop outside Kate's apartment before they continued slowly toward the stairs. Suddenly, Kate jumped to her feet and hurried into the hall, realizing it had to be Linda.

She leaned on the wall at the stop of the stairs, trying to see down the stairwell. She could see a woman with dark hair, walking slowly on the landing below.

"Linda?" Kate whispered. "Linda, is that you?"

Startled, Linda started walking more quickly, reaching the stairs and starting down. "Wait!" Kate continued, following halfway down the stairs, trying to keep her voice subdued so that she would not wake Jenny. The door to her apartment was still open. She didn't have her keys. "It's me. It's Kate."

Kate couldn't see Linda, but she knew she had paused on the stairs below her.

"Sally said you wanted to talk to me." Linda replied. Her voice was hoarse and weak. Kate strained to hear. "But I didn't see a light in your apartment. It's late anyway."

"No, no. We *have* to talk. Please, will you come up?"

Kate took another few steps down the stairs.

"I don't want to wake Jenny. I don't want her to see me like this. I..."

"She won't wake up. And if she does, it doesn't matter. We have to talk about what to do. I can't continue taking care of her."

"I'm grateful to you, Kate. Sally's been telling me what you've done. You've been a saint in this..." She had to stop to collect herself. Kate could hear her muffled crying. "I'm such a fuck-up. I know it, Kate. And you're like an angel sent from God, Kate.

"I was just trying to help out for a while," Kate said. "But I can't keep taking care of Jenny. Next week, you have to get someone else. Okay?"

She heard the sounds of Linda's steps as she started walking again.

Kate rushed after her. She opened the foyer door to the street and stopped, worried it would lock behind her. Linda was halfway to the corner, where she paused and turned. Despite the weather, she was dressed in a long cape that was wrapped around her in a vain attempt to hide her pregnancy. Her face was one that Kate felt she knew, only older, paler, more frightened—Jenny's face, twenty-five years in the future.

"Linda, I'm sorry, but I can't keep Jenny much longer."

At the corner the light changed and the waiting traffic roared away down Lexington or turned onto 92nd Street. Kate's words were swallowed up and she waited for the quiet again. Linda spoke first.

"They wanted to take her away from me," she said. "First I lost my job and then my lousy apartment, and that miserable whore wanted to take her away. That *whore*."

"Who tried to take her away? What are you saying?"

"The social worker for CPS. She has it in for me!"

"I don't understand. Please come upstairs."

"I can't bring her to CPS, okay? That's why this is so important to me. I'll lose Jenny and never get her back."

Linda started to walk laboriously up the hill to Lexington. Kate wondered if she had heard any part of what she had said.

"Don't think I don't appreciate this, Kate. You're a saint. I mean it, a saint..."

"But you don't understand. I *can't* keep doing this. There has to be someone else. Linda, wait! You can't go!"

The traffic came down 92nd Street this time, muffling her voice.

Linda kept walking, the cape swirling behind her as she slowly strode toward a waiting car.

Kate pulled off one of her sneakers and used it to prop open the door to the building. Then she raced toward the car, reaching it just as the door slammed shut and it accelerated away. The windows were tinted. She couldn't see inside.

"Linda! Dammit, your kid needs you!! Linda!!!"

In that chaotic moment, she saw only the first few letters of the license plate. It did not have the T prefix a radio cab would have had. Where did she get a car and driver?

Just then, a smaller car that had been parked across the street pulled out, its tires squealing. At a distance, she glimpsed a man's profile. She was sure it was Anthony.

Her mind raced. Should she follow also? What would happen if Jenny woke up? It wasn't likely, but it was possible. She couldn't leave the girl.

She waved at a yellow cab. It screeched to a halt. The cab driver's arm hung out the window.

She pulled a twenty-dollar bill from her pocket and tossed it into the man's lap.

"That car that just left. I need you to follow it. Find out where it stops and come back here again."

The cab driver was a dark-skinned black man with a cap pushed back on his head. He looked at her blankly.

"You a cop?"

"No. But this is important. I live in that building right over there. My name is Kate. Just come back and tell me where the car went. But you have to hurry!"

"You crazy, Lady," he said.

He threw the rolled up twenty back onto the sidewalk and floored the cab. In minutes, it had disappeared.

Eleven

Kate fell asleep on the window seat, and Jenny found her there the next morning. It had rained heavily during the night, and the sky was still thick with low, dark clouds. Jenny climbed onto the cushion beside Kate, sitting up on her knees, looking out. Kate wondered if she had heard some part of the conversation from the night before. Was she thinking that Linda might still be around? Was she feeling sad that her mother hadn't bothered to come in to see her and kiss her goodnight?

Then Kate noticed that the girl's solemn eyes were fixed upon the sky and those looming clouds. The reason, Kate realized, was her nearly forgotten promise to bring Jenny to Carl Schurz Park on the East River. There was a large playground, she had told her, and grassy places to have a picnic and benches to sit on and watch the boats go by on the river. They could take a walk afterward and feed the seagulls.

She listened to the radio and was encouraged to make the trip by a weatherman's forecast of gradual clearing through the morning. But as they got off the cross-town bus and walked into the playground, it seemed to Kate that she was the only person on the Upper East Side who had been naive enough to believe such nonsense. Not another soul was to be seen. Although it was not raining at the moment, there were huge puddles everywhere. Droplets of water hung ponderously from tree limbs and metal climbing equipment. The seesaws, swings, and benches were completely wet. A heavy mist rose off the river, and the disconsolate sound of foghorns pierced the chilly air as tugboats pulled and pushed their barges past Hell's Gate.

It was dismal, but when Kate suggested they leave and have the picnic in their warm, dry living room, Jenny blinked hard and her eyes grew red as if she would start crying on the spot.

"But you're going to get soaked and catch a cold," Kate said.

"I *won't*."

Jenny held Miranda tight against her chest and bowed her head. She had the sense not to stamp her foot, which would have caused a splash and settled the question.

"But look at this place, Jenny. You can't *help* but get wet."

"I *won't*! Please!!"

"C'mon, Jenny..."

"Please! Please! Please!"

Kate searched her mind for a response, but couldn't come up with any except that if the kid got her feet wet, she would die of pneumonia in a lonely hospital bed (as a friend's mother had always warned). But it didn't seem a likely scenario in the dead of summer, with the temperature already in the upper seventies. And it never occurred to Kate that she should simply lie.

"Okay," Kate said, finally. "But if you get too wet, we're going to go. Agreed?"

"Yes, yes."

"And if it starts to rain, even a little bit..."

But Jenny was already racing across the asphalt, anxious to prove she could stay dry. She skirted the puddles as though they were land mines and raced toward the see-saws, a preeminent "sharing" toy in any playground except for a child of Jenny's ingenuity, who had learned to amuse herself or not play at all. She had realized that if she walked up the plank from one side toward the other, sooner or later her weight would make it tilt in the opposite direction, and, by scampering backward at exactly the right moment, she could balance and play a very respectable game of see-saw all by herself. Not only that, she could accomplish this gymnastics stunt without a drop of rainwater touching her pants.

"See, Katy?! See? Look at me, Katy!"

"O-kaaay!" Kate called back.

Given Kate's phobia about heights, the images of possible disaster flowed rather too easily when Jenny's feet were not firmly in contact with the ground. Jenny could lose her footing on the wet wooden surface, inevitably clipping her head on the metal supports on the way to the ground. She would crack her skull. Blood would flow. There would be a need for stitches...

"It's probably slippery! Be careful!"

Jenny hopped off, sure-footed as a mountain goat, and ran across to the swings. Here, too, the problem of a wet seat clearly was not going to stop someone so determined. To Kate's dismay, Jenny simply stood up on the swing and began to propel herself forward and back, higher and higher, quickly bringing her slight body parallel to the ground at the top of her arc.

"Katy! Watch!"

"Just be careful!"

Kate wiped off the water from one small corner of a bench and huddled there. She wasn't cold. And it wasn't actually raining. But the fact remained that she and Jenny were here all alone, in humidity that had given her hair the texture and bounce of a Brillo pad. Among all the adults with children in this area of the Upper East Side, only Kate had failed to convince her allotted kid that this was a day to stay indoors and watch a movie.

She imagined Roger standing beside her, speaking in his calm voice. "So how did it go with old Linda, last night? When will she be making new arrangements for Jenny? She won't be? Now, there is a surprise." And then, with a "tsk" and a sigh and a telling pause, he'd ask, "And what's with this playground thing in the rain? Aren't you the one who's supposed to be in charge? Maybe you're not so hot at this childcare business after all?"

Just then, as luck would have it, a few other hardy adventurers came through the playground's wrought iron gate. First was a woman in her early thirties, dressed in a white uniform from the cap in her hair down to her stockings and sneakers. She was on the heavy side and walked with a nanny's sturdy gait, toting on her left arm a canvas bag bulging with toys and on her right, another bag that apparently contained their ample picnic lunch. A checkered tablecloth peeked out the top, along with a heavy towel.

Close behind this mountain of a woman, carrying nothing, were two little girls who Kate thought at first were twins, since they were about the same size and were dressed in identical powder blue outfits from some ridiculously expensive East Side shop and all-weather shoes that had not yet been introduced to mud, or dirt in any other form. Even without the nanny they looked wealthy, Kate thought, with a twinge in the region near her heart that could only be jealousy. Was it any wonder that Linda might have wanted to steal or commit any kind of fraud to have nice clothes for her daughter?

Jenny came over to the bench and stood beside Kate. Gently, she put her arm around Kate's shoulder and patted it rhythmically with her fingertips. It was a friendly, even loving gesture, but one, Kate knew, that also betrayed her nervousness. The arrival of those two princesses might have caused it. Kate had never seen Jenny play with another child her own age.

The nanny had pulled two fluffy towels from one of the bags and now was meticulously wiping every last trace of moisture from a bench. Briefly, Kate imagined that she would start mopping up the puddles on the ground too, so that the all-weather shoes could remain pristine. Instead, the young woman wrung out the towels as though they were handkerchiefs, folded them neatly, and put them back in the bag. Her forearms were the size of a sumo wrestler's.

"Go on, Jenny," Kate said. "Go over and ask them if they want to play."

At this point, Jenny was using Kate as a kind of shield, ducking behind her, peering out.

"That woman over there is staring at me," Jenny said finally.

"Jenny, please cut it out."

"She *is*, Katy. Look over there."

When Kate followed the angle of Jenny's pointed finger, she saw that a tall, brown-haired woman had entered the playground and was sitting on a bench. She was wearing a long, tan raincoat, and a man's floppy hat shadowed her face.

"She's not looking at you," Kate said. "No more than at any other kid, anyway. She's allowed. Lots of people come to the park to watch the kids play with each other. It's natural."

She almost added that it was also natural for kids at the *play*ground to actually *play* with each other and that Jenny should try it sometime in the next five years or so, but she bit her tongue.

Jenny took another quick look toward the woman.

"I don't like her looking at me," she said, and then ran back across the playground to the seesaws and resumed her balancing act.

She was quite good at it, Kate thought, wondering if Jenny might actually be showing off for the new kids. She was almost dancing back and forth along the teetering board, nimble as a leprechaun.

"Look at her, you rich little twits," Kate whispered to herself. "That's a nice game she's invented for herself over there."

Out of the corner of her eye, Kate noticed that the woman in the raincoat had moved to a bench that was closer to Kate. The other bench had been under a tree that had been dripping water from its leaves and branches, even though it was not raining. Still, Kate took a closer look. The sleeves and collar of the raincoat she wore were a bit tattered at the edges, and her sneakers had seen better days. She was in her early fifties, Kate guessed, and her face had a pleasantly angular quality, with deep and plentiful lines in the skin, as if she might have spent a lot of time outdoors in the sun. Kate tried to decide whether she was a borderline bag lady or a slightly eccentric bird-watcher or simply a lonely housewife who liked to sit in the park and wear comfortable old things. Whatever she was, she seemed to be focused on Jenny.

Kate stood and walked across the playground to Jenny.

"Are you ready to go home?" Kate asked in a calm voice. She didn't want to betray the sense of anxiety she felt about the woman. "I just remembered I have some calls to make."

Jenny pursed her lips and took Miranda into her arms for a hug.

"Can't we stay a while, please?"

To Kate's surprise, Jenny gave a sidelong glance in the direction of the two girls. Either the kid was on the verge of a behavioral breakthrough, or she was simply being more stubborn than Kate could imagine. The two girls had removed a veritable general assembly of dolls from one of the canvas bags and were busy arranging them on the bench. Their parents had obviously collected them from around the world, and each had an intricately tailored costume and hair in an authentic coiffure.

"They have a pretty nice group of dolls, huh?" Kate asked. "Of course, none of them can match Miranda. And they have zero personality."

Jenny smiled, but was not totally convinced

"Would you like us to go over there and ask if they want to play?"

Jenny gave an almost imperceptible movement of her head in assent, and they set off together, holding hands. This seemed like a major step for Jenny, and Kate was eager to help make it work. Jenny had to learn to reach out to other kids. What would happen when school started?

"Hi, there," Kate said to the nanny. "Nice weather, huh? If you're a duck."

She hadn't expected wild guffaws, but a smile or a little chuckle would have been nice. The nanny's only response was a curt nod of the head, accomplished without taking her eyes off the magazine she was reading, *Spring Wedding.* Its pages were open to an article on color coordination in bridesmaid dresses. The two girls barely paid attention to Kate, or to Jenny.

Undeterred, Kate pressed on, introducing herself and Jenny and somehow gleaning the information that the two girls were sisters, a year apart in age. Their names were Heather and Kimberly. The nanny was *Miss* Stone.

"Maybe the three of them would like to play together," Kate said. "Jenny has her doll with her, too. Her name's Miranda."

Jenny stepped forward toward their bench and preened Miranda's dress and hair, which had suffered somewhat from being held in Jenny's fist while she had played earlier. It was a brave attempt to show that, with love, the most battered possession can become precious. But this sentiment did not carry much weight with Kimberly and Heather, and Kate had the sinking sensation that this was not going to work out, even as she left Jenny with the two princesses and retreated across the playground.

From where she stood, it was apparent that as far as those two girls were concerned, Jenny could play with them, but only if she kept herself and Miranda in certain designated areas (like on the very edge of the bench) and limited herself to the roles they deemed appropriate: servant girl, maid-in-waiting, attendant to the queen, and so on. Kate took a deep breath to control the anger she was beginning to feel.

"Hello," a quiet voice said beside her.

Quickly, Kate turned and saw that the woman with the raincoat was standing beside her.

"I'm very sorry I startled you. My name is Haddie Mills and I just had to come over and tell you how wonderful Jenny looks."

"You know Jenny?" Kate asked. Ms. Mills was smiling and her voice was friendly and causal, but alarm bells were going off deep inside Kate.

"Yes, I was a social worker with Child Protective Services in Manhattan at the time. I'm at a private hospital now. Believe me, the hours are *much* better. I could tell you stories..."

Kate nodded. "I'll bet."

"No comparison." The woman glanced at Jenny and smiled again broadly. "But little Jenny! She seems to be thriving. So vibrant! I can hardly believe it. How long have you had her?"

"Not long," Kate replied. The woman had said she didn't work at CPS anymore, but Kate still remembered what Linda had said, and her uneasiness continued to grow. "Not *very* long. I mean it seems like just yesterday…"

Trying not to be rude, Kate turned slightly away in Jenny's direction and pretended to focus on the dynamics of play. Jenny did not like the arrangement suggested by the Czarinas. Center bench was the place to be, and she saw no reason why Miranda should not assume her rightful position there.

"Excuse me for asking," Haddie asked. "But are you a temporary or permanent home?

"What was that?" Kate asked in an absent manner, desperately trying not to seem nervous. "Oh… temporary. Just temporary."

"I see." Haddie seemed disappointed. "And what agency are you working through?"

Kate felt she was sinking deeper and deeper into quicksand.

Meanwhile, Jenny made room on the bench and placed her doll right in the middle of the debutantes' receiving line.

"Atta girl," Kate said.

"Pardon?" Haddie asked.

"She's asserting herself. That's good, right? I mean if you knew Jenny, you'd know how shy she is."

"Yes, *very* nice," the woman replied, put off her game momentarily by the remark. "But what agency did you say you were with?"

"The Peterson Home," Kate answered. This was the only foster care agency she could think of that was vaguely in the neighborhood. Carla had been on the Board years ago. It had started as a home for unwed mothers in the Depression.

Haddie was puzzled.

"I thought Jenny was a Catholic. Peterson is still Protestant, isn't it?"

"I think I heard that her mother converted last Christmas," Kate said, wishing she could stop talking. "She's Pentecostal now."

"Really?"

"Something like that. They didn't give out every detail, of course. A woman is entitled to a little bit of privacy."

"But surely…"

Kate shrugged and gave her best polite Upper East Side young matron smile.

Across the playground, Jenny stepped back to absorb the full effect of Miranda in the midst of so many beauties. Heather, who was two years older and a head taller than Jenny picked up Miranda between thumb and forefinger and dropped the doll onto the ground. Sanitation men treat garbage cans with more respect.

"You shouldn't have done that," Kate whispered.

She was expecting the nanny to raise her head from the magazine at the sounds of discord and either tell Heather to apologize and restore Miranda to the bench, or give the brat a healthy smack across the rear end. The nanny never moved. Jenny did.

With the lightning speed of a commando raid, she swooped in, grabbed the doll closest to her, a spicy little Mexican *señorita*, dressed in a magnificently embroidered costume—and tossed her into the biggest and muddiest puddle in the playground. The act, for all its swiftness, seemed to transpire in slow motion. It took Kate's breath away.

The doll made a soft "bloop" noise as it landed and its skirt and stuffing began to absorb the brownish puddle water. The girls' mouths fell open, they looked at each other, and then fell into hysterics, flailing their arms and screaming at the top of their lungs.

Jenny retrieved Miranda and held her safely in her arms, gaping at the two of them.

"Miss Stone!!" they cried. "Look what she did!!"

"Jenny, come here!" Kate called.

Aroused, the nanny rolled her magazine into a weapon and took a swipe at Jenny. Miss Stone was agile for her size, but no match for Jenny, who slipped beneath her arms and snatched another doll, flinging it wildly into the air. This one caught in the branches of a locust tree and hung there by its thick blond chignon.

"Stop her!" shrieked the girls. "Stop her!!"

"Monster!" the nanny yelled. "Criminal!"

"Jenny, stop!"

Miss Stone lunged and swung again, but Jenny eluded her, circling in as though the dolls were fresh meat and she was a hungry hyena.

Kate rushed across the playground and planted herself between Jenny and Miss Stone.

"You leave her alone!" Kate said.

"I'll see her fanny smacked!" snarled the nanny.

"Over my dead body!"

Kate was feeling fairly wild with adrenaline herself, but aware nonetheless that she was no match for a woman with forearms the width of stout trees. With Jenny safely behind her, Kate was looking for a chance to turn and run, when she saw the concentric circles widening in the puddles. Then the gray skies began to open in earnest. Kate had never been so happy to see rain.

The two girls went crazy all over again.

"Our dolls! Miss Stone, our dolls are getting wet!"

Screeching, they launched an assault on Miss Stone, hitting her with their fists and kicking her in the legs as though she were an obstinate mule that was not moving fast enough. Kate didn't hesitate another second. She grabbed Jenny and hurried out the gate to the street. Jenny seemed in awe of the commotion she had created and kept glancing back at the girls, who were running in tight circles beneath the locust tree, still screaming, their arms stretched ineffectually toward their doll which suddenly dropped, leaving its hair stuck among the leaves and falling to their feet, bald as a billiard ball.

Kate and Jenny were headed for the 86th Street cross-town bus stop when Kate noticed that the social worker was watching the two of them and gesturing animatedly as she talked on a cell phone.

Kate couldn't hear what she was saying, but she was sure that they were the subjects of the conversation. Who was she calling—CPS, or the police?

At that moment, a cab came by and Kate hailed it, bundling herself and Jenny inside.

A block away on 86th, she suggested to Jenny that she try and rest for a few minutes, and pushed the girl's head down into her lap as a police car sped past in the opposite direction. Kate chastened herself for her paranoia, but as they reached Second Avenue, she told the driver that she had changed her mind about the destination and wanted to be left instead at 79th and Lexington.

They stood at that corner until the cabby had driven away. Then Kate led Jenny into the subway station at 77th Street and took the local to 96th. They had emerged into the humid air again and were nearly up the hill before Kate was aware of Jenny crying hard beside her, holding Miranda by the neck and hissing at her.

"Bad girl! You're such a *bad* girl!"

The sun poked through the thinning clouds. A light breeze hinted that the rain was over and dry air was on its way. Kate found a deli and bought Jenny a fruit drink and cinnamon bun, and they sat on a stoop nearby.

As never before, she was aware of the vulnerability of any child, and of her growing affection for this one. She wrapped her arm around those bony shoulders and smiled at the memory of her dodging Miss Stone, of her own confrontation with that young behemoth, and the prospect of the two of them wrestling in the mud.

The police? Had they been called to break up the fight, or to take Jenny off to a welfare agency? Or perhaps it had been a coincidence and they were headed to some other place entirely. Who could say? One thing was sure: she was not taking Jenny to that playground again. She would stick with the playground at 96th and Fifth, where they had never been bothered.

"Listen to me, Jenny," she said, hugging the child gently. "I don't know what you are thinking about, or what went on in that playground, but it was not your fault. Blame me, or blame that stupid babysitter, or those two *prima donnas,* but leave yourself alone." She paused and picked up Miranda, who had been placed haphazardly on the step between them. She straightened the doll's dress and finger-combed her hair. "Number two," she said, causing Jenny to stop chewing on her straw and look over. "I'm not sure why this is, but you seem to think that everything that happens is your fault because you are 'bad.' This is not true. You are not bad and I will not listen to you say so anymore. Your mother had to leave for a little while, but that was not your fault in any way. I don't know all that has happened in your life, but I do know to a certainty that it was not your fault either. You are not bad. You are a sweet and pretty little person and you should not be thinking anything else. Please try to remember that. Even if you don't understand why stuff happens, you must not believe it was because of anything you did. You are not bad. You are good. Extremely, fantastically good. And so is Miranda."

The girl sat still for a few seconds. Kate could hear the sound of fruit juice being drained through the straw, and the girl's chest heaved once inside the curl of Kate's arm. Then, quick as a young frisky cub, she spun and threw her arms around Kate's neck. Tears were streaming down her cheeks and her face was contorted with the effort not to cry. She nuzzled awkwardly against Kate and kissed her over and over with little pecks that covered her forehead and eyes and chin.

"I love you, Katy," she said in her high-pitched voice. "I love you so much."

Twelve

They ate their picnic lunch at home and relaxed for the rest of the afternoon. A reissue of *Bambi* was playing at a nearby movie theater, and Kate planned an early dinner so they could make the 6:30 show.

The rice was almost finished cooking and she had put the vegetables on to steam, when Jenny came into the kitchen with a big grin on her face.

"What's funny?" Kate asked.

"There's a cab driver out front on the sidewalk," she said. "And Sally's yelling at him."

Kate turned down the burners and walked to the front window.

The driver and Sally had moved their argument onto the stoop, close to the front of the building and out of sight from Kate's viewpoint. As far as she could tell, Sally had been bagging the trash and leaving it at the curb for tomorrow's pick-up, and now was assuming the position of guard dog in front of the building's entrance.

"Let me by," she could hear the man say. His voice had a West Indian lilt and had a tendency to become high-pitched when excited. "I want to go inside this building."

"I told you there ain't nobody here that meets your description. So go away or I'll knock your lights out."

"Don't be foolish," he said. "The young lady told me she lived right here. I'm telling you."

"And I'm telling you that she *don't* live here. Now beat it."

"Then I will call the police."

"Call the freakin' National Guard, if you want. You ain't coming in."

He took a step back, thwarted for the moment. His voice rose another octave.

"But this was very important to her. She asked me to follow a car. She gave me money."

Kate threw open the sash and stuck her head out as far as she could without feeling she would throw up.

"Wait! I'll be right down!"

When Kate reached the sidewalk, she recognized the cab driver she had spoken to the night before. He was standing with his arms folded across his chest, his chin jutting into space, and a frown on his lips as his eyes bored into Sally. He waved one large black hand as Kate appeared.

"You see! I told you. Francis knows what he's talking about."

"You described her all wrong," Sally replied. "You said she was tall and thin. Kate ain't tall."

The man pointed his finger at Sally.

"You just don't like black people!"

"Go to freakin' hell!"

"Please stop fighting, guys," Kate said. "Francis, I'm very glad you came back. I didn't expect to see you again after you threw my money out the window."

"Franies don't take money unless he earn it."

"Here we go," Sally said. "Spare me from freakin' honest cab drivers."

"Sally, please!" Kate said. "Francis, were you able to follow the car?"

The driver had a face that seemed made of rubber. He grimaced now, and it was as if someone had just kicked him hard on the shin.

"I think we can take that as a 'no'," said Sally.

"Hah!" said Francis. "Francis tell you exactly what he do. Each step of the way. Boom, boom, boom." He hit his palm with soft karate chops to emphasize his intention. "You remember Francis got a late start."

"Here comes the con," Sally said. "I can smell it."

"Sally, hush! Please, continue, Francis. I do remember."

"The lights were changing to yellow even as Francis started. He made it through one after another with his foot to the floor." He held out his hands as though holding a steering wheel, his eyes fixed with determination. "But at 79th, there is a very short light. It's not synchronized properly. And Francis had to stop. A truck was already crossing in front of the cab." His shoulders slumped in disappointment. But just as quickly, he revived, his hand extended, pointing into the distance. "But Francis could see the car you told him to watch going down Lexington. It turned right somewhere before 72nd Street. But Francis can't be sure if it was 73rd or 75th. I think it was 73rd. Francis guess the car's destination was between Lexington and 5th."

"And maybe,' Sally interjected. "Maybe the car continued over to 5th and then down to 67th and through the freakin' park."

"Francis don't think so," the man said solemnly.

"Francis don't *think* so," Sally said.

134

Francis waved his finger in front of Sally as though it were a metronome.

"You listen to Francis. If that driver was going across town, he had plenty of time to go down to 67th Street and turn there. That's the direct route for the cabbie. It doesn't make sense the other way. Too many lights."

"Yeah, bullshit."

The driver raised his head a little higher so that he was looking at Sally past his nostrils. He didn't reply to her otherwise.

"Thank you for your help," Kate said. "Here's twenty dollars. Is that okay?"

"No, no. It was only a four dollar fare."

"But you came back. That doubles it. Here's a ten. Are we square?"

"Fair and square," the cab driver said, clapping his hands twice to seal the arrangement. He gave her a wide smile and pulled a business card from his shirt pocket. "You call Francis if you need a trip to the airport. Or send a text. Francis will take good care of you."

"Thank you, Francis," she said.

"And you," he said to Sally. "You *walk* to the airport."

He left, and she and Sally went upstairs. As they reached their landing, Sally turned to her.

"You know, you oughta treat your friends a little better, Katy. I'm trying to save you from a freakin' con man and you come off all over *me.*"

Kate hesitated, and then led Sally to the far end of the hall where she was sure Jenny could not overhear.

"You must think I'm really stupid."

"What are you talking about now?" Sally asked.

"You think I don't know what was going on downstairs? You don't want me talking to Linda and you don't want me finding out where she lives. That's what's going on."

"You are losing your freakin' mind."

"I don't think so. You say you're my friend. Well, my *friend* would have told me Linda was at her apartment last night. My *friend* would have remembered that I wanted to talk to her about making arrangements for her daughter. Right, *friend*?"

Sally's face turned red and she rushed at Kate like a bull that had just been skewered by a *piccadore*. She bumped her chest up against Kate's, knocking her backward a step.

"Don't start with the freakin' sarcastic bullshit to *me*, Katy."

"What are you going to do, punch me? Go ahead. Show me what a friend you are."

"Goddamn your ass, I *should* punch your freakin' face. What the hell did you want me to do? Handcuff her to the freakin' heating pipes? Can't you tell when someone doesn't want to talk?"

"I wanted the *chance*."

"You got the chance and what did it get you? She calls you a freakin' saint and you go to freakin' mush."

"You *were* listening then?"

"I heard bits. I heard enough."

"Damn you!"

"Yeah, damn me! I spent two hours arguing with Linda! Okay? Was it for me? Huh? Does it matter a rat's ass to me, if the kid goes to stay in a freakin' foster home? I was arguing for *you*, Katy. She says she needs four weeks more. Four weeks! I told her she ain't got four *days* left. I told her you were at the end of your rope with the Creephead."

"I never said that."

"'I never *said* that.' You really are a beauty sometimes, Katy. You think if you don't actually say the words it ain't so."

"I happen to like Jenny. But I have to look for a job. And Roger is coming home soon. I *can't* keep taking care of her. There's a difference, Sally."

"However you want to say it is okay with me. The point is that you weren't put on God's green earth to take care of somebody else's kid. I told Linda all this. For two freakin' hours I told her. And for another thirty minutes after she called me back later."

"And what did she say?"

Sally paused. She took a deep breath. "She said she called a few people she knew, just like you suggested. But nobody could help her. She said to thank you, Katy. She knows you did all you could."

"Oh, Christ..."

"It ain't as bad as all that. Linda's due real soon. You saw her, she's as big and ripe as a freakin' watermelon. Two weeks is her date. Then you got a few days after. You know, you don't have a kid and then walk out the next day and go dancing. She ain't a freakin' farm animal. So anyway, I *told* her. You see, I was thinking about you. She's ready for this now."

"And what about Jenny? Is she ready?"

"Jenny ain't never going to be ready as you want her to be, Katy. But she can take it. She's made of freakin' galvanized steel. She don't even rust."

Kate felt tears slipping out of her eyelids, down her cheek. "I'm sorry, Sally."

Sally put her arm around her and hugged her. "Sorry? You freakin' wimp. You got nothin' to be sorry about. Linda was right. You've been real good to the kid."

"I could do for another week. Ten days, maybe. That'll give her more time to find a place for Jenny. Not a foster home."

"You're nuts. Give it up, Katy. Give it up."

"I want you to tell Linda for me, Sally. You're tougher than me. This is the end of the line. One more week. Tell her!"

She was trying to make her voice firm, but the tears made it waver and break.

"Of course I'll tell her. If that's what you want."

"It's what I want."

Sally wrapped her arms around Kate and hugged her, kissing her tenderly on the cheek.

"But don't go looking for her, huh? No more of the freakin' Perry Mason and Paul Adams routine? Give Linda that much respect."

"I wasn't following Linda."

"Katy, I was just with you downstairs. Remember the cabby?"

"That's not what was going on. Anthony was waiting for Linda last night."

"Anthony? What are you talking about?!"

"He must have known she comes to your place to visit sometimes. I didn't notice him until she got in a car and he took off after her. I wanted to tell her. I couldn't just leave Jenny. That's why I called the cab."

"Oh, Jesus. You should have let me know this before."

Sally started to pace back and forth in the narrow hall as Kate described the conversation she'd had in the park with Anthony.

"I meant to tell you, but the cabby didn't come back and I…"

Sally cut her off with a wave of her hand.

"She's gotta hear about this. Anthony's dangerous. You don't know this guy like I do."

"What can we do? Should we go down there now?"

"No. Just hold tight. She left me a number last night where I can leave a message. I'll take care of it."

"What do you think he's going to do?"

"I don't know. He's crazy. I keep telling you that. He used to beat her up pretty bad, I know that."

"Maybe we should call the police."

"No. Let me handle this, Katy. Okay? No freakin' police. I'll tell her about you and Jenny and I'll tell her about Anthony. She'll know what to do. She's been taking care of herself for a long time. Just promise me you'll stay out of this. Okay?"

"Okay, I promise."

Thirteen

Kate had planned to take Gail out to lunch the next day, both to thank her for getting Jenny's birth certificate and to catch up on the intervening events of their lives. Mrs. Morley was supposed to take care of Jenny for the few hours when Kate would be gone, but she had forgotten that she had to go to a funeral for an old friend from the neighborhood who had died earlier in the week.

Sally was at work. Mrs. Morley had no suggestions for stand-in baby-sitters. Every other person Kate could think of would be working.

"Jenny," she said finally, as the noon hour approached. "Put on something nice and comb Miranda's hair. We're going out to lunch."

They took the No. Six train to Canal Street. Along the way, Kate explained that Gail was an old friend from the days when Kate had delivered papers to Family Court for her mother, Carla, whose practice had always specialized in matrimonial law.

Apparently, Jenny had never considered the possibility that Kate had a mother or a father, and she had many questions, which were difficult to answer, starting with the name of her father, which Kate had never known. Carla had raised Kate without the help of any man, and whether because of her fierce pride or some other buried reason, she had never given Kate any information about him, or even explained why there had never been any contact. He was dead, and that was all she would say on the subject. As Kate got older, she stopped believing Carla and this became a source of continuing friction. What could be the harm in giving her his name? Had there been an affair? Was he someone important, or someone she'd met for a sordid one-night stand? Infinite fantasies were spun around this mystery.

When Kate became a teenager, Carla's refusal to answer seemed especially perverse and just another way for Carla to control her, the way she controlled other aspects of her life. She never had liked any of the guys Kate had dated. And the idea that she might work in publishing or become a writer was treated as a frivolous waste of time in a world where so many people needed help. Carla did not say it in so many words, but Kate knew that law school was the preferred path and that a life of penury and hardship working for the poor was the ideal. Carla & Daughter, the sign would say on the storefront window. No thanks. No way.

To Jenny, Kate tried to explain that her father was dead (which is what Carla had always told her) and that she didn't see her mother much anymore. Kate had hoped that this would be enough to cut off further questions. But what works in the adult world does not always work with a guileless child.

"Why, Katy?" she asked. "Was she mean to you?"

Kate smiled slightly, wondering how to answer and close off the subject quickly.

"No," she said finally. "She wasn't mean to me." Kate stopped herself. Jenny was sitting beside her on the subway seat, pressed between Kate and a young man reading the newspaper who was taking up more than his fair share of the space. She turned her shimmering eyes upward to look at Kate's face, searching it for something Kate didn't want to discuss with a child, or think about herself for that matter. Had she been mean? Certainly not in any way that Jenny was likely to understand. She had never abandoned her. Never made her live in squalor. Never hit her. "Let me just put it this way. She's a lawyer and she likes to help people. She's a great person that way. There are thousands of clients of hers around the city that would tell you how great she is and the tremendous effort she puts out for them. I used to hear it all the time. But she wasn't such a great mommy. Okay?"

Jenny nodded, working her way through this puzzle as the train stopped at Spring Street and started up again. Then she put her hand on Kate's.

"Do you *hate* her, Katy?" As she spoke that word, her voice rose in pitch and five thin fingers curled around Kate's hand and squeezed hard.

The little stab of pain that resulted seemed to be matched with one Kate felt inside. She lifted her arm and draped it over Jenny's shoulder and hugged her.

"No, I don't hate her, Jenny," Kate said. "She's my mother."

She wondered if it were really true.

~ * ~

The Canal Street stop was on the edge of Chinatown, and it was not easy to keep Jenny moving past the stores. Fish of all shapes and colors glistened on mounds of ice, bakery windows were filled with cookies and small cakes, variety shops sold slippers and embroidered bags and ingenious fold-out fans and jackets of colorful silk, and so wide a range of gadgets and toys that adults paused to admire the display.

"We'll stop later, I promise," Kate said. "But we have to hurry now."

In a few minutes, they reached the black granite structure that was the Family Court for the County of New York. As Kate led her inside, Jenny pulled back sharply. A look of dread came over her face.

"Katy?" she said in a pathetic voice. "Katy…"

"What is it? What's wrong?"

"I don't like this place."

"What's not to like? It's just a building. Come on. You're being silly."

"Please, Katy."

"We have to meet Gail on the eighth floor. She's waiting for us."

Kate got her past the front door, but Jenny was trembling with fear as they started through the maze of ropes and stanchions set up in the lobby to accommodate the long lines of visitors and litigants. When they reached the metal detectors, and saw the uniformed court officer standing there like a colossus, elbows akimbo, feet planted, Jenny lost it. Gasping, she wrapped her arms tight around Kate's waist.

"Jenny, *stop*," she whispered, trying at the same time to smile at the court officer whose gun and nightstick bulged at his hips.

Kate emptied her pockets and opened her pocketbook for examination, shrugging in Jenny's direction as if to show that it was no big deal. He nodded at her and she moved forward with Jenny still clinging to her. The court officer stopped their progress.

"Sorry, lady. You have to go through one at a time."

"But…"

"I've got rules, lady. I'm sorry."

"Okay. Jenny, did you hear the man?" She felt her tone becoming impatient, and convinced herself that a bit of anger might not be a bad thing. Maybe it would snap Jenny out of this odd behavior. She peeled Jenny's arms off and stepped through the detector. "Now it's your turn. Come on now."

Jenny shook her head and stood rooted to the spot.

"Jenny! Now!!"

Tears started to fall down the girl's cheeks.

"I could use the wand on her," the officer said. He held up a portable metal detector as he spoke. He was trying to be helpful, but Jenny seemed to think he would hit her. She let out a cry of anguish and fell to the floor, screaming,

"No, Katy. Don't let him take me. Don't let him hurt me. I want to stay with you. Please, Katy. Please, please, please."

Kate swept the still crying child up in her arms and began walking to the exit. One of the other court officers helped her with the door.

"Would you do me a favor?" Kate said. "We're supposed to have lunch with Gail Harding from the eighth floor record room. If I call, I'm going to be put into voicemail. Maybe you could get through and tell her we're here? We'll be in that park across the street."

The officer agreed and they went outside to wait. Jenny wasn't crying any more, but her breathing was still jagged and she sat as close as she could to Kate. Her gaze traveled anxiously over those around them. To distract her, Kate started talking about the place where they were sitting.

It wasn't much of a park: there were a few trees and benches and some especially bedraggled pigeons. But deep beneath the surrounding concrete and asphalt were the remains of the Collect Pond. Once it had been a beautiful body of fresh water in the middle of lower Manhattan. Fulton tried out a model of his steamboat there. Newspaper stories told of men and women sitting on the hills in the winter watching ice skaters do their stuff. By the early 1800s, it had become polluted with dead animals and trash and the refuse of leather tanning shops. Over several years, it had been filled in with the soil and rock of the hills that used to surround it and others that were leveled in the name of New York development. Now there was only a small memorial plaque and a dirty park and an asphalt lot for cars.

While Kate was talking, Gail emerged smiling and waving. She wasn't wearing any sort of uniform, but Jenny was not quite ready to trust anyone who emerged from that looming building. All the same, as they started up Lafayette to Chinatown, Jenny no longer had to cling to Kate. Gail had a friendly manner and a hearty laugh, and it was hard for Jenny not to give any response whatsoever when Gail made incessant small talk about her favorite restaurant, asking what they wanted for lunch and whether Jenny knew enough Chinese to order the food.

Jenny shook her head, shyly, looking up at Kate. A hint of a smile was creeping back onto her face.

"No? Then how are we going to eat if you can't talk Chinese? Oh, Lord, Kate, I told you we needed *somebody* who can order."

Jenny giggled.

"Wait!" Gail said. "I just remembered. You can count, right? Yeah? We'll be all right then."

They went into a restaurant that Gail frequented. The owner and the waiters all bowed and made a special fuss over Jenny, pinching her cheeks gently and telling Kate how pretty she was.

"They got that right," Gail said, after Jenny had solemnly given the numbers of the lunch specials they wanted and the waiter had bowed and disappeared into the kitchen. "I know you've got some boys after you. How many boyfriends you got, Jenny? Ten? Twelve?"

Jenny giggled again and turned red this time.

"Nooooo," she said.

"More?! You got more than twelve boyfriends? Girrrlllllll!"

So it went through lunch. Gail expertly drew her into a conversation in which Jenny said that Miranda was her favorite doll, going to the playground was her favorite thing to do and Kate was her best friend in the whole world.

"So how come you don't like the place where I work?" Gail asked.

They had laid out the money for the bill and were walking to the door, nodding and smiling at the staff.

"I just don't," Jenny said.

"You've been there before?" Kate asked.

They continued for a few steps. Tears began to fall down Jenny's face.

Gail bent over and gave the girl a hug.

"No more questions, baby. That's okay. I'm sorry to bother you like this. But you'll come down and see me again, won't you? I don't want to wait too long to go eat Chinese food again. Okay, Jenny?"

Jenny managed an almost imperceptible nod of her head.

"Okay," she said.

Gail and Kate said goodbye, and as they embraced, Gail whispered,

"I'm going to do a little more checking in the file room. Something isn't right."

Kate just nodded and felt the knot in her stomach throb at the thought of what she might find.

~ * ~

Afterward, Kate took Jenny on the 6 train to 68th Street and walked north from there through Central Park, retracing their steps backward from their earlier visit and ending up at the 85th Street playground at Fifth Avenue. They'd never been there and Jenny

146

enjoyed climbing the sides of the brick pyramid and crawling through the tunnel and, most of all, hurtling down the slide. She didn't want to leave and Kate was in no hurry either. Around 6:00 p.m. she bought them both a couple of Sabrett's hotdogs and a bag of chips and water (not every meal can be healthy). The food was spread out on a bench and Jenny interrupted her running and climbing to eat a mouthful here or there. They stayed until the sun had fallen beyond the buildings at the west of Central Park. The only person left was a homeless man who had been going through the trash for soda cans and bottles and any scraps he could feed to his dog, a "mixed breed," to put it charitably. Despite the temperature, a wool cap was pulled low over his forehead. Dirt caked his face and hands.

He gestured to Kate as they were walking past him through the front gate.

"I found this in the sand just now," he said in a raspy voice. "Would you like it for your daughter?"

He handed her a barrette made of a silver-colored metal with blue and red cut glass set in an alternating pattern. It sparkled even in the fading light.

"Thank you," Kate said, thinking that the piece couldn't have been lying there very long. The metal showed no sign of weathering.

"Thank you," Jenny repeated.

"You're welcome, little one," the man said. It sounded as though someone had taken sand paper to his vocal cords.

They passed through the gates and were starting up Fifth Avenue when Kate gave Jenny a few dollars and asked her to bring it to the man in the playground.

Without a word, Jenny took the money and raced to where he was sitting and back out to the street again.

"My mother once told me that you should always give kindness for kindness," Kate said to her. "I guess we should add that to our book about rules and exceptions."

Jenny didn't say anything, just held Kate's hand tight in hers and swung it, humming as they walked the rest of the way home.

~ * ~

The answering machine was blinking when they got to the apartment. Roger's voice promised both good news and bad news, and while Jenny got ready for bed, Kate called him.

Kate opted for the bad news first.

"Okay, here's what's happening," he said. "We submitted our briefs today and argued our case before the judge, who, by the way, is one of the most crotchety old so-and-so's that ever sat on the federal bench. Anyway, he was supposed to decide whether the client gets a preliminary injunction or not, and he was supposed to tell us this afternoon. Only, he has a bright idea. A big trial he was supposed to start next week just got settled unexpectedly. So he has a block of time opening up, and he says he wants us to do all the preparation in the next week and we can have a trial the week after. So instead of coming home tonight, I have to stay out here and start doing depositions. The first one is tomorrow."

"Saturday?"

"Saturday. I'm going to be preparing most of the night. I'm looking at two weeks of hell."

"So, what's the good news?"

"I talked to the partner in charge. He said he was going to fly his wife out here and have her stay with him at the hotel for the duration. Client pays, airfare and all. So I asked if I could do the same thing and he said yes."

"Why would you want his wife staying in your hotel room?"

"Very funny, Kate. I'm so glad to see your wit is as sharp as ever. So, how about it? San Francisco is beautiful with the hills and the fog rolling in. And we have a great view of it from our hotel."

"I don't think so, Roger. I'm still trying to find a job, remember?"

"That's why this is so perfect. You don't have to worry about getting time off. You can just get on a plane. Relax for a while. The classified ads will still be there when you return."

"I really don't believe you'd be saying that if you were the one looking for a job. It's not something you can just not think about. It's always there in the back of my mind. Every morning when I wake up, the first thing I do is go online to look for new ads. Then I go buy the paper and check those ads."

"So you can get the *Times* out here and the room is wired. You can send resumes by e-mail."

"You know that's not going to work."

"It will if you want it to."

"C'mon, Roger. What am I supposed to do all day, go sightseeing with the partner's wife?"

"Don't be ridiculous. We'll see each other."

"When? You're going to be working fifteen, eighteen hours a day. I'll be lucky if I see you for a half hour dinner, you know that."

"I did intend to sleep sometimes."

"Lovely. I'm sure if you look in the Yellow Pages you'll find some girl who'll fill your needs. Maybe the firm will even pay."

"Why are you getting so nasty?"

"Why can't you understand that I might not want to sit in a hotel all day—even in San Francisco—for the privilege of seeing you for an hour during your free time? I have a life too."

There was a silence then. Kate realized that her hands were shaking. Moisture coated her forehead, her palms.

"You know this is all bullshit, don't you?" he asked. "This is all about that kid. She's still there living with you. You're giving up a free two-week vacation in San Francisco with me because you have to take care of that goddamned kid."

"Her name is Jenny."

"Of course. *Jenny*. Excuse me for not remembering her given name; we were so close at one time. No, wait, I must be confusing her with someone I'm actually related to."

"That's enough, Roger."

"Right. It's plenty. I agree." Silence ensued. She didn't want to fight with him. She felt a headache starting. Abruptly, he continued. "So it's decided, I guess, that you're not coming out here. But tell me. What happens when I return to New York? Is this something I'm supposed to be looking forward to? Are we going to be sleeping on that wreck of a sofa in your living room? Or am I expected to move her into my place until the great and wonderful Linda deigns to retrieve her offspring?"

"God forbid you should be inconvenienced for a terribly sad little girl, Roger."

"A terribly sad girl with problems you can't begin to understand. You don't know what's right for a kid like this. You don't even know if you're helping her."

"I know she's happier today than she was two weeks ago."

"Yeah, and *I* know you've been conned. Linda has found a sucker and is laughing her ass off somewhere."

"No, Roger. That's where you are totally wrong. I wasn't conned by anyone. That was the excuse. I admit that I would say that Sally dumped her in my lap. Or that Linda wouldn't come back. I made it sound as if I had no will at all. But I realize now that it was not true. I was saying all these things because I felt I needed an excuse to explain what I was doing. Taking in a kid? How foolish! But the fact is, I *wanted* to take care of Jenny. If I didn't, I would have found a way to stop it a long time ago. I don't know *why* I wanted this. Maybe it was because I realized somewhere inside of me just how selfish I had become. I'm not sure. Maybe I had a need, too. Maybe I needed someone to give love to unconditionally, to give something, just because it is *right* to give. So let me finally get it straight with you, Roger, because this is very important. I don't blame Sally. I don't blame Linda. I don't blame the fates that conspired to put Jenny into my care. I'm not looking for sympathy from you or anyone. I made the decision to take care of Jenny, and I'm going to continue to take care of her until her mom returns for her. That's it."

"I see. And I can like it or lump it? Is that about it?"

"No. You can accommodate it, the way I accommodate your trip to San Francisco."

"That's just a little different, my dear."

"So you say. But I don't think so, except that it was a decision *you* made."

"And now you've made yours."

She drew in a deep breath and let it out again. "Yes, I guess you're right. I made mine."

There was another long silence. She could hear the hum of the wires and the faint sound of another conversation going on over some crossed wires. But now she realized that she had stopped trembling. Her headache had eased. She felt a deep calm.

"I'm going to be very busy over the next week or so," Roger said. "It may be hard to talk every day."

"Call when you can. That's all."

"Okay. I just wanted you to know. And when I get back, we'll sort through this. Or not, I guess."

"I hope we do," she said. "I love you, Roger."

"Goodbye, Kate."

"Goodbye."

She got off the phone and went into the bedroom. Her hands were still trembling and her head felt as though a nail had been driven into her temple.

She was glad to see that Jenny had fallen asleep on her futon. Beside her was the latest *Frog and Toad* book that Kate had borrowed from the library. It was open to one of their favorite stories: Toad sent Frog a card, only he gave it to the snail to deliver and it took forever to arrive. But when the card did come, finally, it was appreciated as if it had been sent via Federal Express.

Gently, she put the book on the shelf and tucked Jenny in beneath the cover, her head on her pillow. As Kate turned off the light, Jenny stirred, smiling with the pleasure of sleep as she snuggled against the pillow.

"I love you, Katy," she said.

"I love you too," Kate replied.

She had turned the phone ringer down, but when she got back into the living room she saw that the answering machine was accepting a call. She let it go until she heard Gail's voice.

"Girl," she was saying. "You better *pick* up this phone. Don't be using that answering machine to screen *my* calls..."

Kate lifted the receiver to her ear. "Okay, mommy," she said."

"Now, look," Gail replied. "You can call me momma if you want. But if I'm your momma, you better be expecting me to come up there and whup your behind when you get smart with me."

"Sorry, Gail. I just this minute got off a call with Roger, and I'm still a little testy."

"Then I'm thinking he must be breaking up furniture someplace."

"I'm not so sure."

"I am. You said he's a smart boy. If he's smart, he won't stay away long. And if he's not that smart, good riddance, baby. The subways stop every ten minutes in New York City. Just get on another one."

Kate paused a moment.

"That's what Carla used to say. But the advice doesn't go down so easy when you're fifteen."

"Advice doesn't go down easy any time when your momma is the one telling you, honey. That's the point. But I didn't call you up to talk about mothers. I did some checking on the computer down in court, just like I said I would. Has to be something makes that little girl so scared of this place."

"You're the best, Gail."

"Yeah, yeah, yeah... Well there's a proceeding for child support that a Linda Gilmour brought a few years ago against a guy by the name of Dilworth. Lawrence Dilworth."

"I've never heard of him."

"According to the caption, it's someone she thought was the father of her kid."

"The father of Jenny? Can we look at the file?"

"It's in storage. I'd have to requisition it."

"I couldn't ask you to do that. Don't worry about it."

"I ain't worried. It just may take a little doing, that's all. I'll let you know if I find out anything."

"Thanks, Gail. You really are the best. I'm serious."

"I'm not close to being the best, baby. But I'll tell you this."

"What?"

"I'm pretty damned good! Yes, Lord."

Kate could hear Gail laughing on the other end of the phone as she hung up. "Yes, Lord," she repeated. "Yes, Lord."

~ * ~

Later that evening, as Kate was getting ready for bed, on an impulse she went into the living room and pulled the Manhattan White Pages off its shelf. There were several listings for Dilworth, only one with the first name Lawrence. She was not surprised to find that he lived on 74th Street between Park and Madison.

When she typed his name into Google on her computer, she found something even more interesting. He worked for the same law firm that Linda had worked for years earlier, before her life had become unglued.

Fourteen

Kate was not surprised that she awoke at 3:00 A.M.—the worry hour, as she called it. Her and Roger's sharp words rattled around in her mind, and she was acutely conscious of the empty space beside her in her bed. She felt as though a line had been crossed. Certainly, her position regarding Jenny had been made very clear. But why exactly she was risking her relationship with Roger to take care of Jenny was still not clear to her. Because it was the right thing to do? Really? How can a person ever know the difference between what is done because it is right and what is done for less savory reasons—for convenience or for pride. As the minutes passed and she tossed and turned, Kate remembered something Carla had once told her: "We can never know what is right in any absolute sense. We can only do what we feel is right. In the morning we look at ourselves in the mirror." Which person do you want to see? The person who made the decision to take care of Jenny or not? Kate knew the answer to that question at least, and with that to calm her, she finally drifted off to sleep.

~ * ~

The next morning, Kate slept later and more deeply than usual and was barely aware of the ringing of the doorbell. Then Jenny was tugging at her arm and begging her to get up.

"Katy, Katy!! There's someone in the hall. He wants to speak to you."

The sudden awakening and the stranger at her door frightened her. There was no cause that she could identify, but she was possessed for the moment with a sense of dread centered around Anthony's name and face.

She pulled a robe around her and opened the door as far as she could with the chain lock still connected. Through the three-inch crack she saw a man in a gray uniform. Was he a policeman? He had no hat, no gun, no badge. Rather, he was holding a clipboard.

She took off the chain and opened the door wide. Jenny peered around her. On the floor was a large arrangement of flowers. Beside it was a smaller, but equally beautiful assortment. Next to that, was a thin glass vase with one perfect rose.

"Kate Andersen? Sign here, please," the man said.

Kate did as she was asked and started to open the card.

"Jenny Gilmour?" the man continued in a crisp tone. "Sign, please."

"I can't write my name yet," Jenny said, giggling. "I can do 'J'."

"That'll be fine," the man said. "And where is Miranda? No last name."

Kate and Jenny stared at each other.

"I'll sign for her," Kate said. "She's still sleeping."

The deliveryman left with a nice tip, and Kate and Jenny brought the flowers inside. Kate read the note aloud.

"To all the girls in my life. (At least I *hope* they are still in my life). With love, accommodatingly, Roger."

"What's it mean, Katy?"

"It means Roger loves us and he hopes we love him."

"Do you love him, Katy?" she asked.

156

"Yes, Jenny. I love him very much."

"Then I love him too!" Jenny said with great determination in her voice. "But not as much as I love you, okay?"

"Okay."

Kate hugged her and felt those thin arms in return, tight around her neck. Tears were lining her cheeks, and she continued hugging the girl until she was able to wipe them away. She was afraid Jenny might not understand why she was crying. She wasn't sure she understood, herself.

It was only 5:00 a.m. San Francisco time, but Kate called anyway. She and Roger spoke briefly. Kate promised him a weekend in Montauk—just the two of them—as soon as he was done with the trial. Roger whispered a few words that made her blush. Then Kate put her hand over the phone.

"Does Miranda want to talk to Roger?" she asked.

Jenny frowned at her.

"Katy," she said, holding out her hands for the receiver. "Miranda is just a *doll*. But I want to say 'thank-you.'"

~ * ~

It took them a while to arrange the flowers just the right way in the apartment. Only then did they sit back to admire their handiwork over a leisurely breakfast. With a cup of fresh brewed coffee and a toasted bagel, Kate realized that for the first time in two weeks she was actually relaxed. She still went out to the newsstand later like clockwork, read the classifieds assiduously, and mailed off her resume to any and every opportunity she saw. The difference was that now she felt unhurried. She was sure that things would work out eventually.

That weekend, they went to the 96th Street playground on the edge of Central Park. This had become Kate's favorite, and not only because it was far away from Carl Schurz Park. Tall trees grew on all sides and the pace of the automobile traffic on upper Fifth Avenue was relatively easy to take, especially in the late afternoon. Sounds were softened by grass and shrubbery and the reservoir to the west. In the quiet, robins could be heard singing in the trees as the daylight waned.

But none of these refinements were important to a kid, Kate was sure. Nor could they explain why Jenny had a special spring to her step as they walked their familiar route that Sunday. As soon as they arrived, Jenny scanned the crowd of children and started off toward a sand area where she had spent a good deal of the previous afternoon. At this point, Kate recognized a girl from the day before who had seemed, if this were possible, to be as shy as Jenny. Somehow, they had found each other, which was surprising to Kate because she had never even been aware that Jenny had been searching for a friend. And yet she must have been all the time.

As the day progressed, Kate had to stop herself more than once from going over to them. Each of the girls maintained her distance in the sand, glancing tentatively in the other's direction every once in a while, mute as stones. Kate ached to have it work out for Jenny. Surely, she told herself, she could help this along without being too obvious. Couldn't she suggest a game? Or offer to buy that taciturn pair a coke? But some instinct told her to stay away, and by the end of that Sunday afternoon, Jenny and the girl, Tricia, were playing a modified version of follow-the-leader: walking across the chain bridge, sliding down the pole, repeating the process a bit faster, but not so fast as to leave the follower too far behind. It wasn't a major social happening. A casual observer might not have known they were playing together at all. But they waved goodbye to one another when it was time to go, Kate introduced herself to Tricia's babysitter, and Jenny's face was bright with pleasure on the way home.

Early the next morning—at the beginning of most people's normal workweek—Kate was checking the refrigerator for the makings of another picnic lunch, when the phone rang. Stevie, from the long-ago days of Hiroth Publishing, was on the line.

"Kate, oh my God," Stevie said, in a rush of words that seemed to erupt from the phone. "I'm sitting on a disaster here. An absolute disaster. I came in this morning, expecting to find a completed article on my desk, and instead I find a putrid mess. Everyone promised me this so-called writer was reliable. Oh my God, *reliable*. Meanwhile, I'm sitting here with a stack of things to do and a deadline in two days."

"Gee, I'm sorry, Stevie," Kate said, for lack of a better response.

"You've got to help me, Kate," Stevie continued. "You've *got* to help me. Promise me you will help me." Before Kate could get a word in edge-wise, Stevie was offering her the equivalent of two unemployment checks to turn the offending article into fine prose on a rush basis. "I know it's short notice. I know it's an imposition. But I remember how good you used to be at this kind of stuff, and if you would just give this a try, Kate, it would be a huge favor. I've made some notes on the copy I have that you might find useful. I don't know. My rear end is really on the line here."

"I'll come right down and pick it up," Kate said.

Jenny gave her a worried look from the doorway.

"Get your sneakers on, Jenny. We've got a short trip downtown and then we'll go on to the playground. We'll be there in time for lunch."

Jenny raced around getting ready while Kate made lunch, then combed Jenny's hair and made sure she brushed her teeth. In less than thirty minutes, they were on the subway headed downtown. It was past rush hour, and they were able to get a seat in a well-air-conditioned car. Dressed in cut-off shorts, tennis shoes and t-shirt, and with child in hand, Kate felt a pleasant detachment from the hustle-and-bustle world of commuters. Her lack of envy was reinforced as they reached Stevie's office suite. The food wagon had just arrived and harried workers were trying to decide whether to buy a stale sandwich or opt for a stale Danish and hope they would have the time to go out later for a more expensive stale sandwich.

When Stevie saw the two of them, she did not even say hello, but immediately went into a frown. For a moment, it seemed that she was debating whether to entrust the bungled manuscript to Kate at all. She held the folder to her chest and gave a long, meaningful glance in Jenny's direction.

"You do understand that I'm really counting on you, right?" Stevie said. "I was not kidding about my ass being on the line here."

"You want me to post bond?" Kate asked.

Stevie was silent, considering her options. She sucked at her lower lip. She looked at Jenny. She looked at Kate.

"I need this back in two days," she said finally. "Wednesday, no later than two. You have e-mail?"

"I'm unemployed, not homeless."

"Jesus… Kate…"

"Yes, I have e-mail. And in a pinch the Wi-Fi is free at Starbucks and the public library."

"Okay, okay. I get the point. I might survive if it's as late as three o'clock. I drop dead completely at three-thirty. I'll be unemployed myself by five-thirty."

Kate took the file from Stevie's clenched hands. It was apparently the only way to stop her from talking.

"Your ass is in good hands."

She and Jenny rode the Madison Avenue bus back uptown, because it brought them just a block from the playground. While Jenny knelt on the seat and looked out the window, Kate had the chance to read the material over, making some preliminary decisions about what was worth keeping. In the playground, while Jenny climbed over, under and around the equipment with Tricia, Kate sat in a shady spot and jotted notes, slashing away with a new blue pencil Stevie had thoughtfully given her. She planned a strategy for how the article had to be written, and the last piece fell into place on the walk home. After dinner, she was ready to pull up to her laptop.

This was the part Jenny enjoyed, the blur of Kate's fingers over the keys and the letters and words magically appearing on the screen. Sensing that something important was going on, Jenny kept very quiet while Kate worked, except to giggle at an exceptionally fast keyboard riff, or to hush Miranda, thereby reminding Kate how very quiet they were. As a result, Kate put in a couple of productive hours.

She stopped before Jenny's bedtime to give her a bath, and then they sat together on the futon in Jenny's corner of the bedroom. With the tensor lamp's narrow beam over her shoulder, a well-plumped cushion wedged behind her back, and Jenny curled beside her, it was a cozy place to read a story or two. And since this had become a bedtime ritual, Jenny's sleep had grown correspondingly sound. So on this evening, despite the specter of Stevie hovering about, reminding her whose ass was on the line, Kate read to Jenny until she drifted off to sleep. After tucking her in, she made a pot of strong tea. Two and a half hours later, she had finished the first re-draft.

~ * ~

In the morning, she did not need an alarm to awaken her. While the coffee perked, she read through the manuscript. By the time Jenny bounced out of bed and ate breakfast, Kate had reworked the last few wrinkles and the manuscript was ready. She sent an e-mail to Stevie with the manuscript attached. The telephone rang within five minutes of Kate hitting the 'send' button.

"You're kidding, right?" Stevie said. "You have another day to work on this."

"No. It's ready. But if you want me to send it tomorrow, that's okay too."

"Kate, c'mon. You know what I'm saying here. If you need more time, please take it. I mean, I really need this to be done well. Not just done."

"It is done well,' Kate snapped. "And if you're that goddamned worried about my work, call somebody else next time."

She hung up the phone and left with Jenny for the playground immediately afterward. Along the way, they purchased a lavish picnic lunch to celebrate the money Kate would be getting—dried papaya and mango, a chunk of watermelon, two glazed donuts. Charmed as all of her decisions seemed to be at this point, no sooner had they arrived than Tricia ran up to Jenny and the two girls hopped around in delight, holding hands and laughing. Tricia explained that she herself had been late and was afraid Jenny wouldn't be coming, and she and her babysitter were almost going to *leave,* and then Jenny had come just in time.

"Oh, *noooooo,*" Jenny squealed. "Did you hear that, Katy? Aren't we lucky?"

Of course we are, Kate thought, unwilling to suspect that the feeling she was experiencing could be ephemeral, or another setup for an even bigger fall. She and Jenny were happy, and they had every reason to be happy. They *deserved* to be happy.

"There is nobody luckier than us, Jenny," she said.

~ * ~

Tricia had to leave early because her parents were going out that evening. But Kate and Jenny felt like staying. Sitting arm in arm on a bench, they watched the babysitters pack up and herd their charges homeward as the day ended. By the time they were ready to start back, pedestrians were heading in the opposite direction toward the park, dressed in jogging outfits but striding along with the determination of people who had not yet let go of the office mindset.

As Kate and Jenny reached their building and walked up the stairs, they heard the phone ringing. They didn't rush. The answering machine was on. When they opened the door, it rang again. The machine indicated eight messages.

"Kate!" Stevie shrieked. "How can you do this to me? For pity's sake, carry your cell phone. This is crazy..."

"Calm down, Stevie. Calm down..."

"But I have work for you. And I can't very well find out if you want the work if I can't talk to you, although I already told everyone that you *would* do it, so you really have to do this for me, Kate. You will, won't you? I mean you did say you wanted work?"

Kate stood beside the window, cradling the receiver against her cheek as Stevie spoke. A breeze tossed the curtains and her shirt and sparked a memory of another day, when she had just moved back to New York from college and was giving her newly-installed phone number to friends. She had felt such confidence, not knowing exactly what she wanted to do, but believing she would find her niche, that she had some ability lying fallow inside her. A novelist? Okay. An editor? Okay. A freelancer working out of her apartment—emphasis on the "free." Her card—*Have Brain, Will Travel.* Of course.

Then weeks and months and years passed. Dreams faded. Confidence waned. Going it alone seemed too much of a chance to take. And now, here was Stevie, asking if she *wanted* that sort of work—wanted to be her own boss, wanted to be free—and the old dream seemed to be moving back into her grasp.

"Yeah," Kate said. The words emerged on a wave of laughter, with the realization that she would never answer an easier question in her lifetime. "Yeah, I want it."

The work was e-mailed to her, but on Thursday morning, Stevie invited Kate to meet a few of the other editors, and one in particular who had a big project coming up that she had not yet assigned to anyone. Kate called Tricia's babysitter and asked her to bring Jenny to the park that day, then took a shower, changed her clothes and hopped on the subway.

Kate shook all the necessary hands and made all the required small talk. As it turned out, one of the editors was trying to get someone to write a series of articles on New York neighborhoods. In Kate's allotted time, the editor sat forward in her chair while Kate outlined an article on Carnegie Hill that wove together the stone carvings and terra cotta figures in Yorkville, the old Beer Barrel Clock that once graced the top of the Ruppert Brewery on Third Avenue, Observatory Place, and, finally, the story of John Purroy Mitchel, the former mayor of this city whose gilded bust stares down 90th Street in front of the reservoir, and who was the only mayor in history, Kate was sure, to have died by falling out of an airplane. The assignment was hers by the time she left, with an advance check for half the fee in her pocket.

After that meeting, Kate took the Madison Avenue bus home and got off when it reached 72nd Street. She didn't have a plan, exactly, at least one that she admitted to herself, except that she was hoping to run into Linda on the street and tell her face to face that she would keep Jenny until Linda got herself together again. She was also curious about the address for Lawrence Dilworth.

It didn't turn out as she'd expected. She wandered along 73rd and 74th from Fifth to Lexington, but did not see Linda. When she reached the address for Mr. Dilworth, she found a hole in the ground where that particular building and the one beside it had been demolished and condominiums were destined to rise. She made a mental note to replace her phone book with a more recent version. Otherwise, she was at a loss as to what to do next, staring at the large poster that had been put up on the wooden fence, containing an artist's rendition of how beautiful the new place would look—an edifice in limestone and brick, it promised. Then she was conscious of a small dog sniffing at her ankle, and an elderly woman trying to pull it away.

"Come along, Desmond," she said. "Leave the young lady alone."

The woman smiled and Kate smiled back. Desmond was a pug that had been fed too many between-meal snacks so that it now had the appearance of a bulldog with shrunken legs. The woman was short and on the heavy side herself. She was exceptionally well dressed. Even Kate could tell that this lady bought at Bergdorf and the high-end shops along Madison.

"That's okay," Kate said. "It's no problem." She bent over and petted the dog. It panted heavily with pleasure, and Kate almost fell over at the blast of amazingly bad breath.

"I hear those condos are going to be selling for a pretty penny," the woman said, pointing at the poster.

"Oh, I guess so," Kate said. "It's out of my range, for sure. I was hoping one of these houses might have an apartment on the first floor that wasn't too expensive. It's a pretty neighborhood."

Kate gazed about. London plane trees overhung the street on both sides. Flowers were planted at their bases. The woman shook her head, a pout forming on her well-defined lips.

165

"Pretty, maybe. But it's going down just like the rest of this city. Right down the drain."

"Really? What do you mean?"

"Drugs! Can you believe it? Right here on these streets? Just the other night, there were shots fired on this very block. I tell you, I've been living here for fifty *years*. Half a *century*. I've never seen or heard of anything like this. Not in this neighborhood."

"It must have been frightening."

"Frightening doesn't begin to tell it. We all called nine-one-one. There must have been five police cars on this block with their lights flashing. And then the next morning, they found bullet shells and *blood*, right over there on that sidewalk. Drug dealers fighting it out, the cops said. They've been chased from the park and they settled here for the time being. Only explanation."

"Amazing." Kate couldn't stop herself from looking in the direction where the woman had been pointing. There was indeed a shadowy spot on the concrete.

"It's mostly gone now," the old woman said. "Washed away by the owner of that house. Couldn't blame him. He's lucky his wife didn't miscarry, with the bang-bang-bang and the police. Oh, my God."

"Oh my *God*," Kate heard herself say, an involuntary echo of the woman. "Pregnant, huh? You know, I just saw a woman over on Madison. Maybe it was her. Very large."

Kate rolled her eyes and used her two hands to describe the shape of a basketball ballooning from her stomach. The woman groaned and let out a cackle.

"Talk about big. *I* was big. The last days with my son, Jeffrey, I felt like I needed a wheelbarrow just to get from here to there. And when he was born, oh my *God*. I thought that little boy was going to split me open and turn me inside out. I told my husband afterward, 'That's it. You better find yourself a good contraceptive, because I'm *not* going through that again.' And believe me, Dearie, that was that."

"I hear you," Kate replied.

"I've tried to tell Amanda what she's in for. But she doesn't want to hear about it. Just brushes me off. 'Oh, no, Mrs. Meyer. I'm not worried.' Of course she's been waiting so long to get pregnant, I guess she doesn't much care about the rest of it."

"She must be very happy."

"Oh, yes. When she told me, we hugged. The tears were streaming down her face. Oh, yes. I haven't seen her as much lately. We used to talk out here on the sidewalk once or twice a week, but she doesn't get out much anymore. A little self-conscious about the belly, I suppose. But maybe she doesn't want to hear what's coming when that baby decides it's time."

The woman nodded firmly, turning toward Amanda's house. It was a red brick building dating to the late nineteenth century, Kate guessed. A flight of brownstone steps led up to the ornately carved front door. The railings were wrought iron, painted black, with impressive curves and shapes.

"Amanda, that's a nice name," Kate said. "She's a big woman, right. Five-ten or so. And very nice dark hair. Pretty green eyes."

The woman made a face.

"That's not Amanda. You must have seen someone else. Amanda is no taller than I am and has short blond hair. She's cute all right, but not much of a figure, if you know what I mean. Nothing up here." The woman put her forearm under her breasts and hefted them for Kate, in case her meaning had been missed. The woman smiled conspiratorially and cackled again. "My husband says she looks like a *boy*."

"There's no accounting for taste," Kate managed to say.

The woman nodded, looking her over with an appraising eye.

"Now, you. You've got a very nice figure. Very nice, indeed."

Kate blushed. The woman came closer. Kate was sure her make-up was recommended by a beauty consultant.

"You're not really looking for an apartment, are you, dearie? You're looking for that girl you described. The tall one with the big belly?"

The woman raised her perfectly plucked eyebrows.

"Well, yes, actually I am. But I'm not a cop or anything. It's sort of a long story. I've been taking care of her daughter for her."

The woman seemed to be assessing her truthfulness. Then she glanced up and down the block as though she did not want to be overheard.

"I've seen her."

"Really?"

"Always at night. The first time was when I was out walking Desmond. She came by in a great hurry, all wrapped up in a cape of some sort, but obviously big already. I didn't think much of it. Why should I? But then, a week later I happened to look out the living room blinds one night late and I saw her again. So I mentioned it to my husband, Harold. He's a doctor, with no imagination, and he told me I should try minding my own business." She lifted her head quickly at the memory. "One more time I saw her, last week. Again at night. Just a day before the shootings. I'm thinking there's a drug lord on the street. Somebody with lots of dirty cash bought up one of the townhouses. Or maybe an apartment on the corner, with the doormen in uniform. She's connected to him, that's what I'm thinking. Some Columbian, or something. Maybe it's his girlfriend. Or maybe he just likes pregnant ladies. There are men like that, you know, Dearie. I told the cops, but they don't want to listen. My husband thinks I'm crazy too, of course."

"That would not be the Linda I know. But I don't think you're crazy."

The woman shrugged. She yanked gently on Desmond's leash.

"Come along, Desmond. Tea time!"

The dog overcame its lassitude to do a little skip, its nails clicking on the sidewalk. Teatime obviously meant cake as well.

"Would you like some tea, Dearie?" she asked Kate. "I live right in that house on the corner."

She pointed at one of the most handsome brownstones on the block. It had an entrance on the side street and many windows, decorated either with flower boxes or with a jungle of plants hanging inside. On the small patio were a white wrought iron table and two chairs.

"Beautiful," Kate said.

"My husband isn't home to bother two girls chatting."

"I can't right now. I have to be getting along."

"Some other time, then, perhaps."

~ * ~

Kate walked thgrough Central Park because she was sure it would be faster than going north to 79th and taking the bus over. Less than ten minutes later, she had reached Anthony's building. It seemed entirely deserted and ready for the wrecking crew. The windows were boarded up. Nailed to the front door was a no-trespassing sign, but the lock was broken and she went inside.

There was not a sound as she climbed the stairs, keeping to the outsides of the runners where the boards did not creak as loudly. At Anthony's apartment, she paused, listening for some noise that would betray his presence inside. She knocked gently, and the door swung open.

"Anthony?" she called. She took a step inside. "Anthony?" she repeated, a little louder. She walked through the living area toward the bedroom. In the short hall, she saw a brownish splotch on the wood. In the hallway near the bathroom, she saw another.

"Anthony?" she called again, just as she heard the entrance door slamming shut three floors below.

She ran through the apartment and froze at the sound of feet coming quickly up the stairs and men talking. She considered running for the roof, but didn't think she would make it in time. And how would that help her anyway?

She retreated back inside. She looked into a closet in the foyer, thinking she would hide there, but it was empty of clothes and provided no cover. The footsteps were nearly on the third floor. Suddenly, she saw a sofa that was placed catty-corner to the walls, leaving a small space behind. She leapt over and crouched down, just as two men came in.

"Yo, Anthony! Anthony, my man! Hey, come out and talk to me wherever-the-fuck-you-are!"

"Man, shut up!" a second voice said.

"Go fuck yourself, Rico. We're wasting our fuckin' time here."

He threw himself down on the sofa, pushing it deeper against the wall. Kate heard his feet being dumped noisily on the coffee table. One hand hung over the back. She could have bitten it.

The one named Rico walked through the apartment. He opened doors and slammed them again. Closets. Bathroom. Bedroom. Then the oven door banged shut.

"You think he's curled up in the fuckin' stove, Rico?" The man on the sofa started laughing.

"No, you goddamned asshole. I'm checking to see if he's been living here. He's living somewhere."

"Yeah, in fuckin' Florida."

"Bullshit. I know Anthony a long time. Anthony don't run away."

"Anthony never had a bullet in him before. How's that? I got him good the other night. I'm telling you, Rico. The man left town. He told his mother he was headed south, man. I got that from the old lady herself. Man, what you scared of?"

Rico had been pacing around the living room. Abruptly, the movement stopped. His voice had a tone as cold as January ice.

"Who you callin' scared? You callin' *me* scared? I'll cut your fuckin' tongue out."

Kate heard the sound of a knife blade flipping open.

"Rico, take it easy, man."

So saying, the one who had been on the sofa leapt to his feet. He circled toward the door.

"Who's scared, Sammy?" Rico asked. "Who's scared?

"Rico, I didn't mean you was *scared*. I was just fuckin' jokin' around. We been up here so many times. I didn't mean nuthin'."

Rico must have given him an opening. She heard Sammy rush out the door and into the hall.

"You are fuckin' crazy, Rico," he yelled.

Rico walked across the room and paused for a moment to look back inside one more time.

"I know you're around, Anthony," he said. "And I'll be ready."

Fifteen

As soon as Kate could hear their footsteps nearing the bottom of the stairs, she rushed to the front window and confirmed her suspicions. The men were the same two she had previously seen exiting Anthony's building, and that "overdose" had indeed been an attempted murder. Shaking from this revelation and from the experience of having hidden from them, she told herself that it shouldn't matter to her what anyone tried to do to Anthony. It did not matter.

She walked across town and arrived at the 96th Street playground in plenty of time to pick up Jenny. The fast pace of her strides eased some of the muscular ache that remained from having been confined, motionless, in that cramped space for so many minutes. But her mind was still buzzing from fear and tension, as well as from the fact that Sally had been correct—Kate knew nothing of the world Anthony inhabited.

The hug she gave Jenny was especially strong.

That evening the routines that had arisen in the past week or so with Jenny proved especially soothing. They'd already bought chicken breasts and stopped at the vegetable stand on the way back for fresh string beans and a pair of sweet potatoes. Jenny always wanted to wash the potatoes and rub on the butter before Kate poked holes in them. While they roasted in the oven, Kate cut off the bean ends and Jenny snapped them in half with a deft flick of the wrists. Cooking the chicken breasts was Kate's job, although Jenny had the *sous-chef* role of sprinkling on the rosemary, salt and pepper.

After dinner, they washed the dishes and took a walk to the bottom of the hill at 91st Street and Second Avenue where a Mr. Frosty truck was parked on most summer evenings. Back home again, Jenny played with Miranda and some of her other toys while Kate reviewed the work she had planned for later. Then she read Jenny stories until the girl curled up on her futon and her eyes fluttered shut in sleep.

Kate was drowsy herself by the time she had tucked the covers around Jenny, turned out the light and sat down in the living room. A cup of tea revived her and she was able to work for an hour with the events of the afternoon like a very distant memory. She was considering an early bedtime herself when she heard a tapping at the door.

It was so soft that she wondered at first if she had been mistaken. Then the sound was repeated, just a little louder.

As she opened the door, she saw Sally's face first. Her body was turned in an odd position, and Kate realized that her arm was pulled backward because she was holding the hand of another woman who apparently did not want to be there. Kate had only seen Linda in the deep shadows of the street, but there was no question in her mind. Aside from the fact that she was very pregnant, her face was remarkably similar to Jenny's—the broad lovely forehead, the thick eyebrows and lashes, the aquiline nose, the well-shaped lips. Linda was clearly exhausted, and the effects of that fatigue dulled her beauty. Still, in a rush of sensation, Kate had a vision both of what Linda had been as a young woman, and what Jenny would be as a teenager. Only the color of their eyes was different. Linda's were an arresting green like jade. Jenny's were a mixture of green and pale brown.

"Did I tell you I would bring her over next time?" Sally asked. "Huh? Did I tell you?"

Sally pulled on Linda's arm but she didn't budge.

"C'mon, Lynnie, for freakin Christ's sake," Sally said.

"No!" Linda wailed. "No, I can't."

Kate stepped into the hall and closed the door to her apartment behind her.

"Shh, please."

Suddenly, Linda fell to her knees in front of Kate and wrapped her arms around Kate's legs and buried her face against her. She was crying. Kate could feel the wet tears through the cloth of her jeans.

"I'm so sorry," Linda said, her voice broken with her sobs. "You've been so good to me and Jenny. I'm so sorry, Kate."

Embarrassed, Kate bent over and stroked Linda's hair and shoulders, looking up briefly at Sally who rolled her eyes and shrugged.

"It's okay," Kate said. "Really, this is no big deal."

"It is! You've been like an angel from God. I swear to you, I prayed to God for His help and then you appeared and took my Jenny in, my baby." She hugged Kate's legs tighter even as Kate tried to loosen her grip. "Every night I pray now, and I thank God first, and ask Him to bless you, Katy. God bless you! Oh, bless you."

She started crying again, harder than before.

"C'mon, Lynnie," Sally said. "You're gonna have the freakin' baby right here on the floor, ya keep up like this. C'mon, get up, will ya?"

Slowly, Sally got Linda to let go of Kate, and helped her to her feet. All the while, Linda kept her eyes averted from Kate, wiping at her tears, as though she couldn't face her.

"I'm so ashamed. I'm sorry…"

"Please, stop talking this way," Kate repeated. She was whispering so as not to awaken Jenny. She came close to Linda and spoke loudly enough to be heard over the sobs. "I'm okay with this, Linda. I'll keep Jenny as long as you need me to. Do you understand what I'm saying?"

Linda's head nodded in response, but she couldn't talk. Her body was wracked with renewed sobbing.

"She's freakin' worn out," Sally said. "That's what's causing this. Plus the baby hormones. Jesus, she's already overdue and the doc said it could be another week or maybe two. The freakin' anxiousness is getting her."

Kate put her arm around her.

"There's nothing to worry about. If it's a week, that's okay. If it's two weeks or even three, I don't care. Are you listening to me?"

In response, Linda nodded quickly again, and embraced Kate. They held each other a few moments. Linda's breasts were large and round and pressed against Kate, as did her belly. Then Kate felt a sharp movement and Linda pulled away, her hands cradling the spot where the baby had moved. There were still tears, but Linda was smiling through them.

"You felt it, right? You felt the kick?"

"Yes," Kate said. "That's amazing. I never knew it was like that."

"You ought to feel it from my end. Oh, God. Jenny was like this. I thought I was growing a soccer player when I had her inside me."

She had a handkerchief that she used to wipe her face.

"I can believe that," Kate said. "She's very athletic. Do you want to see Jenny?"

"Not now," Linda said. "I'm afraid I'll start crying again and wake her up. I don't want her to know about the baby. You understand."

Tears trickled down her cheeks again.

"Sure," Kate said.

"I just wanted to meet you finally. And thank you…"

"It's okay…"

"C'mon, Lynnie," Sally said. "Before you start crying again. I'll help you down to the car."

They started for the stairs.

"You're sure it's safe?" Kate asked. "I heard about Anthony."

Sally turned and stared at her silently before speaking.

"You heard what about Anthony?"

"That he got shot! You must have known, Linda. It happened right down in the neighborhood where you're staying. A woman told me just today. On 74th Street."

Linda's tears finally ceased. Her face bore an expression of puzzlement and something else that Kate couldn't quite decipher.

"Honey," she said. "Where in the world did you get the idea I was living on 74th Street?"

"The cabby said he saw your car the last time. Remember, Sally?"

"Yeah, yeah," Sally said. "Remember I told you it was nonsense…"

"But then I went down there today and I heard about Anthony. The police think it was a drug deal or something, but he got shot. And the two guys who shot him are still after him."

Linda just stood there, hands at her hips. Her face revealed no emotion at all. The tears were all gone.

"Katy, if Anthony got shot, then that's fine with me. He's a bloodsucker. A parasite. But I have not been living on the Upper East Side." She laughed lightly as though the very concept were amusing. "I've been in a building on 9th Street between Avenues B and C for the past two months. The agency set me up there temporarily. After the baby is born and I give him over for adoption, I'm going to get an apartment nearby there and three months free rent, and a few bucks to tide me over until I can get a job. Get back to normal, you know? I can't wait to have my little Jenny back."

"What agency is this?" Kate asked.

"Here we go with the freakin' twenty questions again," Sally said.

"Hush, Sally," said Linda. "Of all people, she certainly has the right to ask. But, Katy, I'm not supposed to give out their name. They are very much against abortion and they try to help people like me have a child, instead of the other, you know. But the way things are, they don't want a lot of publicity because it scares girls off. Believe me, they are legit, though. They get money from the Church. I know that for a fact. My priest put me on to them…"

"I told you not to believe that freakin' cab driver," Sally said. "Ten bucks you wasted."

"But, there was a woman I spoke to today who thought she had seen you."

Linda made a face. Her hands settled on her belly, and she patted it firmly.

"I guess we all look alike, huh?"

She winked at Kate then.

"I guess," Kate said.

~ * ~

In the end, Kate decided it didn't matter where Linda lived. The important thing was that Linda was anxious to have Jenny back again, and that she would have an apartment to help her re-establish a normal life for the child. In the meantime, Kate would care for Jenny.

So she and Jenny followed the patterns of their life through that week and Kate did the work that Stevie arranged for her. And she thought about Roger as well. She wasn't sure how *exactly* things would work out when he returned, but she was sure they would get through it. He didn't call every night. They both had agreed there was something deadening about the requirement that one person call the other *every* 24 hours, without fail. Also, she knew that after a few days of intensive preparatory work, there was going to be a trial, which would cut his free time to zero. So it wasn't a big surprise when she did not hear from him on Wednesday, and then on Thursday. But by the time that Friday rolled by, she began to tell herself that the phone has two ends and maybe it was time for her to spring for the few bucks and show some interest by calling him.

She wished she hadn't when the woman at the hotel switchboard told her that the lawyers had moved out two days earlier.

She figured there must have been a mistake in communication somewhere. She called his apartment and got his answering machine. She tried to remember if it was the same message he had always had. It sounded different, somehow. Had he come home and simply not called her?

She tried his firm in New York. It was after business hours, but there were always people working in the secretarial pool. She said she was looking for Roger Adams. She hoped someone might say he was out of town, or give her another bit of information that would help her solve this riddle. The first woman had never heard of him. When Kate assured her that he was an associate with the firm, she put her on hold and then came back on to say that Kate was, indeed, right that Roger was an associate with the firm, but that he was not there.

"Is he still out of town?" Kate asked.

She was put on hold again.

"I'm not at liberty to discuss the whereabouts of Mr. Adams," she said.

Then Kate remembered the name of the firm in San Francisco that was helping them as local counsel on the case. She called and asked if she could speak to Roger Adams.

"One moment," a nice young voice said. In the interval, Kate listened to much more of a Mozart symphony than she wished to. "Is this Mrs. Adams?" She asked upon her return.

"No, it's not *Mrs.* Adams," Kate said. "Even if I were married to him I would not be *Mrs.* Adams. My name is Andersen. Kate Andersen."

"I'll see that he gets the message, Miss Andersen."

"*Ms.* Not *Miss.* What century are you living in? Don't you know what women have gone through not to be merely appendages of men?!"

It was one of Carla's favorite rants.

The line went dead.

Kate called back and apologized, but the icy tone on the other end did not melt even a little bit, and she knew no more than she had when she started.

The whole sequence put her into a bad mood that carried over into the next day, Saturday morning. Kate was still hoping he might be on the red eye flight and getting ready either to call or to drop over as he had before, so Kate persuaded Jenny that it might be fun to spend the day on the roof the way they used to do.

While Sally hung out her laundry, Jerry slept off the results of drinking a case of beer, perspiring in the sun and licking his dry, cracked lips, and generally giving Kate a headache just to look at him. For the amusement of all, Sally placed a fluff of pigeon down on Jerry's upper lip at one point and mimicked the various faces he made in his sleep as he tried to brush it away. Good clean fun. However, the fact that Jenny thought this marital love-play was the funniest thing that she had ever seen annoyed Kate no end. Jenny's close attention to Sally's suggestions about how *she* would be welcoming good old Roger home if he were *her* man merely fed the fire.

Finally, the phone rang and Kate raced down the stairs to answer. In the background, Sally loudly imitated a breathy Cosmo girl, "Oh, Roger, what a sur*prise*! Oh, Roger, you want to do *what*? *Where*? Oh, *Roger*!"

The call was from a telemarketer, soliciting Kate's business for a discount brokerage firm. To the unfortunate caller and to his supervisor, she vowed that she, her children, and her children's children would not give them business, ever, even if they were the last brokerage firm on earth and she and her children would be forced to eat acorns in Central Park.

"Aren't we overreacting a little bit?" the man asked.

Kate hung up, but at least her sense of inertia had been broken. She called for Jenny to come down so they could pack a lunch and get over to the playground in the park. The hell with the roof. The hell with Sally. And, mostly, the hell with Roger. She wasn't waiting around anymore.

She achieved a moderate sense of calm while sitting on a park bench, working through the latest assignment from Stevie, but her bad mood got a fresh start when Jenny sat down beside her with Miranda bouncing on her knee. Kate realized that Jenny's best friend, Tricia, was away. As a result, Jenny had no apparent interest in playing with anyone except Kate, and Kate was not about to budge from her seat in the shade, even if Jenny pouted so much that the shape of her lower lip was permanently altered.

Kate's pencil scraped across the page in such a fever of concentration that the point broke.

"Are you mad at me?" Jenny asked. Her voice had a particularly sweet ring in the humid summer air. "Was I bad?"

"Of course I'm not mad at you," Kate replied briskly. "Why in the world would I be mad at you? I *do* think you should try to find someone to play with."

"Yes, Katy," Jenny said sadly and walked away.

Kate watched Jenny sit on the edge of the sandbox, dip out a handful, and let the grains sift through her fingers.

With a sigh of regret, she slipped her work back into its folder and crossed the playground, leaning down to give Jenny a hug. Jenny reached up and squeezed her back.

"You're nice, Katy," Jenny said.

"Would you like a ride on the tire swing?" Kate asked.

They raced each other over and Kate pushed Jenny high in the air and around so fast that she thought her own stomach might not make it to dinner. Jenny's cries of pleasure soon drew a crowd of girls who, no doubt, knew when a parent was on the ropes. Jenny invited them on with her and soon the swing appeared to be a writhing mass of small arms and legs and hair and mouths all squealing at once as the tire reached its apogee and returned for another shove.

"EeeeeeEEEEEEEEE. EeeeeeEEEEEEEEEEEEEEEE!!"

To Kate's relief, they stopped before anyone actually threw up. Then, with the crowd of children showing no inclination to disperse, she started a game of "follow-the-old-fool" around, under and over various slides and benches and climbing devices. Finally, having exhausted herself, she led her entourage to the tree house at the far end of the playground for the purpose of giving Miranda her nap.

"Shall we sing her to sleep?" Kate asked.

"Yes! Yes!!"

So they launched into those old lullabies, *Bingo the Dog*, *Old MacDonald*, and, a personal favorite from Kate's youth, *Mrs. Leary's Cow*.

The tree house had walls but no ceiling, and it was cool in the shade of a large willow oak, breezy and pleasantly relaxing amidst the hubbub. She did not care if the song took half an hour to finish, and the refrain—a promise that the second verse would not only be louder, but a little bit worse than the first—never seemed so funny.

"Ohhhh, OOOHHHHHHH, THE COW KICKED NELLY IN THE BELLY IN THE BARN..."

Eventually, there was a pause, filled with giggles. Footsteps could be heard coming up the ladder to their platform and a head popped into view.

"Hi," Roger said.

The girl nearest the opening eyed him suspiciously.

"No boys allowed!" she said.

"No boys allowed!" came the echo of many voices.

Roger made a face that was soft and droopy and sad as a beagle. Opinion began to shift. Kate stayed quiet.

"Well," said a girl with a thick braid of red hair, "he's not *really* a boy."

"Then what is he?" a skeptic asked.

"Good question," Kate said.

"Very good question," Roger agreed. He seemed as interested as anyone there in the answer.

"He's a DADDY!" Jenny exclaimed to a pandemonium of agreement.

"A daddy! A daddy!"

"God help me," Roger muttered. He disappeared from sight, only to reappear with a picnic basket filled with enough food even for that army of children. As he spread it in front of them, cutting things up into small bits so everyone could share, he looked over at Kate.

"They're not all yours, right? You've still got just the one?"

Kate laughed and kissed him on the cheek.

"Just the one," she said.

"Looks like I got back just in time."

Sixteen

Roger's stay in California had ended with unexpected swiftness. After a week of hearings, the judge had invited their client to make a motion and then ruled from the bench at the end of their session on Friday. Afterward, there had been a rush to pack and get to the airport in time for the overnight flight home. The hotel? It seemed that the partner's wife had gotten into some sort of tiff with the staff and arranged a move to another "more professional" establishment mid-week. Kate decided not to hold a grudge over that.

Roger had played a large part in the successful end to the case and, as a result, his stock with the firm was particularly high. Partners were maneuvering to have him assigned to their cases. His lunch calendar filled up. First year associates were greeting him as "Mr. Adams" in the hallway. His secretary was moved closer to him *and* given more space (which had everyone on the floor talking).

To top it all off, his bosses were practically begging him to take some of his accrued vacation. Following the long hours and travel of the San Francisco assignment, he deserved it, they insisted, and because he had no pressing matters, the timing was perfect to shuffle off for a couple of weeks to the beach house in Montauk. But, as Roger's father used to remind him, some things are not possible in life. Therefore, he passed on a formal vacation at that point and rose still higher in the eyes of those who keep track of such details. Instead, during the week following his return, he and Kate had one long afternoon at Coney Island (with Jenny), an evening picnic and outdoor concert on the Great Lawn (at which Jenny dozed off in the middle) and the prospect of a weekend entirely alone in Montauk written on his calendar in big red letters.

"We are still going, aren't we?" Roger would ask from time to time. "Nothing new to stop us?"

"It's all set. Mrs. Morley has promised to keep her for the weekend. Sally has said that she'll take Jenny over to the playground on Saturday."

"You're depending on Sally? Isn't that how this whole thing got started?"

"If Sally doesn't show up, Jenny will simply have to stay with Mrs. Morley. I've explained everything to her. Believe me, she's a very smart girl. She understands we want some time together."

"You explained *every*thing?"

"Okay. Almost everything."

They had these conversations mostly late at night after a certain smart and very understanding six year old had fallen asleep in her corner of Kate's bedroom. One of the first things Roger had done upon his return was to buy a brand-new convertible sofa for Kate's living room.

With their love nest in the living room, they had a modicum of privacy, although there were moments of some frustration when Kate abruptly wriggled out of his arms, the better to listen and decide if the noise she heard was Jenny awakening or merely stirring.

"I feel like I'm in high school," Roger said one night, "and my girlfriend's parents are watching TV upstairs and walking the hallway every ten minutes just to keep us in our clothes."

"I'm sorry, Roger," Kate said. "It won't be forever."

"Don't get me wrong," he said with a grin. "I *liked* high school."

When that special Friday finally arrived, they packed Roger's car and left around noon to beat the weekend exodus. It was their plan to arrive early enough in Montauk to buy take-out fish and chips and a chilled bottle of wine and enjoy their dinner along with the setting sun at the lighthouse five miles past the town. Their anticipation was such that, in the final several minutes of their trip, they barely spoke as the radio poured out favorite oldies. At the lighthouse parking lot, there was no need for discussion either. As other arrivals headed toward the terraced walkway down to the "point" by the lighthouse proper, Kate and Roger, with furtive glances behind them, hopped a guardrail and followed a partially concealed footpath leading to the ocean side.

They emerged from the scrub oak and blueberry bushes to see the deep blue water fifty yards away. Because of the rough surf and currents so close to the convergence of bay and ocean, this was not a place where anyone chose to swim or sunbathe. Apart from a narrow strip of sand near the edge of the bushes, the shore was covered everywhere by an amazing array of stones: large stones and small stones, boulders, tennis balls and marbles, stones of a seemingly infinite variety of shapes and colors, all worn smooth by the glacier that had brought them here many thousands of years before and, more recently, by the ceaseless pounding of the waves at high tide. Beneath their feet, the sensation was of a strange sort of sand as the stones shifted at each step.

Kate and Roger smiled as a stiff wind off the ocean tossed their hair and clothes and teased them with bits of spray. They spread their blanket and ate their dinner and watched as the sun flattened into a disc and dropped lower and lower toward the horizon. Thin clouds to the west caught the changing light, spreading it across the huge expanse of sky. The pinks and purples were reflected by the water in the troughs of the surf and again farther out as far as the eye could see. The sand and stones and cliffs had a rose patina. The sound of water pounding on the shore melted into utter silence between the patterns of the waves. As daylight turned to dusk, their sole companion, a fisherman up the beach, threw his remaining bait to the gulls and left. As if taking this as a cue, the birds also called it a day and departed, circling high over the warm wind rising off the parking lot before gliding off to points unknown. Now this small part of Long Island was theirs alone to enjoy.

It was easy to imagine with the curve of the shore that they were alone together on a small island, marooned by choice beyond the reach of the rest of the world, accessible by kayak only... no party boats, cell phones strictly prohibited and no talk of deadlines or work that had to be done.

Roger interrupted her thoughts with a gentle touch on her arm. He held out a glass of wine to her and silently proposed a toast.

"Alone at last," he said, kissing her.

"Alone at last."

~ * ~

The next day they were up early—unmercifully early, according to Roger. Kate had them at Ditch Plains beach while the lifeguards were still sipping their coffee and huddled in sweatshirts against the morning chill. She pointed to the surfers, bobbing on their boards a hundred yards from shore. Most were wearing wet suits.

"See them," she said. "They don't think it's too early."

"Surfers are crazy. Everybody knows that."

"I thought you had a surfboard in high school."

"I did, but that was just to impress girls. You, on the other hand, are a woman. Women tend to be impressed by sunset dinners. Stuff like that."

"Thanks for the insight."

A walk up on the cliffs and an impromptu race back to the blanket got them warm enough for a swim. A hunt for seashells and pretty rocks and a best-of-five paddleball match led to an invigorating mid-morning nap in the sand and more swimming. They returned to the house at noon for a sandwich and a change of bathing suits. This proved distracting. She asked for help fastening the back of her top and he found it so easy an assignment that he repeated it. Open. Closed. Open.

"Impressionable man," Kate said.

"Alone at last," Roger said.

It was three o'clock before they emerged, telling themselves what a good idea it was to avoid the harmful rays of the midday sun—doctors all agreed. Besides, they both believed the late afternoon hours were among the best to be at the beach, with the shadows lengthening and the sand emptying of sunbathers, the wind off the water raising a slight mist and the seabirds looking for the remains of picnics, emboldened by hunger to come close and stare down the humans. Roger had robes of thick, soft cotton at the house and they wore those and stayed until the first star appeared in the darkening sky, and Roger demanded that Kate make a silent wish. ('If you tell, it won't come true.') Afterward, they showered and had a drink and got dressed to go out to dinner. At that point, Kate thought it would be the perfect time to squeeze in a quick call to New York.

From the instant Mrs. Morley answered, Kate knew something was wrong.

"No, no," Mrs. Morley insisted. "Not at all. Jenny's just fine. Enjoy your weekend."

In the background, Kate could hear Jenny. First the child asked who was on the phone, and then she called out for Kate to come back.

"Hush now," Mrs. Morley said. "Hush."

"Let me speak to her," Kate said.

Mrs. Morley held the phone up to Jenny's mouth and ear, but the girl did not say what was causing her to cry. She simply kept repeating her plea for Kate to come home. "I miss you. I miss you."

"You see," Mrs. Morley said. "She's just being a little girl. You stay right where you are."

"But Mrs. Morley…"

"I know what I'm saying here, my dear," she replied. "She's been okay all day and now we're getting ready for bedtime and a story and she misses you. That's all. You just enjoy yourself there and we'll see you tomorrow, regular time. Everything is fine."

The line went dead with Kate still holding the receiver. Roger had to remind her twice that they needed to leave or they would risk losing their dinner reservations.

"Of course," she said. "Let's go."

During dinner, Kate held his hand across the table and smiled when he joked about the *maitre d'* and the waiter who both hovered nearby, grieving as she picked at her food and barely sipped the wine. ("You're going to ruin their evening," Roger said.)

Over dessert, he told her a story of when he was a child and his mother went away, leaving him with his older brother and his father, and he'd cried his eyes out before going to bed. She agreed that such a reaction was normal for a kid and spent the next few minutes lost in thought, until Roger asked if she wanted to go back to New York. He was hoping she would say 'no, certainly not.' It was a three-hour drive, after all, assuming little traffic. The little angel would be asleep when they arrived. Whatever had been troubling her would be a distant memory.

Kate treated his suggestion as the greatest idea since midday breaks from the sun.

"Do you mean it, Roger?" she asked. "I don't want to ruin our weekend."

She leaned forward across the elegantly set table. An embroidered linen napkin was crushed between her hands. Her expression was filled with such trust that he found he had to lie.

"Of course I mean it," he said. "Let's get out of here."

He hid his anger along the drive back. An oldies station filled the conversational gaps. He reminded himself that he loved Kate, that the past twenty-four hours were better than a week with anyone else, that this disruption of their lives was not forever—Jenny would be gone soon enough.

He reminded himself to act like a grown-up! Disappointments are a part of life. This is important to Kate. And as they pulled through the mid-town tunnel onto the soil of Manhattan, when she grabbed his hand and held it to her lips and her cheek, caressing it with her singular sensuality, and she thanked him again and told him how much she appreciated this act, he was able to reply with equanimity, at least on the surface.

"No big deal, Kate. Really. It's okay."

The building was quiet as they entered and climbed the stairs. Mrs. Morley had agreed to stay in Kate's apartment for the two nights involved. Food that Jenny liked was in the refrigerator. Jenny could sleep in her own bed.

As Kate turned the key in the door, she began to feel that she had been too impulsive. She tapped lightly at the door as she swung it open. To her relief, Mrs. Morley was sitting up still. She rose to greet Kate, a frown of disapproval on her face.

"You shouldn't have come," she said.

But less than a minute after they arrived, the bedroom door flew open and a bare-footed child was racing across the room into Kate's outstretched arms. Jenny held her tight without speaking, her little body heaving visibly and small muffled sobs escaping against Kate's breast.

"You came back!" she said, as though a miracle had occurred.

"Silly, I told you I would." With her free hand, she stroked the child's head. It was only when Jenny stepped away slightly that Kate saw the ugly purple bruise rising on her right cheek.

Kate stared at Mrs. Morley. The old woman was still in her chair. She wiped her hands on her apron over and over.

Kate eased Jenny away so that she could examine the bruise. When the girl winced at Kate's hand touching her left shoulder, Kate unbuttoned her pajamas. Here was a second bruise, larger and uglier than the first. It appeared to hurt just to move the arm.

Roger stepped toward the child.

"My God, Kate."

"Not now, Roger."

"But Kate, really. This is terrible."

He glanced from the child to Mrs. Morley, whose gaze was fixed on her ever-moving hands.

"Who did this?" Roger asked. "Sally?"

Kate stood and guided Jenny back to the bedroom. At the door, she turned back to him.

"It wasn't Sally," she said.

Roger waited with Mrs. Morley. By his watch only five minutes passed before Kate returned, but it seemed like an hour. Kate sat on the sofa closest to Mrs. Morley. Roger stood.

"There's no point hidin' it," Mrs. Morley said. "You know it was Linda."

Kate nodded.

"The bruises are always on the right side of Jenny's face. Linda's left-handed."

She glanced quickly at Roger. He said nothing.

"Linda came by for a visit this afternoon," Mrs. Morley continued. "I guess Sally told her you were gone for the weekend. It was just before Jenny was to go to the Park…" Mrs. Morley shook her head, apparently full of sorrow for the trip that had never occurred. "I couldn't very well tell her she couldn't see her own child. Even if I were sure what would happen, which I wasn't. So she called and I got Jenny ready and we waited for her to show up. Then we waited some more, and Jenny wanted to go over to the Park, of course, but I said no, she had to wait to see her mother. It's more important than seeing her friend… Well, Linda was two hours late getting here. And that should have told me, I guess. When my husband was late, it usually meant one thing. He'd been with the boys, so to speak. Tossing a few back. One drink would lead to another and another and another…

"So she finally walked up the stairs and she had a big bag from the toy store there on 86th Street. The doll still had the sticker on it. I don't know what Jenny was thinking, but it seemed to me Linda had stumbled out of the damned bar and grabbed the first thing she saw in the store and bought it. Well, Jenny didn't want any part of her mother. You could see it from the minute Linda walked into the place. Maybe it was the liquor on her breath. She was stinking of booze. Big smile. Lipstick smeared on. Whatever it was, Jenny would not take that doll. When Linda tried to put it into her arms, she let it drop right there on the floor and then looked up at her mother with that gleam in her eyes. You know the one I'm talking about. You must've seen it yourself once or twice."

"Once or twice," Kate whispered.

"'Pick it up!' Linda said. 'Pick it up, Jenny, or you'll be sorry. I'll smack you good!' But Jenny set that jaw of hers and that was that. Linda swung and hit her on the shoulder with her fist. Of course, Jenny didn't budge. Just stared at her. 'Pick it up!' Linda screamed again. 'You listen to your mother. Pick it up!'

"Then she stood there over Jenny, screaming at the top of her lungs, face all red and ugly. I thought she'd have a stroke on the spot. Bust a blood vessel or something. And what did Jenny do? Didn't she start right in again? 'You're not my mother,' she said."

"Oh my God," Kate muttered.

"'Damn you!' Linda said and grabbed her by that left shoulder, like she wanted to spin her around and spank her. Jenny was squirming then, yelling that she's not her mother, not her mother! Somehow the shoulder twisted, she let out a howl and fell to the ground. Linda was swinging again and hit her in the face. That was probably an accident. But there Jenny was, lying on the floor crying, and Linda was standing over her. Linda looked like *she* was going to start crying. Because something is always happening between the two of them. The one drunk, the other one hard as nails.

"Sally must have heard. Heaven knows the whole building could have heard the screaming. She came in and took Linda away. I don't know what all else went on. Linda didn't come back. Not that it would have helped."

Mrs. Morley got to her feet and walked to the door. She hesitated, hand on the knob as if she had something else to say. But she simply promised they'd talk more about it later, and left.

Kate and Roger got ready for bed, each with their own thoughts, and when the lights were out they lay there quietly. Roger listened to the sounds from the city's life below, the sounds of hurried footsteps, of young men exchanging epithets with alcohol heartiness, of cars squealing around the corner and thrusting recklessly down the street. Everything was ominous, full of danger. He wondered if the whole mood of the city had changed in forty-eight hours.

On the edge of sleep, a thought slipped into his mind that was so clear and unadorned it seemed someone else had spoken it. This situation was going to end badly. He could not insulate himself from what was happening. Nor could he alter or control in any way Kate's involvement with the kid, or shield her from being hurt. He had one choice, and that was to get up from the bed and walk down the stairs and join that unappealing world outside and to begin the process of forgetting Kate and the problem she had visited upon herself.

He moved closer to her, the length of his body pressed lightly against hers. The tips of his fingers grazed her cheek.

He was afraid. A distance was opening between them. As a child holds a charm to keep the monster away, so Roger was sure that if he could touch her through the night, his fears would pass. Love would conquer? But did he really believe it had such power?

"You know what this means?' Kate asked finally.

"Yeah. Jenny's mother is a royal bitch with a drinking problem."

Kate squeezed his hand and pulled it onto her stomach.

"Don't be too hard on Linda. It's going to take a while for them to adjust again. Jenny can be very difficult. It's not easy raising a girl by yourself."

"You're defending her? She hit her kid. She hit her hard."

"I know what she did, Roger. And believe me, I'm not defending that. As bad as Carla ever was, she never hit me. But the point is, Linda's her mother. And the fact that she came over here shows that she loves her daughter." Kate's voice caught. "And something else as well."

"What's that?"

There was a pause. Roger could feel a tremor run through her.

"It means that she's had the baby. She wouldn't have let Jenny see her otherwise. And she wouldn't be drinking."

"And that means…"

"Yes," Kate said, and this time Roger knew she was crying. "Yes."

Seventeen

The next day, Kate was happy to see that the bruise on Jenny's face was far less red and swollen. In its place was an area of skin on her cheekbone that had a pale yellowish color, reminding Kate of the first time she had seen the girl through Mrs. Morley's window and thought someone needed to give her a once-over with soap and water.

Less quick to heal was Jenny's shoulder. Throughout breakfast and afterward, Jenny held her arm stiffly at her side the way a child does who has been given an injection and is trying to protect the arm from further harm. Finally, Kate suggested that maybe they should stop by the emergency room and have a doctor examine it. At this prospect, Jenny became visibly agitated, and to prove that nothing so extreme was necessary, she rotated the arm gingerly in a circle. To Kate, this was an indication that, at least, nothing was broken or seriously damaged. At the playground later in the day, Jenny still seemed to favor the arm somewhat at first, but any lack of mobility was virtually undetectable once she met her friend, Tricia, and they went off to play together.

That week, the promise of Jenny's imminent return to Linda hung in the air. Sally swore she had still not been given any means to contact Linda. She speculated that Linda was probably busy moving into the new apartment she had been promised. There were things to buy, certainly—beds, chairs, a table, pots and pans and utensils. The demolition of Anthony's building had begun. Nothing was left to take from that rat hole.

Kate's freelance business continued to flourish. One of the editors from Stevie's magazine left for greener pastures at another publisher and contacted Kate for assignments. She was seriously considering purchasing a data plan and a smartphone so she could field email from the playground. Roger kidded her that she would soon be driving a BMW. Kate didn't think that was funny.

Roger himself got busy again quickly. A new trial was beginning and he was being courted for a responsible role, as though it were a kind of honor to spend eighteen hours a day in the office in endless strategy meetings and frenzies of work when briefs were due or depositions were scheduled. The surprise was that the work was a kind of relief, since then he didn't have to worry about what was going to happen when Jenny had to leave.

Both Kate and Roger realized they would not be returning to Montauk soon, and as if to taunt them, the weather turned onerously hot and humid, the kind of bad-air days that seem to define August in New York and cause those with money to flee. But for Kate, Roger and Jenny, it was business as usual. The 96th Street playground was the order of the day for the two ladies, and a nightly trip to the Mister Softee truck down the hill at Second Avenue became the entire group's after-supper protocol. So their lives continued, in a kind of holding pattern that everyone knew could not continue but that no one could foresee would end so badly.

~ * ~

The trouble began on a day that Kate was preoccupied with an article she was trying to write on the large and small monuments in

Central Park that had been dedicated to people who had slipped completely from society's collective memory. What did it mean that John Purroy Mitchell had once been loved so much that his gilt bust was placed in prominence at the reservoir, and then was forgotten, a curiosity at best? And in such extreme heat, who could care?

Add to her mental state the fact that New York City streets are always a parent's nightmare. Cabs race down the streets, veering from lane to lane without warning. Deliverymen on bicycles careen at lightning speed in the opposite direction from supposed one-way traffic. Private cars are no better than the cabs, and even the average driver can erupt in a bout of crazy horn-blasting aggression. As a result, Jenny had been instructed over and over again that she was never to cross the street without Kate first saying it was okay.

Of course, Jenny did not always listen, and on this particular morning, the traffic had mostly passed, but the light on Lexington Avenue and 92nd had not yet changed from red to green when Jenny started across immediately on her own. Kate was in a semi-trance, preoccupied with an article, and saw the blur of the girl's shape out of the corner of her eye and, at the same time, accelerating quickly after letting off a passenger, the yellow mass of a taxi with the driver concentrating on the truck to *his* right, which was trying to cut him off and make the light.

Somehow, Kate reached out and grabbed Jenny's left hand in a grip of steel and yanked her backward, just as the cab screeched to a halt and the truck barreled on, belching smoke like the winner it was.

The cab driver stuck his head out of the window.

"Ya oughta put that kid on a leash, lady," he said genially. A hairy arm hung over the door. A cigar that looked three days old clung to his lower lip.

"And you should have some driving lessons," Kate said. "You almost hit her."

"Jesus, lady! I almost went to med school once too, but I didn't. I had the light, anyway."

"The light was red!"

The cabby shrugged as though it wasn't his fault that she couldn't take a joke and slammed the accelerator to the floor. He was a block away before Kate noticed that Jenny was crying.

She knelt beside the girl, hugging and soothing her. At first, Kate thought Jenny was upset and scared. Then she realized that the girl's left arm hung limply at her side.

"You hurt me here," she said, pointing at her shoulder. It wasn't exactly an accusation, but close enough.

"Jenny, I didn't mean to hurt you. You were walking right in front of that car. I had to stop you."

This was certainly true. But mixed with the relief of having saved Jenny had been that special level of self-righteous anger that a parent feels when her child does the very thing he or she had been told a million times not to do and only narrowly escapes dire consequences. Had Kate needed to pull on her arm quite so hard?

"I didn't mean to hurt your arm," she repeated.

"It hurts. It hurts."

Kate was not sure if Jenny was really in pain or simply milking the event, trying to make Kate feel guilty. The light changed again and Jenny stood rooted to the spot, rubbing her shoulder with conscientious gentleness. The sun blasted down upon them. Heat rose off the asphalt and concrete. The air was brown with smog on the edge of the horizon down Lexington Avenue. None of this helped Kate's already tenuous mood.

"Well then, if it hurts as you say it does, we should go to the emergency room right now. Let's get a cab. There's one."

She stuck out her arm and started waving.

"No!" screamed Jenny.

Kate struggled not to smile. She felt very wicked.

"But Jenny, if your shoulder hurts so much..."

"It doesn't hurt *now*. It just hurt before. When you *pulled* on it."

"I've already told you I'm sorry. You must know I didn't mean to hurt you. But I'm very glad you are feeling better."

"All right," Jenny said.

Although the apology was accepted in an official sense, Jenny could not quite let go of the leverage the incident afforded her. At each corner, she refused to hold hands, and a compromise was finally struck whereby Jenny would grasp the bottom of Kate's t-shirt as they crossed the street, thus keeping her close enough that Kate could grab her if necessary, but giving Jenny a sense of control.

The effort of working out this negotiation gave Kate a monumental headache and, of course, she had not brought any Tylenol. To top it off, the heat was not reduced one iota as they neared Central Park. Nor was there the faintest breeze. The leaves seemed to wilt as she looked at them. The sidewalks were empty except for people trying to hail cabs. Even the pigeons seemed to think it was too hot to waste energy on flying. They walked around in packs, pecking at the ground and at each other.

In the playground, Kate settled herself onto a bench in the shade and swore that she would not move for any reason until the sun went down. The one exception would occur if Jenny decided to be smart and return home to their air-conditioned apartment.

"No!"

"Suit yourself. Go find something to do."

To be fair, there really were very few other children around. The fact was that sane people stayed inside when the weather was this bad, and grown-ups with any sort of child-rearing ability were not bullied by six year olds. Even the sprinkler at the far end of the playground seemed to be doing nothing but adding another layer of humidity to the sodden air.

"Where's Tricia?" Jenny asked.

She knew very well that Tricia was at her grandparents' house in the Catskills for the week. It was her way of saying 'How am I supposed to play without my best friend?'

"Why don't you go play in the tree house? Maybe someone will follow you over and you can play."

"I don't want to."

Sweat oozed from Kate's skin. She figured she should be happy it was not flowing in tiny rivulets any more. *Patience*, she advised herself.

"Jenny, if you can find something to do for a little while so I can get through some reading, I'll push you on the swing. Then we'll get a cold drink at the deli and go home. Maybe we can find a movie on 86th Street."

Jenny hopped off the bench.

"Okay. How long?"

"Give me half an hour. Then we'll do the swing. Okay?"

"Okay," Jenny said. She gave Kate a nice, solid kiss on the cheek and ran off.

Kate felt good about this arrangement for approximately two seconds, until it became obvious that Jenny's destination was the playground's climbing apparatus. This was a wooden structure in the rough shape of a pyramid with the top lopped off to create a platform. Four by four beams provided footholds on two sides. A slide afforded a means to get off the top, along with a footbridge to a second, smaller climbing area. But, worst of all, the designer of this plaything (who must not have ever had children) had left the sides of the platform itself completely open with a six-foot drop to the pavement. Granted, the ground was covered with a rubber mat. However, in Kate's mind, this did as much good as a wool blanket beneath a high-wire act.

Apparently, some other parents had agreed with Kate's assessment. Recently, the Parks Department had constructed a metal railing at the top to guard against children accidentally falling off in a rush for the slide. The problem was that many kids assumed the railing was simply a new part of the play apparatus. It was no surprise that Jenny had taken to perching on the bar with legs dangling over the front and backside hanging over the rear. The railing no doubt dug into her thighs. It could not have been comfortable. And yet Jenny and the others gravitated there like starlings to an electric wire, content to spend the afternoon.

"Katy, watch me!" she called.

Kate did not *want* to watch her. Kate wanted to smack that little rear end of hers. But before Kate could even articulate a cogent threat, Jenny escalated her play.

"Look, Katy!! No hands!!!"

Kate glanced over and, suddenly, Jenny started to fall backward. Kate jumped off the bench and watched as Jenny calmly grabbed the bar with both hands, hooked her knees around it, and swung upside down to hang like a monkey. At her leisure, she dropped lightly to the top of the platform and took the slide down to mother earth. This was a trick Jenny had perfected on many previous afternoons, and she was not about to quit, even if Kate had yet to appreciate properly the skill involved.

Today, following the incident with the cab, Kate couldn't stand it. She was close to fainting in the heat already.

"I don't want you on the rail today, Jenny," Kate called to her.

Kate kept her eyes glued on the pages in her lap, watching Jenny with peripheral vision as she went up the pyramid and hesitated at the top, one hand on the railing, then went down the slide.

"Thank you!" Kate said in a motherly singsong. Inside, she breathed slowly to soothe the erratic beat of her heart. A drop of sweat fell onto her notes and the ink began to run. Kate closed her eyes. 'I *am* getting better at this,' she told herself.

While Jenny repeated the cycle, climbing up to the top and sliding down again, Kate tried to get back to her work. Her mind refused to focus. She fidgeted, changing positions on the bench. She reread the same paragraphs twice, three times. She simply could not stop watching the girl from the corner of her eye, going up and down and up and down. So it was that when the repetition of play ended, Kate looked over immediately to see what was happening, although the exact sequence of the events that followed would never be clear.

Whether from boredom or just to aggravate Kate, Jenny had gotten onto the railing again. Her cheeks were the color of a well-cooked lobster and there was a sly grin on her face as she balanced, no hands. It was all in good fun. The question that Kate asked herself afterward, over and over again, was whether her own scream of fear and anger made the difference. In her nightmares, the sound itself has a tangible quality. It seemed to hit the girl like an ocean wave.

Jenny swung backward and reached out to grab the rail as she always did. This time, however, perhaps there was something about the angle of her arm that put a different strain on her shoulder—the one that had been injured by Linda, and hurt again that morning. A jolt of pain coursed through the length of her arm. The fingers loosened. She dangled from the rail for a fraction of a second, let out a forlorn cry, and dropped to the pavement. She landed with an unforgettable, inanimate thud and lay motionless.

"Jennnyyyyyy!!!!"

Kate rushed to the girl and turned her over. A reddish mark had formed on her forehead, close to the remnants of the bruise left by her mother days before. Her arm was twisted at her side. Kate kissed the hurt spots and whispered her name.

"Jenny, wake up. Please, Jenny!"

The girl seemed to mumble something in response. A trace of spittle was visible at the corner of her mouth. Panicked, Kate thought that she might go into convulsions and tried to get her finger into her mouth to hold her tongue. The girl fought her at first, and then relaxed. There were no convulsions. Kate succeeded only in scratching Jenny's cheek.

She glanced frantically around the playground. A nanny for one of the youngest children approached them.

"Would you please call an ambulance?" Kate asked.

The woman smiled agreeably, but it was obvious she didn't understand the request. The woman pointed at herself and at Jenny, apparently trying to suggest that she would stay with Jenny while Kate went for help. This was not an alternative Kate would consider.

She picked up Jenny carefully and cradled that limp body against her chest. It was a relief that she was able to hear the girl's breathing. She remembered a pay phone at the corner where she could call an ambulance.

As she reached the sidewalk, a cab seemed like a better option, but in this kind of heat empty cabs were non-existent. One after another, the yellow sedans whizzed by her, already full. She decided to carry Jenny to the hospital six blocks north along Fifth Avenue.

She whispered Jenny's name as she walked. In response, Jenny mumbled a few incomprehensible words and her eyelids fluttered as though she were asleep and dreaming. After three blocks, Kate's arm muscles felt raw with pain. Soon, her hands turned numb, and she was afraid she would drop Jenny. When she got to the emergency room and kicked open the door, she almost cried with relief.

Inside, the air was cool and the light seemed dim in comparison to the blazing August sun. Dazed with pain and worry, Kate handed the girl over to a blur of helpful hands as a stretcher was rolled out and two nurses placed Jenny onto it. At that point, aware that Kate was no longer holding her, Jenny opened her eyes.

"Katy?" she said weakly. Her voice had never seemed so sweet and small. Love and concern for Jenny, and happiness that she was awake, caused tears to well up in Kate's eyes.

"Jenny, everything's going to be okay."

Kate tried to stay close and hold Jenny's hand, but a platoon of workers surrounded the girl, attaching straps across her lower limbs, taking her blood pressure, firing questions at Kate.

"She fell and hit her head,' Kate said in response to one of them. "It's all my fault."

"No, Katy."

"Don't talk, Jenny."

"The side of her mouth is swollen," a nurse remarked.

"Oh, God. I did that too. I didn't mean to. Jenny, I'm sorry."

"My arm hurts, Katy."

As Jenny struggled to sit up, a male orderly stopped her with an arm laid across her chest. A nurse fastened a wide strap in place. Until that point, Jenny had appeared simply confused. Now she was frightened. She moved her head to keep Kate in sight.

"Katy!"

A tall thin woman entered the room, dressed in a white coat and with a stethoscope hanging down her front like a necklace. Kate hoped she was as competent as she seemed efficient. Her hair was all of two inches long. Even her steps had a clipped rhythm as she approached.

"Better use the head restraints until we have an x-ray," she told the orderly.

"Wait," Kate interjected. "Maybe I could hold her hand and keep her from moving."

Her words bounced off the backs of those huddled over Jenny. They were having trouble adjusting the straps because she was so small.

"Katy!!" Jenny called. She wasn't crying. Rather, her voice had that familiar tone of fear and panic that Kate remembered from their earliest days together. It seemed so long ago.

"This is important," the doctor said sternly. "You must cooperate."

To Kate it was obvious that Jenny thought the restraints were a form of punishment for failing to follow instructions. Couldn't they simply explain why it was important not to move? Or soothe her with a stroke of the hand on her forehead? Didn't they see how frightened she was? Had they no idea what went on inside the mind of a sensitive child?

"They won't hurt you, Jenny," Kate said. "They just want to make sure you're okay. You have to be still so they can check. Understand?"

Kate had hoped that the young doctor would take this as her cue to say a few words to comfort the poor kid, but she was too intent on staring into Jenny's eyes with a light. From the way Jenny squirmed, it might have been a laser. The doctor was losing what little patience she possessed. Kate reached out to hold Jenny's hand. The doctor bumped into her as she moved from the stretcher.

"You'll have to stay back!" she snapped. "Let's get some x-rays, here."

Jenny glanced mutely in Kate's direction. Only her eyes were not bound. They flickered from face to face, her abundant energy concentrated in that worried stare.

"I'll come too," Kate said. "It's okay, Jenny."

As they began to wheel Jenny down the hall, the doctor motioned to Kate.

"I think it will go better if you're not in the room to distract her."

"You don't understand. Jenny is very scared right now, in ways that go beyond this fall. Strangers frighten her..."

"Please, we do this all the time. We know how to deal with children."

"But Jenny is different."

"*Please...*" the doctor interrupted. It was obvious she believed she had heard this story a thousand times. Her pale blue eyes said that whatever uniqueness an individual has outside is left at the door. Here, Jenny was a young person with a plastic bracelet on her wrist who had suffered a fall. She had potential spinal injuries, maybe a concussion. She didn't want to be examined? None of them did.

The doctor walked away briskly and disappeared through a doorway. Kate was still staring after her when she felt a new presence at her side.

"Excuse me."

Kate turned and saw an elderly woman, dressed in white like a nurse but with a printed card attached to her blouse that announced she was a volunteer named Marge. She was barely five feet tall, with a round face that seemed almost completely covered by her pale green glasses and a smile.

She had such a kindly expression that Kate felt emboldened to ask whether there was someone she could talk to who would allow her to accompany Jenny.

"I'll inquire for you," Marge said. "But first let's please go into this room over here and just sit down by the desk. There are a few things we need. Now, what is your daughter's name?"

~ * ~

What's my daughter's name? Kate would think afterward that if she had only lied to that first question, everything else would have turned out differently. A simple lie, the best kind. 'She's my daughter, Jenny Andersen. I'm not covered by insurance right now because I'm out of work. But here's my credit card. I'm good for it.'

Instead, believing that someone with such a decent face could be trusted, she told the woman that she was not Jenny's mother.

"Well, we're going to have to reach her, of course. Would you like to use our phone?"

In her cheerful way, Marge turned the desk phone so Kate could dial.

"That's a problem," Kate said. "I mean I have a vague idea where she's living, but I don't have a phone number for her. I can't even give you an exact address."

"Are you a relative?"

"No. Jenny's just living with me for a while. It's kind of complicated..." Without even knowing precisely why, Kate could feel herself getting nervous. Marge's face seemed to stiffen in response. She reminded Kate of the proprietress of a cottage she and Roger once rented in the mountains. The lady was the heart and soul of hospitality when they were being shown the place, and as tough as granite the minute there was a problem. Kate wished that Roger were there with her.

"Who is the child's physician?"

"There isn't one at the moment," Kate replied with a sigh. "You see, it really is very complicated. I started taking care of Jenny sort of on the spur of the moment and I never had the chance to get this information from her mother. To tell you the truth, I've barely *met* her mother."

As Kate talked, the arrangement seemed more and more odd. Why *hadn't* she found out the name of her doctor? If there were one, of course. And it seemed unforgivably stupid not to have had a phone number for Linda for a circumstance like this. But what difference should that make in an emergency, anyway? Were they going to refuse her care?

Kate was about to ask these questions when the volunteer excused herself. Her clipboard seemed as large as a shield against her chest as she left. After several minutes, a nurse appeared. She was considerably younger than Marge, and Kate decided to be more careful this time in what she did and did not say. The edges of the woman's white uniform seemed to crackle as she sat down behind the desk.

"Hello, Miss Andersen," she said. "My name is Samantha Travis. I know how tired you must be feeling now, but there are a few more questions we have to answer."

Kate gave her a harried look, as if to ask for mercy. She managed a smile.

"How many times do I have to do this?"

The woman reached over and touched Kate on the hand. Without thinking, Kate pulled away, but the gesture made it seem that she was hiding something. She started to move her hand back, only that seemed wrong too. Had the nurse even noticed?

"I know how you must feel," Miss Travis said. "And I'm very sorry. As you know, Marge is just a volunteer here. This is sort of a special circumstance, I'm sure you'll agree. So they asked me to chat with you."

Kate took a deep breath and proceeded to cover the ground previously gone over. The answers did not change, but she could feel herself growing defensive.

"I don't really know where her mother is at the moment. And I have no idea who her doctor is. It wasn't something I was very worried about. Maybe I should have been. It's possible that her mother used the emergency room as her doctor. People do that, don't they? In any event, you are taking care of Jenny, aren't you? You're not waiting for Linda?"

"No, no, we're not waiting. In an emergency we can do what's necessary. And the x-rays indicate that nothing is broken. So that's not a problem."

Kate's shoulders slumped with relief.

"Thank God."

"We do need to know how she was hurt, just to make sure we've checked everything out properly. Would you go over that with me?"

"Of course. We were at the playground—the one down at 96th and 5th—and she fell off the climbing thing there. I think she fell on her head and face. She has that mark."

The nurse wrote furiously. It seemed important to get every word.

"Weren't you there?" she asked.

"I was on a bench and on the opposite side of the apparatus. It blocked my view as she fell."

"Oh. Someone thought they heard you say that it was your fault."

Kate felt a sudden wave of warmth rise within her, as though her heart had shifted into high gear and fresh hot blood were coursing through her body.

"I didn't mean it that way. She was sitting on a railing where she wasn't supposed to be and when I yelled at her, she seemed to lose her balance. That's what I meant. She tried to grab the railing but she couldn't hold on. I think her shoulder was bothering her from where I had grabbed her earlier."

The nurse continued to take down every word. Kate wished she could stop talking, except she wanted to explain and felt that it would all become clear if only someone really listened—someone with compassion and half a brain to go with her white uniform and officious manner.

"I see," the nurse said. "When was that?"

"When was what?"

"The 'grabbing' you mentioned."

"You make it sound as though I deliberately manhandled her."

"I'm simply using your own words, Miss Andersen. Please."

"Okay. It was much earlier. While we were walking to the playground. She started to run in front of a cab and I grabbed her. I think she might have hurt the shoulder then."

"What about the laceration on her mouth."

Kate was silent. The nurse finally looked up from the pad. There was something in Miss Travis' manner that was beginning to annoy Kate. Laceration? It was barely a scratch.

"After she fell, I was afraid she might be going into convulsions. I tried to get my finger into her mouth to clear her tongue. I nicked her cheek with my nail. *Mea culpa.*"

The nurse finished writing and looked up.

"By the way," Kate said. "You might want to take this down too. Her shoulder was already hurting her. Linda, her mother, did that when she visited."

"Now I'm confused," the nurse said, tilting her head. "I thought you said you didn't know where her mother was."

"Right. But I didn't say she didn't know where *Jenny* was. She came for a visit."

"I see."

"I went away for the weekend and left Jenny with a woman in my building, Mrs. Morley. Is her name enough, or would you like her rank and serial number?"

"Miss Andersen, please don't be angry with me. I'm only trying to find out what happened."

"Her mother came over and there was some kind of accident and Jenny's shoulder got hurt. That's what happened. It was *already* hurt when I got back from the beach. I would never hurt Jenny."

"I'm sure you wouldn't. But she is hurt now." A brief pause followed. "Was the shoulder ever examined by a physician?"

"Jesus *Christ...*"

Again, the nurse waited. Once it was obvious that there would be no further response, the words appeared, neatly printed on the pad— '*no examination.*'

"It seemed okay the next morning. Jenny promised me it didn't hurt. Who the hell knew she needed a doctor?"

Miss Travis thanked her and left the room. She told Kate she would be back soon, but that was an obvious lie. As time passed, Kate became progressively more nervous. Twice she got up to call Roger and sat down at the sound of footsteps in the hall. New emergencies were brought in and Kate could hear the flurry of activity that accompanied them. Finally, after a half hour or so, yet another woman entered the room. She was dressed in street clothes, a dark blue conservative suit with a skirt cut to below the knee and a white blouse buttoned to her neck. She was of an indeterminate age, somewhere between thirty-five and fifty-five. Her black hair had carefully placed silver streaks around her face.

The third generation of idiots, Kate thought.

"Hello," this woman said. "I'm Rena Bracton and I'm a social worker here at the hospital.

Kate couldn't say that this new woman was lacking in sympathy. But she had that modulated tone that is reserved by authority figures for crazy people and small children. Kate thought about the woman she had met at Carl Schurz Park and hated her immediately.

"Look," Kate said. "I want to see Jenny. I'm really worried about her."

"I can understand that," Rena said, nodding earnestly. Her brown eyes tried to engage Kate's. "They're nearly done examining her. Would you please sit down?"

"No, I will not sit down. I have to see Jenny. I know her very well and I know she is very frightened by all of this."

"I just saw her," the social worker said soothingly. Her lips were turned upward in a smile that did not affect the rest of her face. "I was talking to her. She's quiet, but she's fine."

Kate struggled for control. She took a deep breath. She reminded herself that this woman did not mean badly.

"Let me explain what I mean. When Jenny is scared, she becomes very quiet. That's her way. When I first met her, she wouldn't talk at all to anyone. She used her doll like a puppet to communicate. I don't want that to start all over again."

The social worker was interested enough in this to make a note. She managed it without looking down at the pad. Kate wondered if she thought it wouldn't be noticed. What a crew!

"I want to see Jenny now," Kate repeated.

"She'll be ready in a minute or two. Then we can both see her. But first, I just have a few questions to ask."

"Ask all you want. Just don't expect any answers until I am in the same room with Jenny. I'm tired of this. You're the third person who's been in here asking me questions, all of which have been dutifully recorded. Is it that they can't write legibly, or that you can't read?"

That smile reappeared.

"I can certainly understand your impatience with us. I'd like to help both you and Jenny get out of here as quickly as possible. But there are a few points I really have to clarify."

"Jesus," Kate muttered. She could feel her jaw clench and imagined the entry that this would inspire. 'When questioned, the subject showed signs of hostility and anxiety.'

She began again, slowly.

"I said the injury was my fault, although it was not. The *reason* I said that is because Jenny thinks *everything* is her fault. If it rains on a day when we're supposed to go on a picnic, she thinks it's her fault. If her mother doesn't visit, that's her fault. So, to make her feel better, if possible, I try to take the blame. Like today. She fell, but why should she think it was her fault? Why should she feel she's being punished for nameless crimes?"

Rena thought this was worthy of a note.

"This is unbelievable!" Kate shouted. "Really. You people are fucking unbelievable!"

"Miss Andersen..."

"I told the other jackass that I was worried I had yelled and scared Jenny and made her fall. I also told her that I might have hurt her arm when I stopped her from getting killed by a cab. I did not happen to remember at the time that her mother had hurt her arm, not me. I'm a little upset that Jenny was lying there in my arms like a dead person."

"I understand."

"Stop saying that!! None of you understand a goddamn thing about this."

"Maybe you would like to tell me the whole story from the beginning."

"It's not a story!"

"I didn't mean to imply that it was. Let's just..."

"Let's just forget the whole thing. I've said as much as I'm going to say. Now, you either tell me where to find Jenny, or I will go screaming her name through the halls until I find her myself. *Capisce*?"

"Ms. Andersen, you can't do that."

"Oh really? Which can't I do? Scream her name, or find her?"

Kate started for the door. The social worker got to the door first and retreated into the hallway to the right of the door. Kate smiled. She hadn't been sure which way to go.

"I can't let you do this, Ms. Andersen," said Rena solemnly.

"As they say in the playground, 'You and what army?'"

Kate pushed her aside and marched along the corridor. Rena ran beside her like a worrisome dog, calling for a guard in a surprisingly loud voice. Kate wondered if two orderlies standing nearby would try to stop her, but she yelled at them and they backed off. She turned another corner and saw a man coming toward her, speaking into a walkie-talkie. He appeared to be the sort who spent most of his free time lifting heavy objects in front of a mirror. His biceps threatened to split the pale blue shirt of his security firm.

Kate stopped and smiled at him, as if to acknowledge that she was trapped. When he came within range, however, she kicked him in the shin as hard as she could and stamped on his other foot. He fell against the wall and she slid by. It seemed easy until she felt an arm clutch her from behind.

"I'm going to sue you if you don't let go of me!" she screamed. "I've got the smartest, nastiest lawyer in New York City and I'm going to sue your damned eyes out! Do you hear me?"

"Grab her legs, will you," her captor said. "Grab both of her legs. Hey, stop it! Stop biting!"

Eighteen

Once Kate recognized the futility of her efforts and ceased to struggle, she was led to an empty office with an outside phone line. A burly security guard was stationed outside in the hall. In thirty minutes or so, Roger appeared. He was escorted by a member of the administrative staff, a man this time, whose polished manner made it appear that he was anxious to please.

"I'd like to speak to my client privately," Roger said. His tone was as crisp as his shirt collar. His stare seemed capable of inflicting pain.

The administrator backed out of the small room, and after the door clicked shut, Roger put his arms around Kate and held her for a few minutes.

"Tell me what happened," he said.

At this point, she was calm enough to explain to Roger the sequence of events from the moment Jenny had nearly run in front of the cab until her last abortive conversation with the social worker. They had taken on a surreal quality, as though she were recounting the scenes of a movie, each full of foreshadowing.

"Why wouldn't they let me see her, Roger? All I wanted was to see her."

"I think they should have. But try to remember what we have here. A young girl is brought in with a bad bruise on her face and a bleeding mouth. These are suspicious marks. They have to ask questions. The law requires them to report the incident if there is any suspicion of child abuse."

"That's crazy! I would never hurt Jenny."

"Kate, they don't know you. They only see a kid who looks like she was in a fight."

"You mean they can take a kid away from a parent? Just like that?"

"You're not her parent, Kate."

"But I'm taking care of her. I'm like her parent right now. Linda put her into my hands."

"This is all true. But if they feel the child is in some imminent danger, they no doubt have the right to hold the child until the police come and sort things out. Still, they have to act reasonably to fulfill their obligations. You and Jenny have your rights. Just how far they overstepped the proper bounds is what a lawsuit is made of."

Kate looked up at Roger quickly.

"I don't want a lawsuit."

He lifted her hand to his lips and kissed it.

"Bless you, my child. But I think I will not tell them that for the moment. Right now, based upon a short conversation I had with them, they are under the very strong impression that I have a client who is a writer with excellent New York media contacts and who is raring to haul their good name into court and through the dirtiest sewer in Manhattan."

"Will that be enough to get us out of here?"

"I'm not sure. But I also asked John Tellum to give the hospital a call and put in a good word. He's the partner I was working with out in San Francisco. He's also part of the family whose donation funded the construction of the hospital wing where we are now sitting. I think they will listen to him."

Kate released a breath. She felt as though she had been holding the air in her lungs for an hour.

"Small world," she said.

"Yes. And sometimes that's a good thing. But please. No more kicking or hitting. Or biting."

"Promise."

With that, Roger left her alone, except for the guard who still sat lazily in a chair outside the door. The sultry afternoon had ended with thunderstorms. Through the window, she could see that the lightning had passed, but a steady rain continued, slowing traffic on Fifth Avenue.

She told herself that soon she and Jenny would be making their way home through that drizzle. Jenny's feet would seek out each slight accumulation of water on the sidewalk. Kate would ask her to stop. Jenny would grudgingly agree. Then Kate would splash *her* at the next opportunity, and they would run home, stamping their soggy sneakers in every single puddle along the way.

She smiled at the thought, but could not escape the uneasiness she felt. Deep inside, beyond the reach of reason, or of Roger's reassurance, she was certain things were not going to work out. She would not walk out of this place with Jenny. Not today. Not tomorrow. Not next week. Never.

She tried again to convince herself that her fears were nonsense. And yet the fatalistic worries crept back into her mind. Her run of good luck was ending and there was nothing she could do about it. No amount of fighting or kicking or screaming would help. At the end of this road, she would lose Jenny. And in her despair, she would lose Roger as well. Her world would contract to the three small rooms of her apartment. But why? What was her tragic flaw? What was there in her that made all of this inevitable from the beginning?

She was startled out of these thoughts by Roger's reappearance. He smiled as he closed the door and stood with her by the window.

"It's all set. They were practically falling over themselves to get rid of this problem. They hoped that you understand now that their only motivation was to protect Jenny. And there isn't going to be any charge for any of the work they did—x-rays, examination—all free. With their compliments."

He made a small bow, obviously pleased with the results.

"Where's Jenny now? I want to see her."

"You will. They're going to bring her down to the lobby. There are some forms that have to be filled out, that's all."

"I want to get out *now*, Roger."

He took her hands in his. They were ice-cold. Her fingers trembled.

"Kate, what's wrong?"

"I just have to get out of here, that's all. It's been a really bad day."

In a few minutes, she and Roger were in the lobby. The administrator was there and so was Rena, as well as a nurse to give her some more information. The doctor believed that Jenny might have had a slight concussion. Despite the fact that they expected no problems, Kate should bring Jenny back immediately if she experienced unusual drowsiness, a severe headache, or nausea. The shoulder was likely to bother Jenny for a few days. Nothing was broken, according to the x-rays, but there was a sprain. Kate could give her children's Tylenol.

Roger had discovered that Rena was best friends with a young associate at his firm. Like people who had met at a cocktail party, they were talking and joking. Then Rena's cell phone rang and she excused herself to take the call.

Kate couldn't take her eyes off Rena as she walked to a quiet corner, listening intently to someone, with her serious eyes, those very serious eyes. In a moment, she was taking notes on a pad of paper, writing feverishly. Why? The knot in Kate's stomach tightened.

"Roger, let's get Jenny. Let's go."

"Kate, will you be patient."

"No! I can't stand this place."

"Kate, come on. Calm down. This is so unlike you."

Rena motioned to Roger and Kate trailed after him, wanting to hear but fearful at the same time. The story came out in fragments. Kate stared at the floor to concentrate and piece them together. Someone in Rena's office had put Jenny's and her mother's names through the computer database. Several months previously, a neglect petition had been filed against Linda. She had been using the last name of Costa, Linda Gilmour Costa. Linda hadn't appeared on the court date and a bench warrant had been issued.

"What has this got to do with Jenny?" Kate asked.

Kate looked from one to the other. Neither seemed willing to meet Kate's gaze.

"A neglect petition can cover a multitude of offenses," Roger said. "We won't know what this one says until tomorrow when Family Court opens. The bottom line is that the Department of Social Services has ordered the hospital to hold Jenny overnight. Tomorrow there will be an emergency hearing before a Family Court judge. Probably in the afternoon."

"She has to stay here overnight? Why can't she just go home and be in her own bed? I'll bring her to court tomorrow."

"I'm afraid we can't do that," Rena said. "They were very specific. We are not permitted to let her out of our sight. Apparently, Linda has pulled this sort of thing before."

"But she will be scared to death. Did you tell them that? Get back on the phone and tell them that!"

"I'm sorry. But there's nothing else I can do."

"And how about you, Roger? Anything else you can do? Or care to do? What about your big-shot friend? Where did he disappear to? The family with all the money!"

Roger's face flushed with embarrassment.

"Kate, please calm down," Roger said. "This is a serious business and they have their rules. You know that."

"I don't know anything of the kind!"

"Kate, we're talking about one night. That's all."

Kate half sat, half fell into a chair nearby. Exhaustion seemed to be a weight on each of her limbs. Already she was beginning to regret her harsh words to Roger. Again, it seemed an inexorable progression. First, she would lose Jenny, then Roger.

"One night is a long time," she said. "Especially for Jenny."

"We'll take good care of her," Rena said. "I'll see to that personally. She's already been told she has to stay. Perhaps you would like to talk to her before you leave."

"Thank you," Kate said. "I would like to do that."

~ * ~

When they reached Jenny's room, the girl was sitting cross-legged on the bed, rigid with mistrust. Miranda was clutched in the crook of one arm. Beside the bed sat a nurse. An uneaten tray of food was between them like a game Jenny refused to play.

"Katy!" she screamed suddenly and raced across the small room, flying into Kate's arms. They clung to each other for several minutes. Kate was afraid that if she spoke, she would start to cry.

"I'm so sorry, Katy," Jenny said finally. She wiped Kate's tears away with the back of her own small hand and touched Kate's cheek, cradling it in her palm. "It's all my fault. I won't do it again."

The comment made Kate aware that Rena and the nurse were there, monitoring the scene. If either of them started taking notes, Kate was afraid that she was going to lose control all over again.

"You didn't do anything," she whispered. "Really."

"Are you going to take me home?"

Kate hesitated. She dropped to one knee.

"I can't tonight."

"Why, Katy? Why?" The girl's voice rose in panic. Kate had expected the question, but she was still not ready to respond.

Roger came over beside them.

"Because they want to keep an eye on you a little while longer," he said. "You had a bad fall."

"Will you stay with me, Katy?"

"I'd like to..."

"You can sleep in my bed with me. I won't take up any room at all."

With Kate's arms around her, she stood ramrod straight, sucking in her breath to show just how little space she would occupy. Her innocent solution was so disarming that Rena and the nurse both smiled. Kate wanted to throw them physically from the room.

"Why can't Katy stay?" Jenny asked, addressing Roger directly. In her eyes, he had assumed a mantle of authority. He was an intermediary who could translate the strange language and customs of this alien place.

"It's the rules, Jenny," Roger said. His voice was soft but firm. The words almost made sense coming from him. "They want to make sure you get a good night's rest and it's important for them to watch you. Besides, I need Kate to help find your mother tonight. We have to talk to her."

"But I don't *want* my mother," she said. "I have Katy."

"Please try to understand that this is the way it has to be."

~ * ~

A few minutes later, they finally had to leave, and this proved the most difficult of all. Despite Kate's quiet cajoling, Jenny would not let go of her, and the nurse and Rena had to pry those thin arms loose, holding Jenny so she wouldn't grab for Kate again. At the moment that the girl lost contact completely, she threw herself back onto the bed and buried her face in the pillow.

They could hear Jenny calling Kate's name until they entered the elevator, and the doors closed behind them.

Rena rode with them to the lobby. She arranged with Roger to find out the name of the judge and call him. At the door, she paused.

"I'm very sorry," she said to Kate. "I know how you must feel."

The young woman seemed genuinely distraught, but the sound of Jenny's cries still echoed in Kate's ears.

"I don't think I'm the one you should be worrying about right now."

"You know that's not fair," Rena said. "I am very concerned about Jenny. And I can see just how much you care about her. I'd like to talk to you about her. I think you could help us help Jenny."

Kate glared at her.

"If you think I'm going to help you take Jenny from her mother, you are out of your mind."

Roger took Kate by the hand and squeezed it, trying to calm her.

"I was hoping you would do what's best for Jenny," Rena said.

"And you and your cronies are the ones who will say what that is, I suppose? What? You'll sit with her for an hour? Read her file? And then you people—geniuses that you are—will make your recommendation? I can't wait to hear that. I can hardly stand it, I want so much to know your opinion."

~ * ~

She and Roger took a cab back to her apartment. The rain had stopped completely. The air was dry and cool with a wind from the north. The change was so abrupt that it felt as though days, not hours, had passed since she had left that morning with Jenny.

"What's going to happen tomorrow, Roger?"

"I don't know, Kate. I'm a corporate litigation lawyer. Ask me about breach of contract and fraudulent stock offerings, not neglect petitions. I've never even been in Family Court."

"Jenny has. I brought her down there to see a friend of mine who works in the clerk's office, Gail Harding. Jenny was so scared she couldn't get to the elevators. I thought it was the court officers and the metal detector. Obviously, there was more to it. We did a search of the records under the name of Gilmour. I didn't think to suggest Costa."

"I'm afraid there's a lot we don't know about Jenny."

The cab pulled up to her building on 92nd Street.

"Roger, I feel as though someone has reached inside of me and ripped out a piece. Jenny is crying and scared and there is nothing I can do to help her. And tomorrow, somebody who doesn't even know her is going to make a decision about her, and she's possibly going to be stuck with some strangers and have to try to learn to trust someone all over again. Do you know how hard that was for her? I just can't even stand the thought of her going through it. I know Linda is not great, but she's better than a stranger for Jenny. And at least if she's with Linda, I'm sure I'll be able to see her. Or is that just selfish, Roger? Is my reasoning all wrong because I can't bear the prospect of *not* seeing her?"

"No, Kate, I..."

"Maybe Rena is right. Maybe I really am unable to see what's right for Jenny, I love her so much. Is that true? Do I love her too much? Is my own selfish desire not to be cut off from her getting in the way of what's right? Is it that twisted now, Roger?"

"I don't know how to answer that, Kate. But I've never thought it was possible to love someone too much. Not with the kind of love you have to give."

She was silent a moment, her arms curled loosely around her middle, rocking slightly forward and backward.

"I can't tell anymore. The pain I'm feeling is so intense. I really wonder if I should just stop now. Like you said before, and like Sally said... let her go. Let it be. There's nothing I can do anyway. Why prolong this pain?"

"Don't give up, Kate."

"I don't want to. But I can't see what there is to do."

"There's plenty to do. It's seven-thirty. There are fourteen hours before the court opens tomorrow morning. I plan to spend those hours finding out everything there is to know about the Family Court. You just described how you were feeling. Well, let me tell you that I think I understand it, because I'm feeling the same way when I see how this is hurting you. You learned something about love from this little girl, Kate. And so have I. So we are going to ride this out together to the very end. Not for you or for me, but for all of us. Okay?"

"Okay, Roger."

She got out of the cab. Roger gave the driver directions to his office.

"What you have to do now is try to find Linda. We need her there tomorrow."

"I'll do whatever I can."

~ * ~

Upstairs, Kate banged on Sally's door with her fist until it opened. Jerry stood there, a beer in his hand, eyes dazed from watching TV in a darkened room.

"Hey, what's the idea?"

"I have to talk to Sally."

"She's in the shower."

"Tell her I need Linda's phone number. Tell her now, Jerry!"

"What's your freakin' problem?"

"Tell her!"

Sally emerged from the back hallway. She had a robe on, but her hair was wet and water dripped onto the floor.

"Katy, what's with the yellin'?"

"I need Linda's number. I took Jenny to the hospital today, and they found out about Linda. They kept Jenny. There's some Family Court proceeding tomorrow morning. I have to talk to Linda. They want to take Jenny."

"Jesus Christ..."

"I need her phone number, Sally."

Sally pushed the wet hair back off of her face.

"I keep telling you. I don't have her number."

"Bullshit. More bullshit!"

"I'm telling you the truth."

"You're lying. You've been lying to me all along. That's fine, Sally. I finally know where I stand with you. But you tell Linda for me, I'm not going to sit around and watch Jenny get hurt all by herself. It's *all* coming down. And it'll come down on her lousy head."

"You're talking crazy stuff."

"Am I?" Kate turned to walk away down the stairs.

"Where the hell are you going?"

"I'm going to the one place where I know they'll tell me something about Linda and her baby."

"Katy stop! God damn it, stop!"

~ * ~

On the street again, the cool air felt good as Kate strode south along Lexington Avenue. She crossed at the first light that stopped her progress, heading west on 89th, then south on Park and west again at the first opportunity, checker-boarding her way to East 74th Street between Madison and Fifth.

Night had fallen by the time she arrived. She found the lot where the condominiums were being put up. Nearby was the house she was seeking. The woman had pointed to one, but which was it?

Kate knocked on the first door she came to, and a woman answered with a toddler in her arms and two other children playing tag on the stairs behind her. Kate apologized.

"I must have the wrong address. I was looking for a friend of mine who just recently had a baby. Her name is Amanda Dilworth."

The woman smiled.

"That would be two doors down. Tell her Meg says hi."

Kate knocked at the front door of the designated address. An older woman answered, dressed in white with a starched apron and cap. In the hall was a large baby pram.

"I'd like to speak to Amanda," Kate said.

"I'm sorry. Mrs. Dilworth is busy at the moment. Was she expecting you?"

"I wouldn't quite put it that way. But just tell her there's someone here looking for Linda. I'm pretty sure she'll want to talk to me."

"I rather think not," the woman said. "She's lying in bed upstairs."

The woman started to close the door but Kate put her foot in the way.

"You tell her what I said and tell her also to get her rear end down here right now, or I'll be coming up."

At that moment, a young woman appeared from a door farther back along the main hall of the house. She walked forward at a brisk pace, apparently trying to act as though she had been coming from some distant part of the house, not simply eavesdropping. In the foyer's light, her appearance was unremarkable—even features, not beautiful, but not unattractive either. It helped that her hair was cut in a flattering way, that her make-up was flawless, and that her nails had recently been manicured. No doubt, upstairs were closets full of clothes from the shops around the corner on Madison Avenue. For now, she was wearing a nightgown that seemed too large, as if to hide her figure.

"I need Linda's phone number," Kate said.

The young woman did not meet Kate's gaze. She picked at a bit of lint on the sleeve of her gown.

"I don't have the slightest idea what you are talking about."

"Yes you do. I want the Linda who lived with you for the past two months. Where did you keep her hidden? Downstairs?"

"We don't use the downstairs. The rooms have to be renovated."

She recited the words mechanically, as if she had memorized them from a script.

"She was pregnant. Does that help you remember?"

The woman winced. Then the distinctive cry of an infant could be heard deep upstairs. The nanny started off in that direction. Kate stepped into the foyer.

"You can't come in here," the woman said.

"That's Linda's baby, isn't it? Where is Linda?!"

Kate had no proof of her accusation other than the expression of panic and despair that covered the woman's face. It was all the proof she needed.

The nanny stood halfway up the stairs, frozen. Above, the baby cried louder and more insistently. The young woman tried to close the door but Kate's foot blocked it. She seemed stunned, wooden. She had no idea why the door wouldn't close or why Kate was there or what she was saying.

"That's *my* baby," she said in the same robotic tone.

"You're lying!" Kate replied and stepped past the woman.

The nanny screamed.

"Stay out! How dare you talk this way!"

"It's my baby," the woman repeated. "My baby."

"Tell me where Linda is!"

Just then, a door opened upstairs, and a man rushed out. He was still dressed in a suit from work, his tie loosened at his neck, his thinning blond hair awry. He came down the stairs two at a time. In his hand was a large umbrella with a wooden handle. He swung it hard against the wall like a club as he approached.

"Get out of here!" he shouted. He had all the fury and determination that his wife had lacked. "Miss Newman, take my wife upstairs."

"I want to know where Linda is!" Kate demanded.

"Get out, or I'll call the police! You are trespassing in this house!"

With each word, the man pounded the umbrella into the floor. He rushed at Kate and swung wildly, smashing a table lamp. Kate stepped backward, closing the door partially as a shield.

"You have Linda's baby. I know you do! The whole world will know if you don't tell me where to find Linda!"

"I'll have you arrested! Do you hear? You'll be thrown in jail! And if you say those things again, I'll sue you for every penny you have. You'll regret coming here! You'll regret you were ever born!"

He swung at where Kate's fingers gripped the door. She let go. He tried to close it, but she pushed back.

Suddenly, Kate felt a pulling from behind her. She lost her footing, and the door closed. Then she was being dragged down the steps to the sidewalk, barely able to keep her balance.

"For crissakes, what the hell's the matter with you?" Sally screamed. She poked her arm through Kate's and held it in an iron grip, guiding her between two parked cars to a cab waiting with the door open.

"Let go of me!"

"Shut up and get in the freakin' car. You want to spend the night trying to get out of the goddamned jail? You think you're going to help anybody in jail?"

They could hear sirens. Two blocks away, a car with flashing lights was approaching.

Sally pushed her into the cab and jumped in after her.

"Get moving, for Christ's sake!" she yelled at the driver. He stamped on the accelerator and they were around the corner before the police came to a halt on the quiet street. "Drive over to the West Side at 67th Street and up Central Park West. Then home to 92nd Street. Got it?"

The cabby just nodded silently. His eyes were on the road in front of him.

"I told you to stay the hell out of this," Sally said. "You remember I told you that?"

She let go of Kate's arm, and at that instant, Kate spun toward her, swinging wildly with her fists in the confines of the back seat. She caught Sally once hard on the side of the face, and again on the shoulder, before Sally could grab both of her wrists and hold them tight. Kate had thought she had no tears left, but she was sobbing again.

"Damn you," she said finally.

"Damn yourself," Sally replied. She rubbed at her cheek, which was turning red.

"You should have told me."

Sally slapped the seat between them with a loud crack that made Kate flinch.

"Am I your freakin' nursemaid? Am I your mother, for Christ's sake?"

Kate stiffened with anger, drawing her legs up beneath her on the seat.

"Just listen to me," Sally continued. "That's your whole freakin' problem, you know. You listen to what you want. You see what you *want* to see. And you act like the world's last virgin when things go wrong."

"What are you talking about?"

"I'm talking about you and your bullshit."

"I didn't know she was selling her baby."

"And you don't know that now, either. You don't know any more than you did two days ago. It's just that suddenly you want to believe it. It suits you."

"That's not true!"

"Bull! I'll bet you a hundred bucks you didn't tell them at the hospital that Linda was pregnant. Did you?"

"It was none of their business."

"And which story did you give them, then? She's working someplace for the summer to get some money together? She's taking care of a sick uncle who'll be leaving her money?

"Sally, I swear I didn't know this was what she was doing."

"All the better, because you don't know any more now than you did before. Leave it that way. If anyone asks, you don't know nuthin'. What pregnancy? What baby? That'll be that."

Sally paused to let her words sink in. She slid across the seat toward Kate, slipping her arm over her shoulder, stroking her hair lightly as she spoke.

"Katy, you know I can hear your freakin' brain working right now. 'How could she? Her own baby?' Katy, I'm telling you, you can't ever understand what this woman is all about. She's from a different world. One that you can't imagine. You think she plans from one minute to the next? You think she worries about what happens *tomorrow*? She thinks she's poor right now and she doesn't want to be poor. She's tired of being behind the eight ball. She's got a kid and the welfare don't cut it at all. The budget they got her on don't buy bubble gum at the bodega. The kid needs clothes. Toys. So she hears about a guy who puts people together. Real quiet. Real well organized. Room and board and doctor bills all paid. And when it's all over, thirty-five thousand dollars cash."

"Is that how it happened?"

"I don't know how it happened, okay. I don't ask questions when I don't need to have answers. It's a *scenario*. The point is, Linda ain't like you or me. You lost your job, but you had Roger to help you.

You had your friends, if necessary. If I'm down, I know I got people to lean on. Right here on this block. But Linda has been hustling for too long. She's got nobody, Kate. Nobody to help her, and nobody to stop her, either. And who's to say in the end? A rich couple has a kid they'll raise with all the best. Linda has money for Jenny and herself. Who the hell knows what's right?"

Kate could see Sally's hand clench into a fist and loosen again.

"Where is she now?"

"Don't start with the questions again. Okay? I've been in touch. She knows the whole story. She'll be in court tomorrow morning."

"I have to talk to her."

"No you don't either. As far as those freakin' busybodies are concerned, you dealt with me, that's all. I got married and couldn't keep the kid anymore, so you volunteered until her mother returned."

"And where exactly is she supposed to have been all that time?"

"Again, you don't know. You heard she was working off the books at some resort on Cape Cod. Trying to get money together to rent a place with Jenny until she could get a job. That's all you have to know or say. Let her do her own lying, Kate. You stay out of it. You don't know nuthin' about any baby. It's the best way to deal with those freakin' agency people. Let Linda do the talking. She doesn't need a lawyer. She does okay. I'm telling you, she's a hustler. Just let her talk and you keep quiet. It's for the best."

Nineteen

The next morning, Kate awoke feeling again as though the events of her life were speeding toward a conclusion that she could not control. She was out of bed early to try to call Jenny at the hospital, but the shift of nurses had changed. Those who had been on duty the evening before were gone and those on the new shift had never heard of Jenny. By the time Kate was transferred to the nursing station on the proper floor, she was told Jenny was on her way to the offices of Child Protective Services downtown. Telephone calls to CPS brought a response first that she was not there yet, and then that she was being seen by professionals and unavailable to talk.

The sense of being in an unreal time and place continued once Kate reached the Family Court building. She arrived at a few minutes after nine and the lobby on the main floor was completely packed with litigants waiting to pass through the metal detectors. The line wound like a well-fed snake, back and forth across the room, three or more abreast. As those at the front left the line to go upstairs to the courtrooms, others joined at the back end. An occasional cry could be heard from a small child. Otherwise the crowd was silent as it inched forward. Eye contact was shunned like a cultural taboo. By the time Kate reached the front of the line, it was close to 9:30 and there were nearly as many people behind her as there had been at the start of her trek. Still, she did not see Linda.

Kate asked a Court Officer where she could find the courtroom for Linda's case and she was pointed to a wall where the computer printouts listed the parties for each judge. A feeling of panic rose in her as she scanned the sheets once, then twice, and could not find Linda's name anywhere. After being directed to the clerk's office, and another five minutes of fruitless searching, a supervisor told her to see Judge Hyatt on the eighth floor. All new matters and emergency hearings that day were going through that judge' scourtroom.

Kate rushed to the eighth floor, and after another wait in line, the clerk said no one connected with the case was there yet, certainly not Linda. She walked around the perimeter of the waiting area and tried to relax, but found it impossible. The building was relatively modern among New York City courts, but it seemed to have been designed with no consideration at all for the comfort of a nervous human being. On one side was a large expanse of glass that looked out on a decrepit building next door. The waiting area itself was roughly pentagonal in shape and served several courtrooms. Within the odd angles of the walls, molded plastic chairs were set in triangular patterns. Above were balconies and setbacks corresponding to the next higher floor. Kate looked in vain for a piece of wood amidst the stone, concrete, plaster, tile and glass.

Finally, she forced herself to take a seat near the courtroom and surveyed the room. The veterans of the process were easy to pick out. They either slept or remained expressionless amidst the ebb and flow of lives around them. The newcomers couldn't sit still. They twisted and turned in their seats. They consulted with the court officers time and again to see when their case would be called or whether the necessary social workers and lawyers had checked in. Others sat alone with disturbed expressions, as if trying to understand what twist of fate—what injustice—had drawn them to this place where a judge would decide a highly personal aspect of their lives.

At one point, Kate saw Rena with another woman talking to the court officer. Kate assumed that this was the lawyer for the Child Protective Services. She had brown hair pulled back into a tight ponytail and wore a gray pantsuit with a fashionable cut. Her single concession to femininity was the collar of her white shirt, which was ruffled and rose high around her neck, causing her already prominent chin to protrude as if it were her first line of defense. Kate thought the woman would have been a bar-storming prohibitionist at the turn of the century. A Puritan was definitely in her family bloodline. Rena pointed discreetly in Kate's direction. But after giving their names to the court officer, Rena and the other woman left.

Shortly before ten o'clock, Roger came in the door. He smiled when he saw Kate, but she knew something was troubling him. He took the seat beside her.

"I've been up in the file room since it opened this morning, looking over the papers in this case. It's a lot more serious than I had thought. This wasn't just a neglect proceeding against Linda. They were trying to terminate her parental rights."

"They want to take Jenny away completely?"

"Yes. And that's really not the worst of it. There had been earlier petitions that were dismissed for various reasons. This last time, from what I understand, Linda didn't show up at all and they went ahead and held a hearing without her. The judge decided that Jenny should be taken from her mother, either to be adopted or to be put in foster care."

"They did this without Linda? That's got to be illegal, right?"

"It's not that simple. If they served her with notice and she chose not to show up, they could proceed without her. Remember, they're trying to look out for the best interest of the kid."

"Yeah, right!" Kate said sarcastically. "I keep hearing how much everybody is looking out for Jenny."

"I don't want to argue with you. I know this is hard, and it's not going to get easier soon. But this is the reality you have to deal with. You knew you were going to have to let her go sometime. That moment may have arrived."

"I thought I would be giving her back to her mother, not to an agency."

"The court may have no choice, if the mother is found to be unfit."

"You can't let that happen, Roger. You have to stop them somehow. Jenny will be so terribly unhappy. I can't stand to think about her feeling that terrible loneliness again, as if she has no one in the world who cares about her."

"I'm doing everything I can, Kate. I promise."

"But what if Linda doesn't show up?"

"That is one thing we don't have to worry about. She was in the file room, trying to look over the same papers as I was. She knows her way around the court system, I'll give her that. She's in the ladies room right now. I told her to meet me here. We'll see if she does."

"What do you mean?"

"I'm not sure she thinks she needs any help. She told me she wanted to do her own talking. I think I persuaded her to at least let me come into the courtroom with her and give her advice."

"I should have warned you about Linda."

"I'm not sure any warning would have helped. She told me how grateful she was to you for everything you've done for Jenny. Then, in the next breath, she asked if I'd like to come down to the East Village and see her new apartment."

"She propositioned you?"

"I don't think she was looking for legal advice."

As they spoke, Rena and the CPS lawyer reappeared and walked over to Judge Hyatt's court officer. He consulted his list.

"Everyone here on Gilmour?" he called. "Parties on Gilmour?"

Roger waved to him and got up.

"We're waiting for Ms. Gilmour," he said.

Then Kate saw Linda enter the room and head directly toward the court officer, where Rena and the CPS lawyer were standing together. She was wearing a short-sleeved white dress with a design of large pastel flowers. Her hair was swept up and back from her face in a simple bun. Her make-up was conservatively applied. She could have passed for a young working mother, off from work for the morning and hoping to get back to the office later. In her hand was a large white handkerchief.

"What is she doing?" Roger asked.

They hurried toward her, but she got to Rena first.

"Where's my daughter?" She pointed her finger into Rena's face. "I want to see my daughter!"

Her voice was loud enough to attract the attention of people sitting nearby. Tears began to fall down her agonized face.

"What's wrong with you people?" she continued. "Can't you ever be satisfied? I try to work and make some money so my daughter and I can live, and while I'm gone, you try to take my child away?"

"You know that isn't accurate at all," Rena said.

"Liar! You wanted me to live in a goddamned welfare hotel with the druggies and the cockroaches." Linda paused, well aware of the people who were listening. "I said no! I won't do that. But you don't like it when people say 'no'."

There was a general murmuring of agreement on this point.

Roger pushed forward.

"Linda, please, let's stop this."

He tried to lead her away a few steps.

"I'd love to stop, but I didn't start it. They started this whole thing. They want to take my daughter away!" Tears fell anew. "Why won't they give her back to me?"

"Because you're unfit," the CPS lawyer said. "And this little act of yours doesn't change anything."

Linda's eyes seemed to glaze over at those words and she started forward with a shout. Kate and Roger together held her back.

The court officer rushed between them.

"Linda, cut it out!" Kate said.

"I'll show you!" Linda continued. "You just love to see people fail. Well, I worked damned hard all summer and I've got money to take care of my daughter now."

"Worked hard doing what, Linda?" asked the CPS lawyer. "That's what I'd like to know."

Kate winced. Linda had to be restrained again.

Roger turned to the lawyer, his face red with anger.

"From this moment forward," he said. "If you have something to say to my client, you'll say it to me. Understand?"

The lawyer didn't respond, but her eyes narrowed as though she were not at all afraid of a fight.

"Okay, calm down everybody," the court officer said. "If we're all here, let's go inside to the judge. All parties on the Gilmour matter."

~ * ~

Rena and the CPS lawyer went in first. Linda collected herself, straightening her dress, as demure in her pose as a lady entering church. She linked her arm in Roger's. Over her shoulder, she winked at Kate and gave her a thumbs up.

Kate didn't know whether to laugh or cry. "Break a leg," she whispered and followed them into the courtroom of Judge Sandra Hyatt.

A tape machine was running to record the proceeding. The courtroom clerk asked the lawyers and the parties to identify themselves. The lawyer for Protective Services, whose name was Cheryl Damian, objected to Kate's presence in the courtroom. Roger explained that Kate had been the child's caregiver for the past month or so and, to Kate's surprise, the judge turned to her and gave her a warm smile.

"Miss Andersen may stay," she said. "And I would like to inform counsel that I have met briefly with the child, Jenny, this morning. It is completely appropriate for Miss Andersen to be here. Let's proceed."

"Your Honor," Roger began. "This is a *pro bono* matter for our firm. I became involved only yesterday afternoon. I spoke to our client, Ms. Gilmour, for the first time this morning. Last night I called up the attorneys for CPS and requested an adjournment for a week to give me a chance to familiarize myself with the proceedings to date. That request was refused, so I would like to make that same request now to Your Honor."

The judge looked toward Ms. Damian.

"What is your position?"

"Our position is that there is no need for an adjournment because there is nothing for the court to do at this point. There has already been an adjudication of neglect. The court has severed the parental rights of Linda Gilmour."

Linda jumped to her feet, screaming.

"Liar! I was never at any proceeding!"

The judge hammered her gavel on the desk in front of her.

"Be seated!"

Linda started crying. Her whole body shook.

"But Your Honor, she's lying about this."

The court officer had rushed to stand between Linda and the judge. His nightstick was in both hands. Roger put his arm around Linda and gently pushed her down into her chair.

"Please, don't do that again," he whispered.

"She's lying," Linda moaned. "Oh God, she's lying."

The judge glared at her angrily, then nodded to Cheryl Damian to continue.

"We don't deny that she wasn't there, Your Honor," the lawyer continued. "It is our contention that she was served with process and deliberately decided not to appear. We have an affidavit of the process server. And there was testimony by him on the day that Ms. Gilmour failed to show up."

Linda was on her feet again.

"I wasn't served with papers! I swear, I never got papers."

The judge banged her gavel again. Then she leaned forward to emphasize her words.

"I will not have you interrupting in my courtroom. One more time and you will be removed, and we will proceed without you. Do you understand my warning?!"

Linda nodded.

"Answer me out loud for the record!" the judge said.

"*Yes,* Judge."

Linda sat down again. Her shoulders were slumped. Her face was cupped in her hands as she stared at the judge. Tears rolled down her cheeks unabated.

"Ms. Damian, do you have a copy of the process server's affidavit?"

"Yes, Your Honor."

She held it out for the clerk to bring up to the judge.

"Show it to Mr. Adams, please."

Roger took the document and read it carefully. It was only a page long. Then he bent over and conferred with Linda. She shook her head violently.

"Your Honor," Roger said. "We would like to have a hearing on service and the opportunity to cross-examine this process server. My client tells me that she was not living at the address listed in this affidavit at the time it was purportedly served."

"Ridiculous!" said Ms. Damian. "Your Honor, she pulls this same act every time. If you were to look at the record of her proceedings in this court—and it is a long one—she never shows up the first time, and then she comes in, crying the way she is today, and swears she wasn't served with papers. It was a lie then and it's a lie now!"

Linda started to get up, but Roger's firm hand on her shoulder held her in her seat.

"I object to counsel's reference to alleged facts that are not in the record here, and I especially object to her *ad hominem* attacks. Those attacks started out in the hall before this case was called, which is one reason why my client is so upset and acted the way she did in this courtroom. I am not trying to excuse her, Your Honor, but I think that an explanation should be made. There is certainly no reason for counsel to continue in this vein now."

The judge nodded in agreement.

"I am directing counsel to be professional and civil at all times. Are you finished with the affidavit?"

"No, Your Honor. There is one more thing. The person who served it, James Prince, is not worthy of belief, at least in our understanding. Within the last month or six weeks, two judges of this court have held that he lied in his service affidavits. Neither of those cases has been reported yet, but they were before Judge Gilbert and Judge Samson."

The judge turned to Cheryl Damian. She appeared angrier than she had been earlier.

"Ms. Damian, were you aware of this?"

The lawyer's chin jutted out. Her back was straight. Kate had to admire her ability to hang tough. She didn't back down at all.

"Both of those matters are being appealed. We contest them."

The judge gave her a look of disgust.

"I want to see counsel for both sides in my chambers immediately. Everyone else stay in the courtroom."

Kate watched the two lawyers follow the judge into her robing room at the rear of the courtroom. Roger held the door. Cheryl Damian nodded slightly at the gesture. No hard feelings, she seemed to say. We're just doing our jobs.

Once they were gone, Linda grinned from ear to ear.

"Kicked her butt, big time, didn't he? Big time!" Linda said. "You know, he told me earlier he had never been inside the Family Court, and I was a little worried. But he sure don't act like somebody who's never been here, does he?"

Kate smiled uneasily.

"No, he seemed like someone who's done this all his life."

"You know," Linda said quietly. "I understand he doesn't want to get paid. I mean I couldn't afford those guys anyway. But that don't mean I couldn't get him something. You talk about it with him, will ya? Maybe a flat screen TV or something. I know a guy who can get me one of those real cheap. Top of the line stuff. Widest screen there is, the works. You talk to him, huh? Find out what he wants and I'll work out the details."

"Sure," Kate said. "I don't think he actually needs a TV, but it's a nice thought. I'll tell him."

Linda leaned back in the chair.

"Hey, Rena, how about you? You need a TV or anything? Toaster? Microwave?"

"No, thank you."

"Cattle prod? Sex toys?"

Linda laughed as Rena's face grew red. The court officer tried not to smile. He turned his back, as though attending to something important in the corner of the room.

"No need for sex toys? That's good. Must mean you're getting it regular, huh? Wouldn't have expected it, but..."

Kate pushed her chair out from the table where she was sitting. The legs scraped loudly across the tile floor.

"Please stop with this," Kate said. "I have a very bad headache."

"Sure, sorry," Linda said. The court officer had turned back around at the noise. Linda rolled her eyes at him and he laughed.

"She's giving you good advice," the officer said.

"Yeah," said Linda. She stretched her arms back over her head, arching her back so her breasts almost escaped the confines of the dress she wore. "But I almost never take good advice."

She laughed at her own joke, giving Kate a playful push with her fist.

Then the back door to the courtroom opened again and the officer called out, "All rise, the Honorable Judge Sandra Hyatt presiding."

Without a word, the two lawyers took their places. Roger's face was a blank mask.

"On the record," Judge Hyatt said, and the officer turned on the tape recorder again. "We have had a short discussion in my chambers among counsel and we have worked out a stipulation which I will read into the record. This matter is adjourned for a period of one week. At that time, the neglect proceeding against Linda Gilmour will be reopened *de novo*. Ms. Gilmour will admit service of process and that will no longer be an issue in the case. Is that acceptable to all concerned?"

Roger leaned across to Linda.

"It's the best I could do," he whispered.

"You rock, baby," she whispered back. "Yes, Your Honor," she said sweetly to the judge.

"Then this matter stands adjourned. Any questions?"

Kate stood up, nearly knocking over her chair.

"What about Jenny?"

The judge looked over at Cheryl Damian and then at Roger.

"I am glad to see that someone cares enough to ask. Temporary custody will be with Kate Andersen. CPS has objected to custody even temporarily with the mother. But I think it would be appropriate. I want overnight visitation at least once in the next week. I will leave it to you folks to work out the details."

"Thank you, Your Honor," Roger said, echoed by Ms. Damian.

"But where is she, Judge?" Kate asked. "I mean, Your Honor."

At that point, the door to the back of the courtroom opened again. Out came Gail Harding, followed by a smaller person with dark hair and the red shirt she'd been wearing the day before at the playground. Her eyes were opened wide, as though unaccustomed to the light. Then she spotted Kate.

"Katy, Katy, Katy!" She screeched happily at the top of her young lungs. "Oh, Katy, we're going home! Gail said so! We're going home!"

Twenty

By the time they all got back to 92nd Street, Sally had bought a lunchmeat platter and put it out on a card table in her living room with crackers and chips and a bottle of wine. Jerry had sprung for a pizza. Mrs. Morley came upstairs with a bowl of cookies.

Roger and Kate were given the seats of honor on the sofa, with Jenny in Kate's lap. Linda poured a glass of wine for Kate and Roger. Sally had a soda for Jenny. Then Linda topped off her own glass and raised it high.

"To the straight-laced but happy couple. God bless you both!" She emptied her glass.

"Here, here!" said Sally. "I always said you were a great guy, Roger baby. Tell him, Katy. Didn't I always say he was the freakin' catch of the century?"

Kate smiled.

"Or words to that effect."

"Right! Ha! Words to that freakin' effect."

Linda came across the room toward them, her glass already half empty.

"You should've seen him, Sally. Spouting Latin just like the nuns at St. Jude's Grammar. Remember Sister Grace? Huh, Sally?"

Sally let out a howl of laughter.

"Sister Grace, with a face from outer space!"

Linda swallowed what was in her glass and went back for a refill.

"Oh, it was sweet, Sally. I swear to Jesus, Mary and Joseph the judge sat up a little straighter when Roger said the name of his firm. Am I right, Katy? I think she had her eye on Roger too. I think maybe she was a little stirred up under the freakin' robes."

"Uh, oh, Katy," Sally teased. She gave Jerry a gentle elbow. He pointed a finger comically at Kate and sipped his beer.

"But not that bitch lawyer for CPS," Linda continued. "Talk about a freakin' ice queen. You'd need a hot poker to drill her."

"Linda!" Sally interrupted with a laugh, gesturing in the direction of Jenny whose little ears were perked up.

"Oops," Linda said. She placed her free hand over her mouth.

Roger sat forward on the couch.

"I really wish I could stay a while longer. But I have to get back to work, folks."

"Oh no! Don't go yet." Linda placed her hand on his shoulder and sat beside him on the couch. It was a tight fit. Her skirt rose up, and her leg was pressed against his. She leaned close. "I'll behave. I promise."

Roger smiled uneasily.

"That's not really the point. I just have stuff to do at the office."

"Just a little while, Rog," Sally pleaded. "You have to eat some lunch. And you barely touched your wine. You deserve a little relaxation."

"Even I agree with that," Kate said.

"Don't get me wrong," Roger replied. "I'm feeling pretty good about the way this is going. It's just that I don't want anyone to think this is over. We still have a hearing. They still want to take away Linda's parental rights."

"Yeah, but that's bullshit at this point," Linda said. "Believe me, I know a little about this Family Court crapola. I got an apartment now for me and Jens. It's clean. It's furnished. The neighborhood ain't half bad. By the time I get back to court, I'm going to be taking some computer courses so I can get a good job. They love that shit. No way the judge is going to take Jenny away. They got nuthin'."

"I wouldn't say they have nothing," he replied.

Linda shifted forward to look at him.

"What the hell do you mean?"

"I'm not sure we should talk about this right now. I don't want to lose any attorney-client privilege."

Linda waved off his concerns.

"Don't worry. Sally has bad hearing and Jerry just left the room, right Jerry?"

"I was never here," Jerry said. "I ain't here now."

Sally slapped him on the shoulder and they both laughed.

"The problem is," Roger continued. "I don't know what they're talking about specifically. But Cheryl Damian made it clear that she had some witnesses to bring in. She wasn't volunteering anything. She's a smart lawyer. But the judge pressed her and she said it had to do with improprieties regarding a sibling of Jenny's."

"That's freakin' ridiculous."

Kate raised up the palm of her hand and stopped Linda from continuing.

"Jenny," she whispered softly. "Would you go downstairs for a few minutes with Mrs. Morley? I'll come for you in a little while and we'll go to the playground."

"I don't want to," Jenny said.

Roger took her by the hand.

"Please, Jenny. The adults have to talk."

Jenny pouted briefly, but got to her feet. After she and Mrs. Morley had left, Kate finally spoke.

"Roger, you didn't tell them Linda was pregnant, did you?"

"No, I didn't say anything about it. When they started talking about a baby recently born, I told them I had just gotten involved in this case."

"You did right," Linda said. "She's blowing smoke."

"I hope so. But I don't think you should underestimate this lawyer. I know you don't like her. And I don't blame you for that. But she is very capable, and very over-worked with a huge caseload. I don't think she would be pursuing this particular matter if she didn't have something substantial to back it up. The judge said as much."

"She ain't got nuthin'!" Linda replied angrily. "Believe me. She ain't got a freakin' thing."

"That ain't true," Sally said. "She could have Anthony."

"Who's Anthony?" Roger asked.

"Anthony's nobody!" Linda shouted. "He's freakin' nobody and if that's what she's got, she's still got nuthin!" Agitated, she sprang to her feet and finished off what was left of her wine. "Excuse me a minute. I gotta go to the little girls' room."

No one said anything while she was gone. Jerry got himself a slice of pizza and one for Sally. Roger and Kate, seeing this as their opportunity to exit, raised themselves laboriously from the depths of the sofa. They said goodbye to Jerry and Sally and were waiting at the open door when Linda reappeared. She rubbed at her nostrils as though trying to stop an incipient sneeze. She stuck out her lower lip in an exaggerated pout. The resemblance to Jenny was striking.

"We've really got to go," Roger said.

"Okay, I know you do. But hey, Roger, I hope you don't take it the wrong way that I blew up a little while ago. I don't mean nuthin' about you. It just pisses me off when they get into my personal life like this. But don't worry about this one bit. I'll take care of Anthony, okay?"

"We'll talk about this again. We have to meet to prepare you for the hearing."

"Okay, Roger. I'll call you. I'm getting my phone tomorrow."

He leaned down to kiss her goodbye, and she took his head in her two hands and kissed him full on the mouth. He pulled away and she laughed.

"You got a great guy here, Kate. You ever get tired of him, you let me know."

~ * ~

Roger and Kate walked down the stairs slowly to Mrs. Morley's.

"Kate," he said. "I know there's something going on that you haven't told me about."

"*If* I haven't, and I do mean, '*if,*' it is because you're better off not knowing. It's for your own protection. Linda doesn't always do what you or I might think is the right thing. I don't want you getting into trouble over her."

"I don't believe I'm hearing this from you, Kate."

"I'm not doing this to help Linda. Remember that. I'm in this for Jenny, period."

"I can't work this way."

"Roger, I understand what you're saying. But just do your job. Treat this like a criminal case where you don't *have* to *know* everything. You make Cheryl Damian prove her case, that's all."

"How do you know so much about it?"

"My mother used to talk about it all the time. She didn't always like it either, but she did it. It was her job."

"Maybe I should talk to her," he said.

"Maybe you already did."

They stopped outside Mrs. Morley's door. He stared into her eyes.

"I'm not very good at keeping secrets, am I?"

"Why should it be a secret?"

"I don't know. Carla is one topic you've never wanted to talk about. I called your friend, Gail, to get some idea of what to expect, and she told me I should talk to the expert."

"And Gail told you not to tell me."

He nodded.

"She wasn't sure how you would take it. But there wasn't a lot of time to waste. I had a hearing that was hours away and a body of law to digest. Carla's the one who told me about that process server. She's a walking encyclopedia when it comes to the Family Court."

Kate's face twisted into a half smile.

"How is the old girl?"

"She's in the hospital. She was diagnosed with breast cancer, but they think they caught it in time. The doctors are optimistic."

Kate took a deep breath and let it out.

"I didn't know."

"She'd like to see you, Kate."

"Did she say that?"

He paused.

"Some things don't have to be *said*, Kate."

"Yeah. That's true. And some things *do* have to be said."

"Kate..."

She put her finger to his lips.

"I'll handle this in my own way, Roger."

"I just don't want you to be mad at me over this."

She smiled.

"I'm not mad. Not even a little bit."

She knocked at Mrs. Morley's door. He took her quickly by the hand.

"We're going to get through this, Kate. I promise you."

I hope so, she thought.

~ * ~

That afternoon, Kate took Jenny to the playground. She asked Linda if she wanted to come with them and was surprised when Linda replied that she would.

The wine had raised Linda's spirits. Half a block over, she took off the shoes she had worn to court and walked barefoot the rest of the way. She held Jenny's hand and talked to her about the apartment she had gotten. There was a room just for Jenny, and although she had gotten her a bed, she was waiting to buy everything else until Jenny could come with her. This would be *her* room, after all.

"And we're going to take this real slow, Jenny. I know how much you love Kate and love living with Kate. And I'm not going to rush you to come back and live with me. Okay? We'll do it a little at a time."

Jenny didn't respond, but the idea seemed to relax her.

"Have you been doing any racing lately?" she asked Jenny.

Jenny giggled.

"No."

Linda smiled back and when they got within a few yards of a corner, she yelled, "Go!" and started running to the curb, raising her arms in triumph, with Jenny yelling and laughing in protest.

Right outside the park, there was a man selling balloons and stuffed animals. Linda bought Jenny one of each. So pleased that she almost forgot to thank her, Jenny set off to play in the sandbox and Linda went with her, digging her bare feet deep into the sand. Kate sat on a bench, holding the toys Linda had purchased. She couldn't hear what Linda was saying to Jenny, but the girl was laughing often, shyly at first and then more openly. It was perfectly obvious to Kate that Linda loved her daughter and that Jenny loved her. She told herself that she was glad Linda and Jenny were enjoying being together. It was the way things were supposed to be between mother and daughter, certainly, and yet it was difficult to keep from crying.

She had brought some work to do, a particularly enervating editing job that she had been putting off. It took all her concentration and so was perfect for such a day as this. As five o'clock approached, Jenny and Linda came over to the bench where Kate had been sitting.

"What the hell is this?"

Linda pointed to the bench a few feet away where an envelope was lying with her name written on it.

"I hadn't seen it before just now," Kate said. She looked behind her, puzzled for a moment. The wrought iron fence that circled the playground was only a foot or two behind the bench. Someone must have stuck his hand through and left the envelope. Thick shrubbery nearby would have provided cover for the approach. She stood to see if the person was still around.

Linda tore the envelope open and read it.

"What is it?" Jenny asked.

"Nuthin', baby. It's a joke, that's all. Why don't you go run to that slide and back and I'll time you."

Jenny raced off.

"It's freakin' Anthony," Linda said. "I told you he wasn't going to testify. He wants money, that's all. That's what the freakin' guy always wants. Money. The grubby bastard. Okay, he'll get his filthy money. And then he'll freakin' leave me alone."

~ * ~

A couple of days later, Kate arranged to bring Jenny down to spend the afternoon with Linda and see their apartment. On the day they were going to visit, a package arrived at about noon. Inside was a new dress for Jenny complete with patent leather shoes, and a small matching handbag. Jenny was beside herself with anticipation as Kate gave her a bath. Her limbs almost quivered with excitement as her hair was brushed and held back with barrettes. And as Kate got ready, Jenny marched back and forth through the apartment at the slightest pretext, just to hear her heels click on the wood floor and stare at her reflection in the mirror on the back of Kate's bedroom door.

The whole outfit couldn't have cost all that much. Kate wondered why she had never thought to buy such a thing for Jenny. Was it proof that a mother, a real mother, has insights into the desires of her child that an outsider never would?

They took the subway to 8th Street and walked east and south again toward the address Linda had given her. The building had been constructed in the early fifties, it appeared, and was six stories high with functional, rather smallish wood-framed windows and a red brick exterior that typified the period. It was thoroughly uninspiring, and yet Kate was sure the rooms would be more than adequate in size, and it was a clean building with little graffiti on the outside walls. In the foyer, Kate checked the list of occupants. The superintendent lived there, which was usually a good sign.

They rang the buzzer to be admitted and took an elevator to the third floor. The walls were thinner than at 92nd street—a couple could be heard arguing from behind closed doors as they climbed the stairs. The air was somewhat stuffy from a lack of ventilation, but the walls had been washed recently and the carpet was swept clean. A stroller was parked at the end of the hall, along with a girl's bicycle of about Jenny's size.

Linda opened the door and waved them in.

"Oh my God, Jenny! You look so beautiful in that dress! Oh, I knew you would look like a doll. Just a beautiful little doll." She dropped onto her knees and gave Jenny a hug. The girl seemed both embarrassed and pleased by the compliments. Kate tried to remember if she had told Jenny even once how very nice she looked. "I'm going to have to put on some more make-up, little baby," Linda continued. "I'll be looking like a dried-up old woman next to you." She laughed and primped her hair. "Come and let me show you around."

The apartment still looked as though it had just been rented. There was furniture, some of it new. But other items were obviously missing—a lamp or two for reading, an end table.

"I bought a rug for the living room," Linda said. "It's coming tomorrow. I still have to get some decent pots and pans and kitchen utensils. I guess we're eating out tonight, Jens."

"It's really very nice," Kate said. "Isn't it nice, Jenny?"

Jenny nodded.

"Let me show you your room."

On the bed was a bright pink bedspread with animals printed all over it that made Jenny smile.

"We can go out and start buying the other stuff today, Jenny. If you want."

They continued down a short hallway. Linda's bedroom was on the right, and as they passed, she stopped to push open the door. A man was sitting on the bed in a short-sleeved t-shirt and boxer shorts. His hair was short and parted neatly. He said nothing while his eyes played lazily over Kate and Jenny without apparent interest. On a table near the bed were a mirror, a razor and a small plastic bag with white powder in it.

"For crissakes, Rico," Linda said. "I told you I had company. Get some freakin' clothes on, willya?"

She closed the door again and whispered to Kate, "He's been helping me move in, but he'll be gone real soon. He's a freakin' freeloader. Like all men."

They went back into the living room. Linda offered Kate a glass of wine, but it was time for her to go, Kate realized, so she declined.

"I'll pick Jenny up after dinner. Say, seven o'clock? Seven-thirty?"

"Sounds great," Linda said. "We'll go down with you. Me and Jenny are going to go do some shopping, okay Jens?"

Jenny nodded and smiled.

"Okay."

~ * ~

Kate walked home and did some work, then went out to pick up a load of dry-cleaning and stop at the store. When she got back it was about five o'clock and the phone was ringing.

"Kate? It's Linda. I'm glad I caught you. We had a great time shopping and then Jenny said she wanted to go to Central Park, so we're here now. We went to the zoo, and we're going to work our way up to you. There are some places she wanted to show me. So you don't have to pick her up. I'll bring her by around seven, I guess. We'll have a picnic dinner."

"Okay, but..."

"Wait, Jenny wants to say hi."

While Linda handed Jenny the cell phone, Kate could hear people walking by and disparate phrases from their conversations.

"Hi, Katy!" Jenny sounded happy and breathless with excitement.

"Hi, Jenny. How are you?"

"I'm okay. I'm going to show mommy the place where you and me went."

"The playground, you mean?"

"Noooo, Katy. I don't mean the playground."

"The reflecting pool? With the boats?"

Noooooo," Jenny laughed. "The *other* place. Where you and me went."

Her voice broke up

"The Egyptian playground?" Kate asked.

"Not a playground," Jenny said, her voice breaking up again.

Linda took the phone back.

"Sorry Kate. The battery's low."

"Where are you?"

"We're in the Park. Just hangin' out a little. I'll have her back around eight-thirty."

"Eight-thirty?" Kate repeated. It was just a little later than Linda had promised. Why was she so worried?

"See ya!"

Kate's shoulders lifted in an exaggerated shrug. She was curious where Jenny wanted to take her mother. It made her feel happy, in a way, that Jenny was trying to go back to some of the places they'd been because it showed that the kid remembered the nice times they'd had together. All of that was soon to end. But it *should* be that way, she told herself.

She settled back down to work until she reached a convenient point to break. Then she made a salad for dinner, frying up a half a chicken breast and chopping it up and putting it on top of mixed greens with a favorite dressing she usually didn't eat because Jenny didn't like the smell.

While she was waiting for the water to boil for tea, she was reading over an article when suddenly it struck her that the place Jenny was thinking of must be the one where they had gone for their barbecue in Central Park when they had seen Anthony. But why would she want to return there with her mother?

Kate ate her dinner with no appetite. Seven o'clock passed and Kate felt more and more nervous that she hadn't heard from them. What would they be doing at this hour? Finally, she could not sit home any longer and put a note on her door, saying that she had to go out and they should wait at Sally's if they returned before her. Then she started over to the park.

She took a cab down Lexington and across 85th. At Fifth Avenue, she paid, leapt out and raced up the long path beside the Metropolitan Museum.

It was nearly dark. There were few people walking along that path, but she crossed the East Drive in the park and continued toward the Great Lawn. She passed one woman with a dog. It barked as she ran by. A young couple sat kissing on a bench, oblivious to the passage of time. Otherwise the paths were empty.

She turned off the path and into the deserted area where she had been with Jenny that first night, straining to see ahead of her in the darkness. Then she spotted Linda and Jenny, sitting on a blanket in the grass. Kate remembered as if it were last week how she and Jenny had eaten their dinner near the very same crooked pine tree.

She walked over to them. Jenny hopped to her feet.

"Oh, Katy. Will you take me home? I hate it here. It's all buggy now and we didn't have marshmallows."

"You're not going anywhere yet," Linda said angrily. She checked her watch. "Where the hell is he? He's a freakin' hour and a half late. The freakin' shit head. Never gets anywhere on freakin' time."

"What are you talking about?" Kate asked.

"Freakin' Anthony. He asked me to meet him here. He wants some bucks and I told him I'd give him some. Then we're done. End of freakin' story."

"You had to bring Jenny for this?"

"Look, stop the freakin' Mother Hubbard routine, okay? I brought my daughter. I'm allowed to bring my freakin' daughter where I want to bring my freakin' daughter."

"I'm taking her home."

"You ain't taking her any freakin' place until I say she goes."

"Look, Linda, I don't want trouble."

"Don't make trouble, there won't be trouble."

As they spoke, a bagman emerged from behind a group of bushes, carrying a huge bag of plastic bottles and cans over his shoulder. His hair stuck out from under a dirty woolen cap. Dust and fragments of leaves covered his face and beard. Kate didn't want to stare at him, but it seemed to be the same man who had once given her the barrette for Jenny after a day in the park.

Jenny let out a cry of fear.

"Get your smelly ass out of here!" Linda said.

"Hello, babe," the man said. He took off his hat and it was obvious then that Anthony was standing in front of them.

"Jesus!" Linda said, laughing nervously. "You freakin' scared me to death. I almost pissed myself, for crissakes. What are you doing?"

"Can't be too careful these days, Linda," he said. "You got the money for me, babe?"

"Sure, I got it. I got it right here in my bag. But Anthony, you were going to give me some paper, right? You were going to write down that you lied to the ice-queen. You remember the paper."

"Give me my money, bitch."

Linda looked around into the darkness.

"I'm going to take Jenny," Kate said.

"You ain't going no place," Anthony replied. From inside one of the coats he wore, he pulled a gun.

"Freakin' Jesus. Rico!"

"You calling Rico, Babe? I don't think Rico hears you right now. Rico is indisposed right now."

"What did you do?"

Anthony laughed.

"You think I would ever trust you again, bitch? Fool me once, shame on you. Fool me twice, shame on me. I knew Rico would be hiding in the freakin' bushes. But Rico wasn't looking for no bagman. I asked him for a light, and Rico got a blade stuck between his ribs."

"You got it all wrong," Linda said. "Rico was just hanging out, Anthony. He was going to bring me home, that's all. He wasn't here for you."

"Just shut up, Babe. And start walking over to the fence. All of you."

"Take my money. It's in the bag, Anthony. Look in the bag."

"Don't put your hand in the bag or you are a dead woman. Just move to the fence."

They obeyed. There was no choice. Kate feared that she understood what he might do. Just beyond the fence was the transverse road. With the traffic going by at this hour, a shot or two would barely be heard. Or maybe he would use his knife. She held Jenny close, waiting for an opportunity for them to run.

As they neared the fence, Linda began to cry.

"Please, Anthony. Don't kill me. I wasn't going to hurt you. I swear, I wasn't going to hurt you. I brought Jenny along. I wouldn't pull nothing with Jenny here."

Anthony laughed.

"Bitch, that's what you wanted me to think. But I know you don't give a shit about nuthin' and nobody but your own ass."

"I'll give you more money," Linda said. "I swear I will."

Anthony pushed her to her knees in front of him. She put her hand on his crotch.

"You want me to do you, Anthony?" she said in a whisper. "I'll do it. I'll do anything."

"You ain't putting that mouth on me," he said. "Put it on this."

He shoved the gun into her mouth hard. Kate could see a piece of a broken tooth fall onto the leaves.

Linda pulled away. Blood streamed from her mouth. She spat on the ground, crying.

"Please, Anthony."

In response, he pointed the gun at her head. Linda grew quiet, sobbing almost noiselessly. Kate took a step backward with Jenny. Two more, she thought, and they could start to run through the trees.

Kate watched Anthony's face as she slowly moved away. Suddenly, there was the sound of a gun firing. Jenny screamed. An odd smile appeared on Anthony's face. His hand flew to his throat, and then slipped down to reveal a dark hole just above his breast bone where the bullet had severed the artery and blood was pouring out. He staggered, dropped the gun, and fell.

Only yards away, Rico appeared, struggling to stand, his own gun held at his side. A knife was sticking out of his chest, and his white shirt had turned black from his lost blood.

He seemed puzzled as to what he should do.

"Rico!" Linda cried. But he had fallen dead before she could reach him.

Kate picked up Jenny and turned and ran. She didn't look back, and this time never had the thought that she should call 911, even when they had made it home.

Twenty-one

Kate didn't tell Roger or anyone else about the incident in the park. A day later, the *Daily News* reported that two bodies had been found beside the 86th Street transverse. The police described them as well-known drug dealers who apparently had killed each other in a turf dispute. *It's close enough to the truth*, Kate thought.

She didn't contact Linda either. Roger met with her to prepare her testimony for the hearing, and Kate begged off, saying she wasn't feeling well. Linda called Kate several times and left messages asking Kate to please call her back. When Kate ignored her, she left a longer message.

"Kate," she said, in her breezy breathless voice. "It's Linda. Look, I'm sorry about what happened. Believe me, it wasn't meant to go down that way. We were going to scare him, that's all. I swear it. Rico promised me. I just wanted Anthony to freakin' go away and leave me alone so I can live my freakin' life, Kate. I had the money in my bag. We were going to scare him and then pay him the money and tell him if he ever came back for more he'd be a dead man. That would be it. You know? I mean I *know* Anthony. If he thinks you're weak, there's no end, he bleeds you freakin' dry. He's a freakin' leech, Katy... *Was* a freakin' leech... So call me, huh? I want to set up a time I can see Jens. I'd like to have her overnight, like we talked about. There's stuff I have to buy for her and..." Kate stopped listening at that point and erased it.

A couple of days later she woke early to see that her message machine was blinking. It was Linda again. This time she had called at two in the morning. Her voice was slurred and her words were interrupted with bouts of crying. Kate wanted to shut it off and go back to sleep, but she forced herself to listen.

"Kate, please call me. Please... I'm asking you on my knees, Katy. I'm at the end of my freakin' rope. Not that I should expect you to care, I know... Listen, Katy, I know I'm a fuck-up. I know I did the wrong thing here. You think I don't see that? You think I don't know what a lousy freakin' mother I am? What a piece of shit I am to do something like that? But Katy, I can't stand that you're mad at me, too. I think about the way you looked at me that night in the park, Katy. You didn't just hate me. Hate I can take. I'm used to hate. I got a lot of people out there who hate me... But you believed in me. Even when you knew I wasn't such a good person, wasn't doing such nice things, you *believed* in me. You thought I could pull myself together and make something for myself and for Jenny. But that night, you had a look in your eye...oh God... it was like you gave up, Katy. Like, finally, you agreed with everyone else. Like I really ain't no freakin' good and never will be any freakin' good..." There was a long pause. In the background was the sound of her sobs. "I know you're not going to help them against me. Maybe you should, but I know you won't. I know what kind of person you are. But Katy, I swear to you, I can't stand having you think about me that way. Not you, too." She started crying again, harder than before. Occasionally, she tried to talk but had to stop. "Katy, please, you were there for Jenny. You helped her when no one wanted her around. Please, Katy, don't give up on me. I ain't got nobody else, Katy. Don't give up on me. Please, Katy. Please…"

~ * ~

On the day of the hearing, Roger arranged to pick Linda up at her apartment. He was aware of her past failures to appear in court and was determined not to let it happen again. He called her the night before and she assured him that she would be ready at 8:30 in the morning.

When he arrived and saw that she was not waiting for him on the sidewalk, he told the driver to sound the horn. After a minute, he went upstairs and pushed the buzzer, holding it down for five and ten second intervals. He pounded on the door. There was still no response. Worried, he put his shoulder against it, and the frame seemed to give. He got a running start across the hallway and crashed into it.

The door flew open, slamming against the inside wall. The place was a mess. An empty vodka bottle stood on a coffee table. Drinking glasses lay broken on the floor where they had apparently been thrown against the wall. He could see a set of bloody footprints. She must have stepped in the glass and been so drunk she hadn't noticed, or hadn't cared.

He went into the bedroom and saw her sprawled on the bed in her nightgown. At first he was afraid that she was dead, but as he felt for her pulse, he heard her breathe.

"Linda," he said. "You have to wake up. We have to get you up to court. Linda!"

He pulled on her arms, and she cooperated, allowing him to raise her into a sitting position. Then he heard a sound in her throat and moved back just in time to avoid the spray of vomit. He used the sheet to wipe her mouth. Her eyes opened partially.

"Lemme, 'lone," she said. "S'okay. Jus' lemme 'lone."

"Linda, we have to get you to court."

"No, lemme 'lone, Roger. Nice guy. Buh lemme 'lone."

"Let me help."

Roger looked behind him and saw that Kate was standing at the door to the bedroom.

"I had a feeling this was going to happen," she said. "Help me get her gown off. And let's get her into the shower."

They peeled off the gown. It reeked of vomit and they tossed it onto the floor. They turned her to the side of the bed and each got under an arm and lifted her up. Again, her eyes opened to slits. She leaned against Roger companionably.

"Lemme 'lone," she muttered. "Lemme 'lone. Lemme die. Wanna die."

"Shut up, Linda," Kate said.

They carried her into the bathroom. Roger held her steady while Kate turned on the water.

"Step up into the tub," Kate said.

"Lemme die. Lemme die."

"Help me, Roger."

They guided her into the tub and sat her down behind the curtain.

"Roger, you make a pot of strong coffee and maybe some toast. I'll see what I can do here. Maybe you should call and tell people we're going to be a little late."

"They aren't going to give an adjournment, Kate. You know that."

"Get us an hour, Roger. Let's just do what we can do."

Kate stripped down to her underwear and stood in the shower to turn it on. Linda sputtered and tried to get away from the water, but Kate grabbed her by the hair and held onto her, first directing the flow to wash off the remains of the vomit, then aiming the water at her face in a vain attempt to make her open her eyes.

Linda threw up again, but this time there was very little left in her. She retched and her body shook with convulsions.

"Lemme die! Will ya?"

She started to sink to her knees, but Kate yanked her by the hair again and made her stand.

"Lemme go."

Kate slapped her and shook her hard.

"Wake up! You have to try to wake up! Damn you!"

She turned off the hot water and left only cold. Linda began to shriek. She slipped and her feet went out from under her. She fell into the tub and Kate nearly landed on top of her, but she held onto the nozzle of the shower and pulled Linda's head back so that the stream of water fell directly onto her face. Finally, Linda stopped struggling, and managed to get to her feet. Kate turned off the water.

Linda was crying again. Her face was contorted with the effort to stop. She put her arms around Kate's neck and leaned against her for a minute, sobbing silently, finally able to mouth the words, "Thank you."

"Don't thank me yet," Kate said. "We've got too much to do."

She wrapped a towel around each of them and helped her walk into the kitchen, where Roger had coffee waiting. While Linda sipped at the cup, Kate combed her hair and arranged it as best she could with barrettes she found in a dresser drawer. Afterward, she found a skirt and blouse and helped her get dressed.

~ * ~

In the cab no one said much. When they got up to the courtroom, the court officer was making a final call of the case. They barely had time to walk in and sit.

They gave their appearances as before. Kate looked over at Rena, who glanced away. The lawyer for CPS seemed confident as ever.

"Are we ready to begin?" the judge asked.

"Your Honor," Roger said. "My client is here, but she is not feeling well. I would request a brief adjournment."

Cheryl Damian stood up.

"I would agree to an adjournment if Ms. Gilmour would have a blood test done to show that this latest sickness is not drug or alcohol related."

"Mr. Adams," the judge said. "I'm not inclined to give any adjournment at all under the circumstances of this case. Are you willing to take Ms. Damian's offer?"

He turned to Linda. She shook her head. Then she started to cry. She put her face in her hands and her body trembled as the tears flowed.

Kate leaned over and patted her on the arm, whispering. "Do you want to take a little break?"

Linda shook her head again, still crying.

"Mr. Adams," the judge said. "Do you want a few minutes? The court will be in recess for five minutes, no more, and then..."

"No!" Linda said, looking up at the judge. "I can do this. I'd just like to say something, please."

"This isn't a time for speeches, Your Honor," Ms. Damian said.

Roger bent over Linda and whispered, "I don't think this is a good idea."

"Please!" Linda said. "I have to do this. I have to tell you, Your Honor. CPS is right. I've been a terrible mother. I've been on booze or on drugs and doing worse than that for years and years. And I know I don't have any right to ask anyone to believe me anymore..." She paused.

Ms. Damian rose from her chair and took a deep breath. "Your Honor, with all due respect, this is exactly the kind of self-serving speech I object to."

"I haven't heard anything self-serving so far," the judge said. "Go on, Ms. Gilmour."

"Your Honor, I've made promises before about what I was going to do with my life, and I've failed every time. And I always had an excuse. I don't have any excuses this time, except that I'm a weak…a very weak person. But the thing is, I've never felt the way I am feeling right now either. And I really do want the chance to try again. Just one more chance."

"Your Honor!" the CPS lawyer said. The judge held up her hand to stop her and gestured for her to sit.

"And what makes you think this time will be any different?" the judge asked Linda.

"I don't know that it will, Your Honor," she said quietly. "But I never had anybody behind me before like Kate, here, and Roger. I never had anybody care for me so much…" She started to sob again. Kate left her chair and stood beside her. Linda's voice broke, but she continued.

"I don't think I could ever do it by myself, Judge. But I think maybe I can now. And here is what I want to ask you to do. Beg you to do, really. And I beg Kate, too. I ask you to let Jenny stay with Kate for the next year. Let Kate be the parent. Let her have the final say in everything. And let me just visit. Let Rena—I mean, Ms. Bracton—come check on me as many times as she wants. Let her see if I'm making any progress. Maybe, if I prove myself after a few months, maybe I can take Jenny overnight once a month. Let me get into a rehab program. Let me find a job and keep a job. Let's just see if I can do it. If I can't, what's the harm? Jenny will be where she's loved. I can give her whatever love I'm capable of. I do love my girl, Your Honor, I swear I do."

This time when she started crying the judge gave a brief recess.

Kate sat down with Linda, moving her chair close enough so they could put their arms around each other. Roger conferred with Rena and the attorney. In ten minutes or so, the deal was struck. Then the court re-convened and the stipulation was read.

~ * ~

Afterward, on the street outside the building, Linda hugged Kate, holding her for a minute.

"I'm going home to get some rest. I'll be in touch, okay?"

"Okay," Kate said.

They got a cab for Linda, and another one for themselves.

"Do you think she'll do what she said?" he asked.

"I don't know. I didn't think she would get this far."

Holding hands in the back seat, Kate and Roger rode uptown to his office, content to be quiet, immersed in thought. When the cab stopped, he hesitated.

"To be honest with you," he said. "I wasn't sure we were going to get through this either."

"Yeah, I know what you mean. But I always liked the odds."

He opened the door and she kissed him.

"Call me if you get a chance," he said. "I'll stop by later at the usual time."

"I will call. But I have something to do first, with Jenny."

"What's that?"

"There's a tough old bird of a woman lying in a hospital bed who I want Jenny to meet. That's what I'm doing first."

Roger smiled.

"Never a dull moment," he said.

"Not in this lifetime, anyway."

Meet

Anne Rothman-Hicks

Anne Rothman-Hicks was born in New York City and, except for a brief exile to the suburbs imposed by her parents, she has lived there all of her life, the latter part of which she has shared with her co-author, Kenneth Hicks, and their three children.

VISIT OUR WEBSITE
FOR THE FULL INVENTORY
OF QUALITY BOOKS:

http://www.books-by-wings-epress.com/

*Quality trade paperbacks and downloads
in multiple formats,
in genres ranging from light romantic comedy
to general fiction and horror.
Wings has something for every reader's taste.
Visit the website, then bookmark it.
We add new titles each month!*